THE SPIRAL AWAKENS

SPIRALS OF AZTALUN (BOOK ONE)

SARA LANGHE

CONTENTS

To those who live life, dream of other worlds,
believe in true love and the everlasting power of friendship

1

THE SPIRAL AWAKENS

The motel room smelled faintly of sage and desert dust. I'd left the window cracked overnight, and the cool Spring Sonoran air rolled in with the distant chatter of doves, quail, and cactus wrens. My phone buzzed loudly against the nightstand, dragging me out of sleep. I reached for it, squinting against the pale morning light filtering through dusty curtains.

"Heidi!" I croaked, swiping to answer. "Don't you ever sleep in?"

Heidi Jensen's laugh poured through the speaker, bright and familiar. "Only when I'm not desperate to hear my best friend's voice. Morning, sunshine. How's Mexico?"

I rubbed my eyes and smiled. "Dry, beautiful, and full of potential. It's also littered with rocks. I will inevitably spend the next few weeks digging around."

"Sounds like heaven to you," she teased.

"Almost, but it's missing one important ingredient." I rolled over and stretched my legs under the scratchy sheets.

"Me?" she asked, mock-shocked.

"Obviously." I sat up and pushed the covers off my legs. "God, I miss you, Heidi. It's not the same being out here without you. We used to do everything together—school and wine-fueled Netflix binge-nights. Now you're in San Diego pretending to be a normal person."

"Normal is highly overrated," she said. "We need to plan another girls' weekend, somewhere weird and full of artifacts."

"Deal. After this dig wraps up, I'll be desperate for margaritas and meaningless banter."

"I'll bring the chips. You bring the ghost stories."

I laughed. "I'll look forward to it."

She hesitated. "So... this is your first time leading the dig?"

I nodded, then realized she couldn't see me. "Yeah. Just call me Principal Investigator. I'll tell you all about it as soon as I get home. You already know I won the grant last fall. It was a proposal focused on linking trade patterns between the Maya lowlands and indigenous tribes in the Southwest. Many people doubted it and still do, but I believe there's something here that could provide that elusive connection."

"Of course you do," Heidi said, gentle and proud. "You've always had the eye for patterns no one else sees. I'm proud of you, Alayna."

The words hit deeply, and I swallowed around a lump in my throat. "Thanks, Heidi. That really means a lot to me."

"Are your students all starting to get Spring Fever yet?" I asked. After getting her master's degree at UCLA, Heidi had landed her dream job as a high school counselor in San Diego.

"Honestly, they're great kids," Heidi paused, "but so many of them seem totally clueless about what direction to take in life. They don't seem to plan beyond what's happening each weekend."

"Well, I can't say I was any different in high school. They're lucky they have you to help them find their way." I had finally started to wake up.

We lingered a bit longer in familiar silence until she said she had to get ready for work. We said our goodbyes—too short as always—and I placed the phone back on the nightstand.

It was time to face the day.

After a quick shower, I changed into field clothes—cargo pants, rust-colored tank top, and weathered hiking boots. Stopping to check in the mirror, I pulled my long, dark, wavy hair up into a quick ponytail, slipped on a light linen long-sleeve shirt, and topped it off with the baseball cap I'd borrowed from my dad years ago and just hadn't gotten around to returning yet. Even though my caramel-colored skin didn't sunburn as fast as my best friend Heidi's lighter skin tone, I knew from experience the Sonoran sun could be brutal even in late February.

I put on my good luck charm, a copper spiral maze pendant my mom had given me, and headed downstairs. My fingers lingered on the small turquoise stone at the center of the symbol and smiled fondly. It always made me feel safe.

My new Graduate Research Assistant, Jacob Sanchez, was already at the tiny motel café, sipping coffee and flipping through his notebook. His long, dark hair was pulled into a braid, and he looked as organized as ever.

"Morning, Jake," I said, grabbing the seat across from him.

"Hey, Dr. Archuleta! Did you sleep okay?"

I nodded even though it wasn't true. "You've been up for hours, haven't you?" I eyed him knowingly.

He grinned. "Just one. I was far too excited to sleep more."

The server came around and poured me some much-needed coffee. I breathed in the warm aroma deeply and exhaled, looking at Jake. "You'll need that excitement since it's your first dig, and Sonora is not exactly forgiving. But it'll be worth it."

"I still can't believe I get to be part of this. How did you even land the research grant?"

"Countless hours of proposal work," I said with a smirk. "A lot of coffee, and a little desperation. Don't worry, next time I'll let you do all the research and proposal writing. And rewriting. I shouldn't have all the fun," I joked. "Seriously, I pitched it as a chance to trace cultural linkages across ancient trade routes. I then highlighted the significance of oral histories, ceramics, and petroglyph patterns. Luckily, it resonated with the review board."

"It's amazing, and probably nerve-wracking. What do you expect from me out there?"

I paused. Jake deserved an honest answer. "Professionalism, attention to detail, and humility. You're not just cataloging objects—you're protecting stories. There's power in that, and responsibility."

Jake nodded seriously. "I won't let you and your team down."

"You'll be fine, just pace yourself, and don't be afraid to ask questions. With your undergrad degree in anthropology, you have a lot to add to this project. Still, if you don't understand a technical term or jargon, speak up and say so."

We finished breakfast and packed up our gear. My Jeep Wrangler gleamed in the sunlight like a desert flame—burnt orange, bold, and utterly mine. We tossed our packs in the back, climbed in, and hit the road.

The hour-long drive to the dig site wound through vast desert valleys and rocky ridges. Golden grasses swayed in the breeze, and the mountains were jagged in the distance. It was the kind of place that kept secrets I wanted to uncover.

Jake gazed out the window. "It's so wild out here. I mean, you read about places like this in textbooks, but actually seeing it is so profound."

"It feels different, doesn't it?" I agreed with a nod as I rounded a wide corner.

He nodded. "It's almost as if the land is watching us."

"Perhaps it is."

We lapsed into silence for a while, the hum of tires on asphalt filling the air. I found myself thinking about my ex-boyfriend, Vincent—his voice, his criticisms disguised as compliments, the way he always had to be right. It had been over a year since our split, and I'd spent so long escaping him, but sometimes the shadow still clung to the edges of moments like this. I clenched the steering wheel tighter and focused on the road.

When Jake and I arrived at the site, my team gathered under the canvas shade canopy. There were about ten of us, including field techs, two undergrads, and a representative from INAH (*Instituto Nacional de Antropología e Historia*), the Mexican archaeological authority. I gave them a nod and stepped into the makeshift command circle.

"Morning, everyone," I said as I took off my sunglasses. There was just something about addressing a group I was leading that made me feel I owed it to them to look them in the eye. "Let's start with safety."

We reviewed the basics—hydration protocols, first aid locations, and radio checks. The heat here could be brutal. This winter had been warm and dry meaning temperatures were higher than expected for this time of year. Plus, the wildlife wasn't always friendly. This was the time of year snakes started coming out of hibernation on warmer days. I gestured toward the map posted beside our equipment tent.

"We're working within these perimeter flags only." I pointed to them on the hanging map. "Artifact zones have been marked with red flags for pottery shards, blue for lithics, and green for organic material. No one touches anything without documentation or my approval. And be aware—this site is culturally sensitive."

Our INAH liaison, a short, bald man named Arturo, stepped in. "The community elders have given conditional approval," he said, stopping to wipe sweat from his brow. "That means full respect. No photos outside the documentation protocol, and no removal of materials without site lead approval."

Jake scribbled notes furiously beside me as we went on to describe the terrain and hand out assignments. I remembered my grad assistant days fondly. I was in his situation just ten years ago when every trip to the field was an adventure. Jake was only about three inches taller than my five-foot, five-inch height and seemed so naive. I needed to make sure I respected that at age 22, he was an adult and didn't need me to be his babysitter.

When the briefing wrapped up, everyone nodded their understanding. The team began breaking into pairs, heading to their designated units.

Jake tugged gently on my sleeve. "Where should I start?"

"You're with me today. We'll be mapping, photographing, and cataloging the northeast grid. I want you to understand how I document before you take your own section."

His eyes lit up. "Seriously? I would love to see how you work, Dr. Archuleta." He grinned, and I admired his enthusiasm.

"Seriously. Let's get our hands dirty, shall we? And, for the record, most of my grad students call me Alayna or Professor A for short." I winked.

As we walked to the marked grid, I felt the familiar buzz —that heady mix of anticipation and reverence I always felt when a dig began. Maybe the land was about to speak to me, and I was certainly ready to listen.

***

By midday, the sun was devastating, beating down on the dig site like a hammer, but Jake and I had hit our stride. Elbow-deep in dry soil, we worked side by side, the soft clink of the trowel against stone the only sound for long stretches of time.

I had been worried that Jake would be talkative, and I liked to work in silence, so I was pleasantly surprised that he wasn't. I still didn't know him well, since he had just transferred to the University at the beginning of the semester a few weeks ago, but everything pointed to him being a solid addition to the program.

We'd found the corner of a platform—possibly ceremonial or maybe even domestic. It was too early to tell at this point. Still, it was the kind of puzzle that kept me going.

"You know," Jake said, swiping sweat from his brow, "I didn't realize how satisfying this would be. It's like grown-up treasure hunting."

"With less gold and more back pain," I reminded him, brushing dirt off a shattered pottery piece.

He laughed, an easy, infectious laugh. I even found my lips curling in response. "Come on, Doctor, I mean Professor A., even you have to admit this is fun."

I smirked, "It's always fun until the paperwork hits." I smiled. "But I guess that will be largely your job now."

"Thanks a lot," he said as he started to whistle. *Oh, no, not whistling.* I sighed to myself. Vincent had been a whistler, unless he was lurking and eavesdropping on conversations. Luckily, I had learned to tune him out.

When I called lunch break, the team migrated toward the shaded tents, where coolers full of sandwiches and water were waiting. Jake lingered a second, nudging me with his boot.

"Are you coming?"

"In a bit," I said. "I'm going to walk and stretch my legs out first. You go ahead."

He nodded, understanding without prying. I liked him already.

The stretching felt good, and I decided I would need to take up yoga someday to balance out my usual routine of rock climbing and trail running. Still, I had managed to keep an athletic build even after my years competing in youth and high-school soccer ended.

I hiked out beyond the site boundary, across the dusty slope toward a rocky outcrop that had caught my eye earlier. The desert here was quiet, save for the wind skimming over the surface, carrying the scent of mesquite and sandstone. I looked forward to the summer rainy season, when the smell of wet creosote back in Tucson would be nearly intoxicating. After a few hundred yards, I spotted something half-buried at the base of a ridge.

It was a large, flat gray stone with an intricate black design and geometric edges. I crouched and began brushing away the packed dirt, my pulse ticking faster with each pass. The slab revealed itself beneath my fingers. It was no larger than a carry-on suitcase but unmistakably carved, not just with *any* symbol.

It was a spiral maze. I froze, and my heart stopped beating. It couldn't be! I would recognize that design anywhere. The same intricate pattern graced the pendant resting against my collarbone.

I reached up instinctively, pulling the necklace from beneath my shirt. My mother had given it to me the day I left for UCLA. She said it was handcrafted in Sedona from copper, silver, and turquoise—the colors of the land, she had told me. The maze etched into its center was tight and hypnotic, with a single path spiraling inward. I'd always thought of it as a metaphor for my career: one long, winding route toward some hidden truth.

Now, here it was, again, but not in jewelry. This time it was etched into stone.

I ran my fingers over the carving, and strangely, the slab was warm. Not sun-warmed, though. It was hot, almost like it radiated from within. The moment my fingertips traced the spiral, something shifted.

The pendant pulsed repetitively. A whisper of wind coiled around me, colder than the desert breeze, circling my body like a breath from the past. The copper maze glowed faintly, heat flaring against my chest. Air caught in my throat as some kind of current buzzed underneath my skin, traveling to every part of my body.

"What the—"

The ground trembled beneath my boots, and my heart slammed hard as my pulse accelerated instantly.

A low hum filled the air, like the resonance of a distant drumbeat. The spiral on the slab began to glow in tandem with my pendant. Light spilled from the grooves, white-gold and blinding. My blood seemed to be thundering in my ears.

Before I could respond, the world cracked open before me.

A colorful vortex spiraled out from the stone—a whirlpool of light, wind, and energy so raw it felt like being scraped clean. The ground buckled, and my scream erupted, but a roar of wind swallowed the sound.

I stumbled backward, but the pull was too strong. Wind rushed past me like freight trains, full of scents I couldn't name—incense, rain on hot stone, wildflowers, and old, old earth. I reached for anything to anchor myself, but there was only light.

The spiral blazed, and then I felt it.

The world became a tunnel of spinning color and blinding motion. Light lashed past me, fragmented and searing, interspersed with flickering visions—a woman cloaked in feathers standing atop a cliff, a temple of obsidian rising from jungle mist, and a boy drawing a spiral in the dirt with a stick.

I didn't recognize them, but their eyes connected with mine as if they knew me.

The spiral was no longer just a symbol. It became a map, a globe, and finally a portal.

The air in the spiraling tunnel spun against my skin. My clothes whipped around me, and my hair lashed out like wildfire. I had no sense of up or down, only forward, uncontrolled, spinning. I felt my stomach churn and clamped my mouth shut.

The light grew brighter, the wind roared. And still, I tumbled, until suddenly, there was no sound at all.

With a jolt like hitting water from a great height, the spinning stopped, and my feet found ground. My knees buckled, and I collapsed on all fours, panting.

The silence was total, and I looked up.

The sky above me was violet, streaked with ribbons of silver. The trees were unlike anything I'd ever seen—tall, silver-barked, their leaves shimmering like mica. A strange energy hummed in the air, and the pendant at my chest glowed faintly.

I was somewhere else. I was no longer in Sonora. I was no longer on Earth.

"Where am I?" I whispered as my body trembled.

I couldn't move at first, and my breathing was so labored that I wondered if I was having an attack of some kind. My eyes felt heavy as my eyelids swished over them, and my head lowered slowly. I felt like I was in a trance or my own daydream, but I knew I would never dream this.

I couldn't fight it anymore. My eyelids closed, and I slumped to the ground as heavy as a sack of corn masa.

I woke to the same silence, not the silence of an early morning in Sonora or the muffled quiet of my motel room. This was thick, heavy, and almost otherworldly. I blinked hard against the glare of silver-blue light and then froze.

Three moons hung above me, and there were no stars or clouds in sight. The three glowing orbs—one the color of bone, one sapphire, and the third a deep, dark red—drifted slowly across the lavender sky. It was mesmerizing.

I sat up, heart still pounding—at least it hadn't stopped beating.

My fingers clutched instinctively at the pendant around my neck. It was still there. Its copper edges pulsed faintly against my skin, still warm, but almost... alive? The spiral maze at its center shimmered with a dull glow, like coals banked under ash, and the small piece of turquoise at the center was now as dark as obsidian. It was the same spiral I'd traced with my finger on the stone slab back in Sonora. That was... what? Minutes ago, or was it hours?

What the hell had happened?

I scrambled to my feet, red sand cascading down my arms and sticking to my palms. Not red like Earth's iron-rich dirt. This was crimson, deep and unnatural, like powdered garnet. It shifted strangely, as if reluctant to stay still. My boots sank slightly with every step. My heart accelerated even more.

Where *was* I?

The horizon was jagged, dominated by enormous black obsidian spires that jutted from the ground like the broken ribs of the world. They glistened even in the moonlight, reflecting faint blue auras. So far, there was no sign of any civilization.

No vehicles. No dig site. No Jake. No Jeep. It was just the sky, the spires, the moons, the sand, and me.

I glanced around, then down at my feet—and let out a breath of relief when I spotted my day pack lying in the sand beside me. Snatching it up, I unzipped it with shaky hands and dug through the contents, silently begging for my cell phone to be there. I'd just call them. Tell them where I was. Get out of here. But after several frantic seconds of rummaging, the truth settled in like a stone in my stomach: my phone wasn't there. I let out a low groan, the memory flashing back—setting it down beside the cooler when I grabbed a water bottle. A water bottle. My fingers closed around it, and I nearly laughed when I pulled it free and saw it was still full. I took a small, grateful sip and tucked it back into the bag. No telling how long I'd be stuck out here. Best to make it last.

"Okay," I whispered, voice hoarse. "This is *not* a dream." I pinched myself just to be sure. *Nope, not a dream!*

The air smelled like minerals and ozone. Like right before a lightning-filled desert monsoon. Yet every breath felt cleaner and easier. I took in a deep lungful and almost laughed. For once, I wasn't congested. No dust or dryness, and no mesquite-tree allergy spike. There was just this strange, heavy magic laced through the atmosphere.

Magic? Did I really just think that?

I brushed sand from my shirt again and glanced down. At least I was still wearing my cargo pants and field boots. My work shirt was half-untucked, my pack was slung over my shoulders, and no phone—not that I expected it to work wherever I was. My fingers trembled as I touched the pendant again.

"Gabriella," I said softly. My mom's name felt like a lifeline. "What did you give me?" Somehow, I knew all of this was directly related to the pendant. There was simply no denying that. She'd always spoken about it as more than jewelry. She had said it was made in Sedona, imbued with vortex-energy. Back then, I'd smiled politely and chalked it up to her spiritual side. But the spiral on that stone in Sonora matched it perfectly. And now I was standing in a place with three damn moons!

I spun slowly, trying to make sense of my new surroundings. The landscape stretched out in all directions like an alien canvas—rolling dunes of red, sharp rocks that sparkled with mica-like veins, tall tufts of dark grass that whispered in the breeze. The sound was low, melodic, almost like a vibrating chant.

One thing I was certain of: I wasn't alone. I could *feel* that.

Goosebumps rose along my arms. The back of my neck tingled the way it did when I sensed rattlesnakes or long-legged spiders nearby on hikes. There was no logical source for the feeling—no rustling of leaves or sound of approach. There was just a presence, like the sensation of being watched.

And yet... I didn't feel afraid, not as I should have. Don't get me wrong, I was *worried*. My mind was racing through possibilities—heat stroke, hallucination, dream states, dimensional folds, or quantum displacement. But underneath the fear was a wave of awe and wonder where there should have been terror.

This was the unknown and unexplored, and I felt more *thrilled* than I felt scared. It must have been the adventurous streak in me, or just plain stupidity. I wasn't sure which.

"Pull it together, Archuleta," I told myself.

Still, I couldn't stop my mind from drifting back. Had Jake already noticed I was gone? Was he pacing the campsite right now, calling my name, and wondering if I wandered too far without water? The thought of him alone out there hit me like a gut punch. He was my responsibility.

And what about the others? Would someone call the ranger station? Would they comb the hills or dismiss it as one of my impromptu solo scouting hikes? How long would it take before they knew I hadn't just wandered off?

Then there were my parents. If this turned into a full-on missing person's case, Mom would lose it. Dad would try to stay calm, to think rationally, but I knew the look that would pass between them—that fragile, wide-eyed fear they shared whenever I told them I was heading out on another expedition.

And Heidi... God, Heidi would panic. We talked at least once a week, usually more. If I missed our regular call, she'd text me a hundred times and start asking around. She never said it, but I knew she always feared something like this would happen—that I'd disappear into the desert and never come back.

I swallowed hard, trying to shake off the weight in my chest. Not guilt exactly, but a sense of detachment, like I'd been ripped from a thread connecting me to home, and that thread was now fraying in the wind.

I needed more information, landmarks perhaps? I had field maps in my pack, but not of this place. I looked around, trying to find something resembling shelter or elevation. I scanned the spires. One, taller than the rest, stood to the northeast. If I could get to higher ground, maybe I'd see a settlement, or at least get my bearings.

I started walking, the crimson sand whispering beneath my steps. My pendant pulsed again, faint but insistent. Was it guiding me and responding to this realm? Was it a realm or another planet altogether?

"This is insane," I said aloud, just to hear my voice. It steadied me.

For a moment, I thought of Heidi—her voice, her laughter, and how she rolled her eyes whenever I went off about glyphs or spiral symbology. *She'd never believe this.* But then again... she might. Heidi was the one who'd always felt that not everything could be understood through science. She would love this sense of magic.

No wonder she had never gotten along with Vincent. His smug and condescending voice flickered in my mind: *You need to see the evidence before jumping to conclusions, Alayna. Emotion clouds logic.*

I clenched my jaw. Screw him. This clearly wasn't just a fantastical dream—this was real. And I didn't need his voice in my head while trying to survive in a surreal dimension, or realm, or whatever this was.

I hiked for what felt like twenty minutes, the terrain rising subtly. As I climbed a low ridge, the wind shifted. It was warmer now and carrying the scent of smoke… no, not smoke—something older, resinous. My fingers twitched, itching for my field journal. I needed to record everything— every sight, sound, and symbol. But Jake had my journal. All I had was my memory.

At the top of the ridge, I stopped.

There it was, etched into the rock below, so large I hadn't seen it from the ground. A spiral maze, just like the pendant and slab in Sonora. Only this one glowed faintly, embedded in the stone like a beacon.

My knees weakened. I dropped into a crouch, breath catching in my throat.

This isn't a coincidence. This is a call.

I touched the pendant. It was hot now and throbbing with energy. And I didn't know what terrified me more— that I might be stuck here forever… or that some part of me *wanted* to stay.

2

RIVER LIGHT

I climbed down the jagged slope, careful not to slip. The twilight had taken on more of a bruised appearance since I had 'landed.' It all felt strangely surreal, like I'd been beamed down from the *Starship Enterprise* into someone's dreamscape gone wrong.

When I reached the rock I had been heading toward, I pressed my fingers against the maze. I wasn't surprised when it was warm. It pulsed under my palm just like my pendant, as if they were syncing, and communing in a language I couldn't understand.

I kept thinking about the dig site—how long had I been gone? It felt like no more than a few hours, but my gut told me time moved differently here. Had it been days or even weeks since I had disappeared? Or was time here faster, and it had only been minutes? The possibilities gnawed at me. This was supposed to be the most important discovery of my career, maybe even of the decade, and I'd vanished in the middle of it. Had Jake or the rest of the team realized I was missing? And if yes, what were they doing or saying now?

This excavation was everything—years of research, months of planning and field prep, and the chance to uncover something truly groundbreaking. I should've been there, cataloging, recording, leading. Instead, I was somewhere else entirely, and I hated the idea that everything might have moved on without me.

What if I could never go home? The thought alone sent a shiver down my spine. I forced myself to take a steady breath, trying to quiet the storm of panic rising in my chest. Worrying wouldn't change anything—not now. What I needed was to find someone, anyone. Some sign of civilization. Maybe then, somehow, they could help me get back home.

In an effort to distract myself, I turned my attention back to the flat lands beneath the monolithic rock formations. A faint hum tugged at my senses, startling me as I turned to look over my shoulder. It sounded oddly like flowing water. A river? I craned my neck to see if there was something there. Not far from the base of a small hill, I could see something glowing in the distance. Curiously, I walked toward it, wondering all the while where my fear or good sense was.

When I came upon it, it was translucent; its currents threaded with veins of hazy blue-green light. It seemed to stretch on forever. The liquid pulsed, and with each throb, my pendant vibrated.

Curiosity eclipsed fear, so I followed it along for a while. "Where are you taking me?" I said aloud, used to talking to myself on my many solo explorations.

The banks were lined with strange flora—tall, reed-like stalks that shimmered when touched by the river's light. I brushed one with the back of my hand. Its surface was slick but dry, like dragonfly wings stretched over bone. It was unbelievably soft, much like the buds of a pussy willow.

It smelled faintly of sage and citrus, much as home outside the window of the little southwestern bungalow where I lived alone with my grey cat, Kiva. I hoped she was a good kitty for my colleague, Sylvia, who was cat-sitting. After this moment of thought for home, I was drawn back to the river.

Further along, bioluminescent ferns arched toward me, their fronds brushing my jeans with a whispery tickle. Each leaf left a faint trace of silver light, like moon dust. I stopped the trail it seemed to leave, which faded after about ten seconds.

The hum of the current became a low thrum in my bones. I decided to call it a river for lack of a better name.

"Am I dreaming?" I asked the river. It didn't answer.

Distant whispers floated on the wind, tugging at my ears. They weren't words, not exactly—more like impressions.

Keep going. Don't stop. You were meant to find this.

I froze. Where had those words come from? It wasn't me thinking them. My heart rate increased as I realized I was moving within this 'realm' like I had been here before. But how could that possibly be?

I stopped to touch the bark of a nearby tree—if you could call it that. It was silver, smooth as marble but warm to the touch. A fine network of veiny light danced beneath the translucent surface skin of bark.

The tree felt alive, not just alive but aware. As I leaned into it, palm flat to its side, a sense of calm rippled through me. The smell of wet stone and wildflower pollen hung in the air, cool, clean, and oddly comforting. I realized then that my sense of smell seemed to be enhanced ever since I arrived here. Wherever here was.

"Why are there three moons?" I asked aloud, staring up. "And where the hell are all the stars?"

The orbs floated in the sky. Their reflections shimmered on the river's surface, giving everything a surreal glow. It was easy to lose track of time here, with no sun or shadows shifting.

I kept walking and kept asking myself why I didn't feel afraid or alone.

The air was pleasantly cool, not cold, like standing in the shade of canyon walls at dawn. Each breath felt easier than the last. It was what a life with no dust must feel like. It was so clean and my lungs seemed to heal every time I inhaled. My lungs had never felt so light and strong. Growing up in New Mexico and living in Arizona, it seemed there was an endless supply of dust in the air.

As I walked, the ground shifted from flat red sand to obsidian shards that jutted from the earth like broken teeth. One stood taller than the rest, maybe six feet high. Its surface was mirror-smooth and black.

I reached out, expecting heat, but it was cold. Colder than any desert night I'd camped through. My fingers recoiled, then returned. I pressed my palm against it and felt nothing —no energy, just cold and smooth.

"I should be terrified," I whispered.

But I wasn't. I felt... anchored. Not safe, exactly, but serene.

A flicker of movement caught my eye. Small, quick—like a lizard darting between the stones.

I crouched. "Hey," I whispered. "It's okay."

It peeked from the shadow—glassy black eyes, iridescent scales that shifted from lavender to green. It blinked slowly, then disappeared behind a glowing mushroom.

I smiled despite myself. But suddenly, I stopped breathing. Where there was one creature, there were many. That would mean there would likely be some unfriendly ones somewhere. I shivered. No, I wouldn't let my mind negatively control my thoughts. I would be just fine.

I sat on a mossy boulder, the thrumming vibration of the river echoing beneath my skin.

Does anyone even know I'm gone?

Would Jake panic? Would my students assume I just bailed on the expedition? Did time pass here like it did back home? Could it have been days there already? Or the blink of an eye?

And if I never made it back…

Would anyone even know where to start looking?

The thought hollowed something inside me. Still, I couldn't shake the certainty that I was meant to be here, at least for now.

I looked down at the pendant, now glowing softly.

"Okay," I breathed. "You brought me here for a reason, so show me."

The wind whispered again, a shiver threading through my spine.

I stood and kept walking.

I felt like I'd been walking for days, but it was probably closer to six hours if I had to guess. Still, my feet throbbed, and my calves ached like I'd just run a marathon. The air here stayed locked in twilight, and I had no idea how time worked in this realm—if it worked at all. My stomach growled in protest, low and hollow like the rumble of distant thunder. That was a definite sign that time had passed.

I needed food and to refill my water bottle. I looked down at the river. I wanted so badly to scoop some of the liquid up and drink it, but I was too unsure of what it actually was. I would wait it out a little longer.

I scanned the glowing underbrush, trying to pick out anything remotely familiar. The vegetation here looked like someone with a cosmic palette had painted it—leaves shimmered with pearlescent sheens, and berries glowed faintly, like bioluminescent jewels. Beautiful? Yes. Safe to eat? Absolutely not.

"Yeah, because radioactive fruit is definitely how I want to go out," I grumbled as I crouched beside a strange vine that twisted up from the red moss like it had grown under moonlight instead of the sun. Its leaves were broad and spade-shaped, edged in a faint glow that pulsed rhythmically. Tiny hairs lined the stems, catching the ambient light and giving them a haloed shimmer. Hanging low from the vine were clusters of iridescent berries, each no bigger than a marble but impossibly vibrant, their surfaces swirling with multiple colors like oil on water. Some were a deep opalescent purple; others shimmered in hues of orange and yellow. They looked soft to the touch, ripe and heavy, but something about them felt deeply wrong. They didn't belong in any ecosystem I recognized. They looked like they belonged in a sci-fi movie or even a cursed fairy tale where one bite steals your name or swaps your soul for something ancient.

I laughed at myself and then glanced down at the pendant hanging from my neck. The copper spiral was warm and pulsing gently, as if it could sense my doubt. I missed the desert. I missed my Jeep. Hell, I even missed Vincent's terrible instant coffee. No—I didn't miss him, just the illusion of stability, and maybe the bad coffee.

My stomach growled again, and I reached out, hesitating just before my fingers brushed one of the berries. Eventually, I would need to eat, so I had to try something. I comforted myself with the fact that I could easily spit it out if it were awful.

"I wouldn't eat that," said a voice from behind me. "Unless you want to spend the night puking your insides into the moss."

I froze, hand mid-air.

The voice was feminine, but slightly raspy. It wasn't hoarse but textured, like it had weathered some things and come out steadier for it. I turned fast, ready to face whatever strange being this place had conjured up.

What I wasn't ready for was *her*.

She stood tall—maybe five-eight—with bronzed caramel skin that shimmered softly in the half-light, not glowing, just radiant. Her Afro was a cascade of tightly wound coils that extended over her slim shoulders and down to her waistline, a dark, dense halo that framed her face with effortless gravity. She wore a sleeveless top, woven from tightly braided cotton with an intricate and utilitarian texture, like rope softened by time. Horizontal stripes ran across the fabric in shifting shades of purple: soft lavender, dusky plum, smoky amethyst, and deep violet. The v-neckline dipped just enough to reveal the graceful slope of her collarbone. It hugged her trim torso with ease. She wore deep wine-colored jeans, and I noticed the subtle strength in her arms as she stepped forward. The way her muscles moved—fluid, quiet, and powerful, like she didn't need to prove herself but could knock you flat if she wanted. Bracelets of braided cord and crystal adorned one wrist. On her right shoulder, the edge of a tattoo curved into view, a raven or a crow, etched in black ink with feathers trailing into lines of script I didn't recognize.

She didn't look threatening, though. If anything, she felt like something sacred, resembling a guardian you'd stumble across in a myth.

"Uh... thanks for the warning," I said, voice catching a bit as I stood. "I've been trying to figure out if anything here won't poison me. Are you, uh... are you from around here?"

Her dark brown eyes found mine and held. There was something almost knowing behind them. Could she see the bruises in my heart without asking where they came from? I wanted to ask her if she was human but figured I would find out soon enough.

"I'm not," she said, voice softening. "My name's Sasha Kahn. I'm from Guyana." She looked around her and added, "From Earth. I feel I need to clarify that."

Earth. My knees went weak with relief.

"I'm Dr. Alayna Archuleta," I said. "From Arizona." I took a deep breath and exhaled. "I also need to clarify that I'm from Earth."

Her eyes flickered with recognition. "Arizona. Southwest, right? Near California?"

I nodded. "I'm an archaeologist. I was working in Sonora, Mexico, before I got... sucked into whatever this is."

"I woke up near a waterfall," offered Sasha, "and I've been wandering ever since."

"I woke up on top of that cliff back there," I said. "I found this river." I jerked my thumb toward the flowing mass a few feet from me. "I've been following it and contemplating drinking from it, but the jury is still out on that one."

We stood in silence for a moment. Two strangers in a world that made no sense, eyeing each other like mirrors tilted at strange angles.

"How long have you been here?" I asked.

"No clue," she replied. "Time's weird. It feels like it stretches when you're alone and collapses when you move. I want to say almost a day, but time feels long when you've been thrown onto another plane of existence, so I'm not entirely sure."

"Sounds about right." I took a breath and looked at the berries again. "So... what do people eat here?"

She smirked and walked past me, gently brushing the berries with the back of her hand. "Not these. They'll mess with your gut and your dreams. There's a root I've found a few times. Doesn't taste great, but it doesn't kill you."

I followed her, a little stunned by how easily she seemed to glide through this strange place, as if she was born from this land or at least belonged here more than I did.

"Do you know what this place is?" I asked, catching up.

She paused. "No. But it feels old, and not in a ruined way. And alive, like it's watching."

I swallowed. "I'm glad I'm not the only one who feels that way."

"Me too," she said, glancing sideways at me. "Feels better not to be alone, doesn't it?"

Our eyes locked again. This time, something unspoken passed between us. It could be the relief, or perhaps the quiet understanding that neither of us had signed up for this, but we were in it now. At least we were experiencing it together.

We stopped near a silver tree, just far enough from the berry bush to feel safe. The twilight never lifted. I couldn't tell if it was evening or morning since it was just the same muted hush blanketing the world. But at least now, I wasn't alone.

Sasha walked ahead of me, her steps sure as we picked our way across the mossy earth and roots that wound like sleeping serpents beneath our feet. "We should find somewhere to sleep before we both fall flat on our faces," she said, glancing over her shoulder at me.

Not long after, we came across the first strange place—a hill covered in tall, reed-like grasses that swayed despite the stillness in the air. When the wind passed through, the stalks sang—not just rustling—singing. The music was high and eerie, like wind chimes in a dream. I tilted my head, listening.

"It actually sounds like real music," I pointed out with a surprised laugh. "This might be a good place to stop."

Sasha crouched and let her fingers drift through the grasses. "This place is too exposed," she said. "We'd be sitting ducks here."

We moved on.

Next came a field of floating stones—wide, flat boulders suspended a few feet off the ground, bobbing gently in the air like lily pads. Sasha picked up a pebble and tossed it onto one. It dipped slightly, then steadied.

"Creepy," she said, head tilted in contemplation. "Like we're invited for dinner."

"Or sacrifice," I said, hugging myself.

We didn't linger.

Then we found a massive silver tree, hollowed at the base, like something sacred had once lived inside and burned a hole in its heart. A shallow, glowing pool reflected the strange moons above us.

"There are stars in the reflection," I whispered, "but not in the sky."

Sasha looked unsettled. "That's too bizarre for me." She straightened. "I'm not comfortable with this place. Come on."

I trusted her instincts for now, so we kept going until we reached a grove of the silver-skinned trees.

Willow-like vines hung from branches so high I couldn't see them, glowing in gentle shades of lavender, turquoise, and seafoam green. The scent in the air was strange but soothing—night-blooming flowers and something like rain on warm stone.

Sasha pushed aside the vines and stepped through. I followed her into the soft, mossy hollow within. As soon as we entered, the vines drifted back into place behind us. The outside sounds faded, like the world had stepped back and left us in a hush.

"I vote we sleep here," Sasha said.

"Agreed."

I dropped my pack on the ground, and Sasha set down a small bundle she had tied to her belt. A small stone knife fell out of the bundle. I raised an eyebrow at the sight of the knife. "I found this near the waterfall," she explained. "I think it's obsidian. It was sharp enough to cut these." She pointed at the bundle, which was a bag made of hand-woven leaves and twisted vines that she must have created.

The moss beneath my hands was springy and warm, almost unnaturally comfortable. I let myself sink into it, stretching my sore legs.

"I think this place chose us," I said, brushing my fingers along one of the glowing vines. It felt alive, pulsing faintly beneath my touch.

"Let's hope it stays friendly."

Sasha opened the bundle of thick, twisted roots wrapped in woven leaves. "Remember that root I told you about? I found a lot of it tucked beneath one of those obsidian spires. Smells earthy, not sweet or slimy. Do you want to try it?"

She cut a piece in half with the stone blade and offered it to me. "You first."

I narrowed my eyes but smiled. "How noble of you." I took a bite. It was bitter and chewy, but it settled in my stomach with a warm, grounding weight. "Not too bad. It has the texture of a beet, but the chewiness of cooked oatmeal."

We sat in silence for a few moments, eating. "Where did you get that blade, again?" I asked, eyeing the jagged edge.

Sasha shrugged. "I made it from the river stones. The crimson ones sharpen easily if you know how."

I reached out and she handed it to me. Surprised by its weight when I turned it over in my hand, I inspected it as it glittered faintly.

"They're not just pretty," Sasha added, watching me carefully. "Something in them stays sharp longer than I thought they would."

"It's really stunning," I complimented her. "You did a great job sculpting it."

"Thank you." She wiped it on her pants and then tucked it away in her belt.

We shared the rest of the roots silently, chewing as the glowing vines swayed overhead. When I looked down to adjust my pendant, Sasha suddenly froze.

"Hey," she said, voice quieter than usual. "That spiral. Where did you get it from?"

I followed her gaze to my chest. My pendant pulsed faintly in the low light, the carved spiral maze glinting.

"My mother gave it to me as a present," I said, hesitating. "It means a lot to me."

She reached up and pulled down the neckline of her sleeveless top just enough to reveal a black tattoo above her heart. I sat up straighter.

It was the exact same spiral pattern. My skin prickled.

"I dreamed it," Sasha said. "About a year ago. I was walking through a carved labyrinth, massive and ancient. I felt like I was being watched, but not in a threatening way. I woke up and sketched the symbol, then had it tattooed here so I would never forget it."

I stared at her. "You dreamed the exact symbol I have on my pendant?"

"Seems like it."

"Do you ever feel like some things are planted in you before you even understand them?" I asked.

"All the time," she replied.

We lay back, the moss cradling us like a living bed. The vines above us made no sound. Something shifted through the grasses somewhere in the distance, but the grove remained still. I probably should have panicked, but oddly, I felt safe.

"So," I said, "where were you before this?"

"Kaieteur Falls," Sasha answered. "It's in Guyana—the tallest single-drop waterfall in the world. I flew in from Georgetown and stayed with the Rewa community at this eco-lodge. They protect the river and its creatures. I saw arapaimas, giant spiders, and frogs that fit in your fingernail.

It's sacred ground. The falls are named after Chief Kai—he sacrificed himself by paddling over the edge to save his people. According to legend, it appeased the great spirit Makonaima."

She paused. "That whole place feels... thin. Like something's pressing against the other side of the world, just waiting to bleed through."

"Is that when it happened?"

"Yeah. I saw a spiral of light in the sky. Everything smelled like rain and old earth. Next thing I knew, I was here."

I swallowed. "I know it's not logical, but I think this might be another realm."

"Could be. Maybe a spirit world," she guessed. "Where time is sideways and the rules are new."

We sat in silence for a long moment, the soft hum of glowing vines the only sound between us. Then I asked quietly, "Do you miss your home?"

Sasha let out a slow breath, like she'd been holding it for hours.

"Honestly? I never really fit in there. My family... they love me, I guess, but they never understood me. I was always the weird one. Always too intense, too curious, too restless. I think they wanted me to settle down, pick something safe, and be someone grounded, but I couldn't. I felt like I was always pressing up against a wall nobody else could see." She looked away, her gaze lost in the violet haze. "Maybe that's why I ended up here. Maybe that wall finally broke."

I nodded slowly, surprised by how much that mirrored my own path. "I know what you mean. I was always chasing answers—buried ruins, ancient scripts, anything that hinted at a bigger picture. I thought if I just found the right fragment, I could decode the truth. But now... I wonder if I was asking questions meant for another world entirely." My voice caught a little. "I left so much behind. My students, my friends... my family. I didn't even get to say goodbye. And now I'm here, in a place I don't understand, under a sky that doesn't feel real, just trying to make sense of it all."

Sasha leaned back. "It's strange," she said softly. "Back home, I always felt like I didn't belong. But here? As terrifying as it is... it almost feels like this is where I'm supposed to be, even though I don't know where that is. Isn't that crazy?"

"Do you think we're supposed to do something here?" I asked, my voice barely above a whisper. My chest heaved as the realization materialized.

She turned to look at me, her dark eyes reflecting the lavender glow of the moons. "Yeah. I'm not sure why I feel this way, but I think we are."

I swallowed as my heart rate quickened at the thought. "I don't know what it is yet... but I don't think we're here by accident."

"Me neither," she said. And in that moment, the silence between us wasn't empty—it was waiting.

We sat in the silence together for a few moments, watching the vines shimmer.

"We need to find water first thing when we wake up," Sasha said at last, breaking the quiet. "We should try to make something—a bowl, maybe a knife and spoon. Anything useful. We don't know how long we'll be out here."

I nodded, my eyelids already drooping. "Good idea."

"We should get some rest. Who knows what we'll need our strength for tomorrow?"

I murmured my agreement, and we exchanged quiet good-nights. As I turned onto my side, I marveled at how surprisingly comfortable this makeshift bed was—like the ground itself had softened just enough to cradle me. We propped our bags under our heads like pillows. It wasn't what I'd call comfortable, but it was better than nothing.

But sleep didn't come easily. My mind buzzed with thoughts—of home, my dig site, my mother, and the stranger lying beside me with my pendant inked into her skin. Could I trust her?

I wasn't sure, but I was glad not to be alone.

My hand curled around the spiral at my throat. The vines above swayed like guardians, whispering lullabies I couldn't quite hear.

Please let this place be kind.

3

THE ARTIST AND THE ASHBEAST

Something tickled my face. I woke up with a start and brushed at my cheek. It wasn't a spider, thank god. It was a leaf. It had fluttered down from the canopy above. A slow-motion reminder that this wasn't a dream. The world, if you could even call it that, was still cast in soft violet twilight. This place didn't seem to care much for the whole day-and-night routine. But then, twilight always was my favorite time of evening, so I could deal with that. Still, I was already missing sunsets.

Nearby, Sasha stirred, her long limbs stretching out over the mossy forest floor. "Is it morning?" she murmured sleepily.

I rubbed sleep from my eyes. "Who knows? Do we even have mornings here?"

Sasha sat up and twisted her thick black curls into a loose knot. "My body says it's time to start moving. How about you?"

"Same," I said, pulling myself up with a satisfying yawn. I felt like I had just had the best sleep in a very long time. I glanced around, considering the eerie silence. There were no apparent threats, just oversized flowers that reminded me of fairy tales. "What time do you think it is back home?"

Sasha looked up through the canopy. "It's hard to say. Maybe late morning?"

I nodded slowly. "So, like… back in Tucson, it would be three hours earlier than Guyana, right? That means it's probably still early morning for me. But for you, it'd be closer to noon."

"Yeah," Sasha said, rubbing her arms. "We're in completely different time zones, but it doesn't matter here. The sky doesn't even look real."

I glanced at the three moons still faintly visible through the lavender haze above us. "It's messing with my sense of time. I keep expecting to hear birds or traffic or something familiar."

"Instead, we get enchanted flowers and silence that feels like it's listening."

Sasha's comment brought me back to my own reality. I tried to picture my place in Tucson. Was Heidi trying to call me? Was my department at the university sending out frantic emails? Were my parents wondering why I hadn't checked in?

"Do you think anyone knows we're gone yet?" I asked, wondering if Sasha was feeling the same way. I wanted to get to know her. I mean, I had little choice since she was the only other person here. But she did intrigue me. She seemed so strong and confident, and I admired her muscular physique when she wasn't looking. Heidi would have called it *'comparanoia.'*

Sasha gave a sad smile. "My best friend, Natalia, probably thinks I'm on some last-minute yoga retreat. She'd give me 72 hours before calling my mom."

I chuckled weakly. "My best friend, Heidi, would start a search party by hour six. Maybe even four."

"Do you have any pets?" Sasha asked, alarm reaching her dark brown eyes.

"Yes. A gray kitten, about 6 months old, named Kiva. One of my colleagues who lives nearby is taking care of her. Do you? Have pets, I mean?"

"Nope, just a ton of plants. They're probably thriving without me hovering. They're very hearty. I hope I get back to rescue them before they give up on life, though."

We packed up the few supplies we had—basically, ourselves and our wits. Hunger gnawed at my stomach, and my tongue felt like it had been sandpapered. "I guess water, food, and shelter are our top priorities. I feel like we're on some kind of survival show."

Sasha nodded, "Let's head toward that ridge over there." She pointed through a dense curtain of vines. "I'm too nervous to try and drink from that strange river. It looks radioactive, but I swear I heard some rushing sounds like water in the opposite direction. I say we try that way first."

I agreed. I wasn't a stranger to surviving in harsh conditions, but Sasha seemed to have a better sense of this place, and it was nice not having to be the one to lead all the time, so I followed in silence.

We moved cautiously, stepping over gnarled silver roots and ducking under glowing fern fronds. The air smelled green, damp, and oddly sweet, like a mix of crushed herbs and alyssum.

"Sasha, what do you think this place is?" I asked, breaking the silence as we skirted some tall obsidian spires.

She hesitated. "I don't know. But it feels like this place has a mysterious personality. We ought to be very watchful."

Thinking of the land having a personality gave me chills. We kept walking until the sound of water grew louder, and then suddenly, we found it—a crystalline stream, glinting with soft blue light like moonlight trapped in motion. I dropped to my knees and cupped water into my hands.

"Just take a tiny mouthful to make sure it doesn't taste metallic," Sasha warned as she knelt beside me in relief.

"Oh, my god," I said between small gulps. "This is probably the best-tasting water I've ever had."

Sasha sipped, then closed her eyes. "It seems very fresh and pure. I hope we can trust it."

We refilled our water bottles before scouting for food. Not far from the water, we discovered strange, melon-sized fruits growing from low bushes. They were salmon-pink, smooth, and smelled like citrus and honey.

"Do you think it's safe?" I asked, eyeing one to my left. My mouth watered just thinking about sinking my teeth into it. I suddenly felt a little weak as I gave in to my hunger.

Sasha crouched and closed her eyes, pressing her hands lightly over one. "The energy feels good, not aggressive."

"Not aggressive? You make it sound like it might attack us."

She smirked. "I'm not sensing anything like that."

We peeled back the thick outer layer and took a small bite. The texture was creamy like banana with a tangy kick. My stomach purred with gratitude. "This is actually really good," I commented as I took another bite. "I could get addicted to this."

"Everything in moderation," Sasha cautioned. "It looks like there are many of them," she pointed out as she stood and looked further ahead. I decided to stash two in my daypack, and Sasha added one to her rope bag.

As we walked deeper into the jungle, we fell into a rhythm. The vines hung like drapery, in almost every shade imaginable, and the trees curved in impossible shapes. Every now and then, something rustled above or scampered across the path, but we didn't actually see what creatures were lurking.

"So," Sasha said, brushing a strange-looking beetle the size of her palm off her shoulder, "what do you think happened? How did you get here?"

"I came through a portal," I said. "I was on an archeological dig site. It opened near a carved spiral, like your tattoo and my pendant. It was almost as if the portal reached out and sucked me through. I didn't even have time to react."

"That sounds like the same portal I came through," Sasha murmured, pausing briefly. "It was like nothing I've ever experienced."

I looked at her. "Does your tattoo ever glow?"

She nodded. "Yes, want to see it?"

I tried not to blush. "Yes. I'm curious on a professional basis."

Sasha grinned and tugged her collar to the side. The spiral was there, just like the one on my pendant. My pulse skipped. What were the odds? "May I touch it?"

She hesitated before saying "I suppose so."

I slowly traced my finger over it. The tattoo itself was slightly raised like a scar. It felt warm to the touch, and I looked down at my pendant. It was glowing in response.

Sasha's eyes widened in disbelief. "I think it's reacting to you."

"It's reacting to *us*," I corrected her.

A faint hum vibrated through my fingertips, as if the spiral beneath her skin echoed something ancient—something alive. She held perfectly still, her breath shallow.

"I can't believe I dreamed it months before I ever saw your pendant," she said softly.

My throat tightened. "I wonder what this all means?"

"I'm don't know," she admitted, her voice trembling. "But it can't just be a coincidence."

We stood there, connected by a symbol neither of us could explain, in a place that made no sense.

We both fell silent until I asked, "Do you think we're supposed to be here?"

Sasha didn't answer right away. "I don't know, but something or someone wants us here. Before meeting you, I kept hearing these soft sounds in the breeze, as if someone were whispering. It was the oddest thing."

"That's not creepy at all," I said sarcastically as I breathed deeply. I had to admit to myself at least that I had heard whispers on the wind both here and back in Sonora.

A sudden chittering noise made us stop. My heart jumped into my throat as my eyes locked with Sasha's. Neither one of us was breathing.

In the underbrush, a trio of small creatures emerged. They had iridescent silver and black fur, too many pink eyes, and long fingers tipped with opalescent claws. They stood on hind legs, stared at us, then chattered among themselves in a rhythm that felt almost like laughter. Then, as quickly as they came, they were gone.

"Did... did they just *gossip* about us?" I asked, bewildered by what I'd just seen.

"One hundred percent," Sasha agreed, her eyes still wide.

A whooshing sound above made us both look up. Massive, dragon-like birds glided overhead, wings spanning easily twenty feet or more. They didn't seem to notice us, but the sight made me shiver.

"Still want to be chosen?" I asked quietly.

"Less and less by the minute," came her response, though she was still looking up in awe. "I mean, were those actually *dragons?*"

"I don't know, but I half expect Toothless to come out of the bushes," I joked as I scoured the space around us.

We walked in uneasy silence before Sasha asked, "Do you think we'll ever get back home?"

I sighed. "I sure hope so. I hate not knowing what is in store for us here. My whole life is schedules, grants, digs, and lectures. Now it's simply survival. There has to be a way out of here."

"I run my own business," she said. "My days are clients, workshops, lessons, and retreats. My calendar was booked solid."

"Did we just vanish? Do you think this is another planet or a different realm?"

Sasha's jaw clenched. "I don't know which would be worse. Neither sounds like it would be easy to get home from."

I slowed, staring at my boots. "My ex, Vincent, would probably spin this into a conspiracy."

Sasha was quiet momentarily, then nudged a pebble with her boot. "Do you mind if I ask... what happened with Vincent?"

I looked away, eyes tracing the trees ahead that swayed despite there being no wind. "It's not a fun story."

"You don't have to tell me if you don't want to," Sasha said, understanding in her voice.

I hesitated. The thought of dredging up old pain made my chest tighten, but there was something steady about Sasha. I only felt curiosity coming from her, not judgment.

"It's fine," I said softly. "We broke up a year ago. He's an archaeological scientist who is particularly interested in the chemistry and physics aspects of the field. He could tell you what a shard of pottery was made of, down to the molecule."

Sasha nodded slowly. "Sounds impressive."

"He is, or was, rather, but was also manipulative as hell." I swallowed hard. "He made me doubt myself constantly. He was always so charming in public, but behind closed doors? Everything was my fault. He twisted my words and made me feel like I was being dramatic or unreasonable for reacting to his childish behaviors."

Sasha walked beside me, quiet but close.

"I didn't even realize how deeply it affected me until after I left," I continued. "He never hit me. It wasn't that kind of abuse. It was psychological—slow erosion. I should be over it by now, but, well, sometimes I know I'm still… recovering from the toxic relationship."

"I'm really sorry you had to go through that," Sasha said gently. "You didn't deserve it."

"Thanks," I sighed. "The point is, I'm not looking for any romantic drama right now. I just want to focus on what I'm building, my career, and my independence."

"Makes sense. You don't have to prove anything to anyone," Sasha commented firmly.

I gave her a small smile. "I only need to worry about my own opinion."

"I'm glad you were smart enough to get out," Sasha shook her head.

"It took me far too long to see it. Vincent was self-involved, charismatic, and disrespectful as hell. It was a dangerous combination."

She was quiet for a moment. "My ex, Leroy, was far too childish. He needed a mother, not a partner. I don't miss him."

"You deserve better, too," I mirrored her words back to her.

"It was easy to break up with him once I realized he wasn't the kind of person I saw myself building a mature life with. I'm not even sure why I stayed with him for two years," she volunteered.

Something warm settled between us as we walked and talked.

"Are you close with your family?" I asked. Trying to get to know Sasha better was taking my mind off the fact that my life may be changed forever since I 'dropped' onto this plane of existence. The thought twisted my stomach and brought on a feeling of anxiety. I quickly pushed it down, knowing it wouldn't help me get through this.

"Very tight. My mom's a herbalist, and my dad used to teach Eastern philosophy. They both taught me a lot of what I know now. I don't have any siblings, which is something I always regretted growing up. I think I felt like I was missing something. You?"

"My parents are both educators too," I said. "My dad teaches high school history, and my mom's a librarian at a community college in New Mexico. My family's Southwest through and through. My little sister, Julia, is probably telling everyone I got abducted by aliens."

"Oh my god!" Sasha gasped as she stopped walking and stared at me. "I never even considered that. You don't think…"

I reached out and touched her arm, hoping to calm her. Her skin was warm and soft. I half expected her to pull back, but she didn't, and I was glad I hadn't invaded her personal space. "If that were the case, I imagine we would be getting poked and observed in some operating room."

"I guess you're right." She seemed to relax, and we kept moving.

We stepped over a fallen tree slick with blue moss. The forest smelled richer here, and the air warmer. I felt sweat trickle down my back, but it wasn't from heat. I think my nerves were just getting the better of me.

"Do you ever think about our life's purpose?" Sasha asked.

"Constantly. That was my whole thesis: that ancient symbols still carry meaning today, and that we need to reconnect with them."

"Maybe this is the universe's way of saying you were right."

It was an interesting thought that stayed with me until we stopped for a small break. We both took a long pull from our water bottles.

"It's so strange that this place never seems to get darker or lighter, like we are forever in twilight. It can't be a planet since we'd have to be rotating, right? Unless this is the dark side of a planet that doesn't rotate. Like the Moon. I hope we don't get a vitamin D deficiency without any sunlight," I commented out loud.

"I never even thought of that." She looked around. "We could walk for days and not know how much time has passed."

"Hopefully, this isn't all that is here. I really hope we stumble on a town or something," I tried to sound confident. "Let's just take it one step at a time."

Sasha's presence grounded me. Her calm was like an anchor, and I didn't even realize I needed it. I could feel the weight of the unknown pressing in from all sides, but it didn't feel so impossible to bear with her beside me.

"Hey," I said. "Thanks for being pulled into your portal so I don't have to be here alone."

She smiled. "Likewise, Alayna. It's been nice getting to know you. I am glad I'm not doing this on my own."

After what seemed to be about thirty minutes of walking, we heard the scream before we saw anything. It was sharp, panicked, and *human*.

Sasha and I locked eyes.

"Someone's in trouble," she said, already moving.

We sprinted through the underbrush, crashing through slick ferns and vines. The jungle thinned into a mossy glade, quiet in a way that made my skin crawl. The air smelled like something nearby was burning.

And then I saw her—a red-haired woman standing in the clearing, surrounded by writhing black smoke and a monster straight out of a nightmare. Its limbs looked like black twisted bone, all jagged edges and spasms. It moved wrong, too fast and almost stiff, like a puppet missing strings.

The woman didn't have a weapon—just a palette knife gripped tight in her hand, glowing with a strange pearly light.

"What the hell?" I breathed as my heart jack-knifed.

Sasha didn't answer; she just charged. Her tattoos shimmered, a faint pulse of blue under her skin. I followed, grabbing the thickest branch I could find.

The creature whipped its head toward us. Its face was hollow, stretched into a permanent scream. My pendant flared—white-hot against my chest—and the branch in my hands started to glow with it.

"Go for the legs!" the woman shouted as soon as she noticed us. Her voice was high but strong.

Sasha sliced through the air, her river stone blade catching a limb mid-strike. It screeched, flickering like smoke, and lunged toward me.

I swung the branch as hard as I could. It connected with a cracking jolt. A ripple of light shot through it, and the creature staggered backward.

"What *is* this thing?" I yelled.

"Deadly!" the redhead snapped, dancing around a tendril. "It came out of my painting."

"Excuse me?"

"I didn't mean to draw it. It just came into my mind like a flash. The painting's unfinished, but the magic's too unstable!"

Magic painting? Sure. Why not? Maybe I'd passed out in the Sonoran Desert, and this was one extended asphyxia-fueled hallucination. Hallucination or not, that beast was coming for me.

Sasha moved, positioning herself between me and the creature, like she'd done this before. Each strike of her blade glimmered. Her hair whipped in the wind, and her muscles were sharp with focus. She shouted, "Alayna, hit it again just below its knees while I'm distracting it!"

I did what she said. The branch lit up brighter this time as I slammed it into the monster's shins. It screamed—no, *cracked*, like something inside it had just shattered.

The redhead darted forward, slashing her glowing palette knife in a clean arc, hitting it right in the chest. And then the thing just unraveled. It didn't die—it dissolved—like someone had blown out a candle made of smoke. Thin black ribbons floated upward, twisting toward the murky sky, and then dissipated, just like that.

Silence dropped over us as our chests heaved.

I leaned on my knees, gasping. My whole body shook with adrenaline. "Okay," I panted. "Okay. What. The actual. Hell. Was that?"

The redhead straightened, brushing ash off her arms. "Thanks for jumping in. I didn't expect it to come out until I finished the painting." Her accent caught me off guard—soft but unmistakably Scottish, each word laced with a rhythm I wasn't expecting.

"You say it came out of your painting. What does that even mean?" I asked, slowly regaining my composure.

She pointed at a small canvas propped against a stone nearby. It was a strange, unfinished painting—dark, abstract, and glowing faintly. "I paint things," she said slowly, "and sometimes they… come alive."

I stared in disbelief. "Alive?" I croaked and took another breath.

Sasha smiled, wide and a little wild. "We don't even know where we are," she told the woman. "But if you can *summon* monsters with your painting, perhaps you could paint us a map next?"

The woman laughed—a tired, breathless sound. "The name's Blair. Blair Grindall."

"Alayna Archuleta," I said, voice still shaky. "This is Sasha."

"Sasha Kahn," Sasha finished.

Blair gave us a look like she wasn't sure if she should be relieved or more alarmed.

I didn't blame her.

Whatever this place was... we weren't in Arizona—or Guyana—or anywhere *normal* anymore.

4

THE FOREST THAT BINDS

We walked silently for a while, our boots crunching over a hard bed of moss and broken silver twigs. The air smelled wet and green. Somewhere behind us, the wind whispered through those massive, twisted trees. At least the creature Blair had summoned, or released, was gone.

My shirt clung to my back with dried sweat and dirt. Sasha walked just ahead, her tall frame purposeful, her arms swinging with that same fluid control she used when she fought. Blair trailed beside me, quiet. Her clear blue eyes kept flicking toward the artist's tote bag at her side, where the edge of a charred canvas peeked out.

Eventually, I broke the silence.

"Are you alright?"

Blair gave a slight nod. "As okay as I can be after unleashing a monster I've never seen before and almost getting us all killed." Her voice was soft, but not fragile. Her Scottish accent was charming. I had always wanted to visit both Scotland and Ireland. Maybe if we ever got back home, I'd prioritize that.

I glanced at her. "You said it came from your painting. You didn't mean that metaphorically, did you?"

"No." She slowed, then stopped. Sasha turned and waited, arms folded, listening.

Blair unsnapped her tote bag and pulled out the canvas. The edges were scorched, the center smeared with wild strokes of shadow and teeth. A thing with too many limbs and a twisted grin still clawed its way across the surface, frozen mid-lunge.

"I didn't create it on purpose," Blair said. "It just… happened. It was like I had no control over what I was painting."

"You didn't draw it from memory?" I asked.

Blair shook her head, her eyes the clear blue of sea glass, looking at the painting as if it might move again. "I'd never seen that thing before in my life. I was sketching something abstract at first—lines, shapes, nothing specific—and then it felt like something crawled into my head. I don't remember finishing it. I was distracted for a moment, and the next thing I knew, it was growling at me."

"That's terrifying," Sasha said as she approached us.

Blair hesitated, then pushed up the sleeve of her shirt. A red birthmark was on the inside of her left arm, near the elbow. I could barely believe my eyes: it was the same spiral maze.

I stared. My fingers went instinctively to the cool metal at my chest. "Where did you get that?"

"I was born with it," she said. "I always thought it was just a weird birthmark. The doctors said it didn't mean anything."

Sasha stepped closer. "I have the same one. Mine's a tattoo, though." She pulled the fabric aside to uncover the spot over her heart. "I saw it in a dream, and it felt... sacred. So, I added it to my collection of inked birds."

Blair exhaled, then looked between us. "I didn't come through the painting." She paused and took a breath. "I came through, don't laugh... I came through what I think was a portal, two nights ago." She looked up at the never-ending twilight sky. "At least I think it was two days ago. I can't tell because there doesn't seem to be night and day here. I was painting near the glen when the air split open. It was like a shimmer—like the canvas tore and I fell through it."

Sasha let out a slow breath. "So, you were pulled here just like us."

"Exactly like us," I said, adding, "I have no idea where we are now."

We all fell silent again. Around us, the woods were beginning to thin, the trees giving way to sloping hills covered in waist-high silver grass. The sky overhead was dusky lavender, and the three moons were still visible, stacked like bruises fading into each other.

"I just know this is definitely not Earth." This time more confident in my statement.

"I keep wondering," Blair said quietly, "if this place chose me."

"Because of your art?" Sasha asked.

Blair nodded. "My canvas reacts to this place. Or maybe the place reacts to it. I can't tell. But it's like everything's charged, and I feel this thrill when I paint, like the land is alive and watching."

"That's how I felt when I meditated before I found Alayna," Sasha said, voice lower. "My tattoos came alive. One of the birds actually *fluttered* on my shoulder. I felt like I was going crazy."

"You're not," I said. "Or if you are, so am I."

They both looked at me. I hesitated, then unclasped the pendant around my neck. "My mom gave this to me long before my trip to Sonora. She said it was handcrafted by a metalworker in Sedona and charged with vortex energy." I turned it in my palm so the spiral maze caught the light. "As crazy as it sounds, I think this… opened something."

"Great," Sasha sighed. "So, we've got a painter, a healer, and an archaeologist—all pulled through spirals."

"It's like we're part of the same pattern," Blair said, more to herself than to us.

We kept walking, the grass brushing against our legs, soft and cold. I noticed Blair still looked uneasy, like the painting had left something inside her that hadn't quite settled.

"You said it got into your head," I prompted gently.

She nodded. "It was like… a whisper but not words exactly, just an emotion. I don't know how, but I felt rage and hunger. I think that's what I painted. Not the creature, but the emotions. And this place, wherever we are, gave it a shape."

A chill skittered down my spine. "That's not how painting works."

"I know," she whispered.

Sasha looked up at the moons. "We have a little water now, but we need to find shelter, food, and people, or at least *something*. Whatever civilization might look like here."

"Agreed," I said. "But until then… we stick together."

Blair gave a hesitant smile. "You really don't think I'm crazy?"

"Lady," I said dryly, "I just survived a fight with a monster from a painting while standing under three moons in a world that feels like a fever dream. Crazy is relative."

Sasha laughed, the sound unexpectedly warm. "Okay, Explorer. What's the plan?"

"We keep walking," I said. "We ask questions. And we talk. If this place is real, we need to understand it and each other."

Blair walked beside me now, her steps steadier. "What's your world like, Alayna? Before all this?"

I took a breath. "Hot and dusty. I live in Tucson, Arizona. I'm an archaeology professor, so when I'm not lecturing. I was working in Sonora before I landed here. My life was mostly dirt, research papers, and arguing with grant boards. But I loved it."

"Any family?" Blair asked.

"Yeah. Mom, Dad, and a younger sister, Julia. They all live near Albuquerque, New Mexico. And my best friend Heidi, who lives in San Diego—she's the one I do girls' trips with. She'd kill me if she knew I vanished without inviting her along."

We all laughed at that one.

"I keep thinking about my parents, too," Sasha said. "And my friend Natalia. She'll be worried sick. Probably already rallied a search party."

Blair sighed. "My brother's probably pacing the cottage, wondering if I ran off to paint the entire world. He always knew I was a bit weird."

"Same," I mumbled. "People don't blink when archaeologists wander into caves, but something else happened here. In this scenario, I disappeared. I hope someone noticed."

"Going on our discussion earlier. What if we really were abducted by aliens?" Sasha said suddenly. "What if we're not even alive in our world anymore?"

Blair stopped walking. "That would be really bad. We need to figure out how to get back."

I glanced at the horizon. "Or we figure out why we were brought here in the first place."

We stood there momentarily, three women with spiral marks and many questions. The air buzzed faintly, like the realm itself was listening. I couldn't shake the feeling that something had started, an unwinding of sorts, and we were standing right at the epicenter.

The forest had been thick for hours, each step a fight through roots, brambles, and hanging vines from the silver trees that seemed intent on slowing us down. Heat pressed against my skin like a wet cloth, and every breath tasted of moss and rot. We were deep in what seemed like a thicket.

Sasha stopped walking. "Hold on," she said, crouching near a tangle of moss at the base of one of the obsidian spires.

I turned, wiping my arm across my damp forehead. "What is it?"

She didn't answer right away. Her hand reached into the warm red sand, and when she stood again, something glittered between her fingers—a crystal the size of a cherry, translucent blue, and laced with thin silver veins. It shimmered faintly, like moonlight caught under water. She held it up to her eye.

"Whoa," she whispered.

Blair leaned in, her fingers brushing Sasha's arm. "What is that?"

Sasha looked dazed, like she'd just seen something too beautiful to describe. "It feels alive and pulsing, a magical egg with the glow of moonlight inside it."

"Let me see," I said. She passed it to me carefully, and I turned it in the light. The core fractured into shifting patterns of silver and blue, dancing like reflections in a river. It was ice-cold against my skin, with several pointed edges, though its surface was smooth. "It's gorgeous, not like any crystal I've seen before, and seems to be sticking with the 'silver' glowing theme here." I handed it back.

"It's beautiful," Blair said, eyes wide with awe. "It looks like a star that fell out of the sky."

Sasha didn't say anything else. She just slipped it into her pocket, fingers lingering, and then we moved on.

The forest changed. The deeper we went, the more it pressed in—not just the plants, but the air itself, tightening around us like a net. That was when I noticed—a flicker of motion in the corner of my eye, and then another. Something wasn't right.

The vines were *moving,* but there was no wind. Long stalks, silver and green, began to twitch from the underbrush. One uncoiled and shot toward Blair's leg.

"Move!" I shouted at her quickly.

She yelped and jumped back as it struck the ground where her foot had been. Another vine hissed past me, so close I felt the air shift. Its tip glistened with a thick, light gray liquid that sizzled as it hit the red sand.

"They're trying to tangle us," my voice tight.

Sasha had already drawn her river blade and slashed through the growth, forcing a narrow path. "I'll cut, but someone needs to keep them distracted!"

Blair dropped to one knee and ripped a canvas from her tote bag. Her brush flew, paint streaking in long, urgent strokes. Within seconds, glowing figures sprang to life—half-formed bodies in motion, radiant with illusion. The vines went for them immediately, snapping at the mirages.

"I've never seen anything like this," I said, ducking a vine that lashed toward my head. My pendant bounced against my chest. I grabbed it instinctively, the cool metal warming against my skin. A nearby vine froze mid-snap, trembling. I pressed the pendant forward, and the stalk recoiled.

"They're responding to this," I said excitedly. "But there are too many!"

One of them caught my ankle while another wrapped around my wrist. I tried to tear free, but they were far too fast. Within seconds, I was tangled in a snare of green and silver, being dragged backward. "Sasha!"

Everything spun. Then there was a sound, like a breath caught between two heartbeats. I twisted to see Sasha frozen mid-step. Her hand closed, she reached into her pocket, and she brought out the crystal. A soft light glowed through her fingers.

It wasn't blue anymore, it was silver. She didn't scream or panic. She just stared at me, calm, steady, and focused.

And then a sharp white light burst out from the crystal, and a wave of radiant frost surged out from where she stood. It swept through the jungle like a breath of winter, flash-freezing everything it touched. The vines stiffened mid-strike, crystallizing in elegant arches. Trees glittered with sudden ice. I felt the grip on my arms dissolve as the vines around me froze solid and shattered like glass when I pulled away.

I dropped to the ground, gasping. The entire jungle had transformed underneath our feet. What was once chaos was now a still, gleaming sanctuary. Every branch, vine, and leaf was encased in silver-blue frost. It was positively breathtaking. Everything was encased in ice like a winter wonderland.

Sasha stood in the center of it all, the crystal in her palm glowing softly, like an ember.

"Are you okay?" she asked me.

I nodded, still catching my breath. "Yeah. I think so."

Blair jumped onto the clearing, eyes wide. "What the hell was that?"

Sasha looked down at the crystal, her brows knit in confusion. "I don't know. I was just so worried the vines would get you two. All I was thinking was that I needed to save you."

I rose to my feet, brushing ice shards from my sleeve. The vines at the edge of the clearing still writhed, but they didn't cross the frost. It was almost as if they couldn't.

"We're safe," I said quietly. "For now."

Blair nodded. "It's like a shield. That could be useful."

There was a feeling of peace and clarity. My thoughts sharpened, and I could think straight for the first time in hours. The three of us stood together, surrounded by glittering stillness, and I couldn't help wondering if it was the crystal or the forest itself that had given us this moment to gather ourselves before it closed in again.

We stared out at the quiet stillness of the frozen clearing, ringed by glittering vines that pulsed and writhed just beyond the frost line. They couldn't reach us, not yet—but I could feel the tension in the air, the moment before glass breaks.

"We need a plan," I said, scanning the forest. "This quiet won't last."

Sasha nodded. "Whatever that crystal did… it bought us time, but I fear it won't last long. We really need to think about how we will get out of here."

Blair stepped forward, her breath puffing in the cold, her porcelain cheeks rosy. "I have an idea."

She pulled a sketchpad out of her tote bag, which was smeared and warped from the damp air. With her thumb, she smeared a streak of glowing paint across a fresh page and began to draw with quick, bold lines. Her hand moved like it knew what to do before she did.

Within seconds, a bridge of light and texture arced from the edge of the clearing across the tangled mass of vines. It didn't look real—more like a watercolor illusion, pale and slightly transparent, with brush-stroked edges that looked like morning fog.

"Do you think that's solid enough to walk on?" I asked, eyebrows raised.

Blair gave a tight smile. "We're about to find out, but we must be fast, as I don't expect it to last long."

Sasha didn't hesitate. She was already moving, boots crunching over the frost, heading for the painted edge. As soon as she stepped onto the bridge, it hardened beneath her feet. I followed. The bridge was solid but strange—like walking on glass with the texture of canvas.

One by one, we stepped tentatively onto it. The frost behind us began to melt when Blair's foot left the clear ice—a slow, creeping thaw.

"Run!" Blair shouted.

We ran as fast as we could, each step making the bridge ripple faintly beneath us. My heart thudded as the path began to unravel behind us, like brushstrokes lifting off the air and dissolving. Sasha was ahead, fast and sure-footed. I was right behind her. I glanced back just once and saw the far end behind Blair—already gone.

"Don't stop!" Blair cried. "It's unraveling faster than I thought!"

The middle held, just barely. But as we neared the opposite side, the far edge of the bridge started to fray, curling upward like burnt paper. Sasha jumped the last few feet onto solid ground, and I leaped after her. Blair's foot landed beside me just as the final piece of the bridge vanished.

We collapsed into a heap, panting and laughing from sheer adrenaline. The jungle behind us boiled with motion as the vines writhed, reaching for us, but it was too late. The bridge was gone, and we were safely out of the thicket.

"Holy shit," Sasha gasped. "Remind me never to doubt your paintings again."

Blair clutched her knees, still catching her breath. "I wouldn't recommend it."

I got to my feet and scanned the terrain. This side of the jungle was somehow denser, darker. The canopy sealed out most of the light, and the shadows felt heavier. Luckily, just ahead, nestled in a rise of moss-covered stone, it looked like there was a cave. A narrow, jagged mouth in the side of the hill was just big enough for us to crawl into.

"Well, that's foreboding," breathed Blair.

"We don't have much choice if we're looking for shelter," I suggested, still trying to catch my breath. "I've explored a lot of caves. If this one's dry and not already occupied, it could be a good place to rest without being disturbed for a while."

We glanced around for other options, and then from the tangle of trees behind us came a new sound—a low, rumbling growl that vibrated the very air. We turned with wild eyes.

And there it was. A creature too massive for logic. It was white with gnarled limbs like tree trunks, its back hunched and plated in bark-like armor. Moss dripped from its haunches, and its face—if you could call it a face—was all shadows and glistening fangs. Its eyes glowed with slow, ancient rage. It didn't chase us; it didn't have to.

We scrambled inside the cave as it lumbered forward, deliberate and terrifying, until it stood right outside the cave mouth. The ceiling was low, and my backpack scraped against damp rock; my heart thudding. I made as much room as possible for Sasha and Blair, then turned to see the creature's eyes glowing dimly through the entrance like twin embers. Thankfully, the thing couldn't follow us—it was too large—but it dropped low and crouched just outside, its eyes twin embers.

It growled, low and restless, as if to tell us we would have to come back out at some point.

"Well, that's comforting," Blair sighed, curling her knees to her chest. "We have our own bodyguard."

We sat silently for a long moment, the sound of the beast's breath a rasp against the jungle's quiet.

Sasha leaned back against the stone and sighed. "We'd better get some rest. We have no idea how much energy we'll need to deal with that thing."

I gave her a look. "You're serious? You can sleep with that thing right there?" My heart was still pounding in my chest.

She shrugged. "Do you have a better idea?"

I didn't. So, we huddled close, using our bags as makeshift pillows. We agreed to take shifts. Sasha fell asleep first, curled like a cat, one hand still resting near the crystal in her pocket.

Blair and I sat shoulder to shoulder in the dark, listening to the slow exhale of the creature outside.

"Any chance it will fall asleep, and we can just inch by it slowly and soundlessly?" I asked, taking a stab in the dark.

Blair shook her head and heaved out a breath. "I don't think so. I don't know, maybe? You can go first." She gave a nervous laugh.

"Thanks. It's nice to know you can use me as bait right after we just met."

Blair laughed. "She's tougher than I thought," Blair said softly, glancing over at the taller woman. "She didn't even flinch when she used that crystal. It's like she just knew what to do."

"Yeah," I agreed with a nod. "She seems to act on instinct."

"She's also got that blade like it's an extension of her arm," Blair added. "I kind of love that about her."

I smiled faintly. "She's got street smarts, that one."

Silence settled again. The cave was narrow but dry, and the rock beneath us was cold but not unbearable.

After a moment, Blair asked, "What did you study before this happened. I mean, I know you said archaeology, but what specifically?"

I hesitated. The answer came slower now, like something from another life. "Mesoamerican civilizations, indigenous cultures. I taught at the University of Arizona. But I do field research as much as I can."

Blair whistled softly. "Wow. So, you're brilliant."

I rolled my eyes. "Depends on who you ask. My students might say otherwise."

"I would've liked to sit in one of your classes," she said. "I went to art school and then started freelancing. I always thought I'd have more time to get serious about things."

I looked at her, this paint-splattered woman with wild red hair and an even wilder imagination. I couldn't help but smile. "I think you're already serious. You're probably the first human on Earth to paint something and have it come alive. How about you paint us a plane so we can get out of here?"

"I guess I could try. There's no harm, right? Do you know how to fly a plane?"

"I was half-joking, but sure, I could give it a whirl."

She shrugged, suddenly shy. "It's weird, right? That we're all here, together like this, in this place."

"Maybe it's fate," I said before I could stop myself, since I've never believed in fate.

Blair glanced at me, then at Sasha sleeping peacefully nearby. "Yeah. That's the word. I'm so glad we ran into each other."

"You mean you're glad we saved your ass?"

She cocked a brow. "I had it handled even before you two arrived, thank you very much."

"I'm glad you'll never have to find out if that were true," I winked, although in the dark she wouldn't have been able to see.

Outside, the creature growled again, but it sounded distant now and less immediate, or maybe I was just too tired to care. "Hey, what happens when you run out of blank canvas?"

"I can just paint white or black over the surface and use it repeatedly," Blair explained. "Or I can switch to the sketchbook I always have in my bag."

"That's good to know. I have a feeling this place will keep trying to kill us."

"Why bring us here only to kill us?" Blair wondered aloud.

"Your guess is as good as mine. Sasha's right. We need some sleep. You go ahead. I'll be good for a while. I will wake Sasha when my eyelids get heavy."

"If you're sure. I am quite tired. Wake me if that thing shrinks and gets inside."

"Seriously? You're going to leave me with a thought like that?"

"I'm just trying to keep you awake, is all," Blair said, and I saw a brief flash of white teeth in a grin.

"Great. I think it will work," I shook my head and added a playful eye roll.

As Blair pulled her knees closer, resting her head lightly on her arms, I kept watch, eyes open, and fear running rampant throughout my body.

5

THE ICEBORN STRANGER

I woke to the sound of something breathing, not just breathing, but *snoring*.

A low, gurgling rasp echoed from the mouth of the cave, so deep and guttural it vibrated the ground beneath me. I froze. For a second, I had no idea where I was. Just darkness, damp air, and the coppery taste of fear on my tongue. Then it all came rushing back—the chase, the cave, the *thing* at the entrance.

I blinked and looked around before I moved a muscle. In the nearly pitch black I could barely make out the shape of Blair curled beside me, her arm draped protectively over her tote bag. Sasha was sitting upright, her brown eyes dark and wide, holding a fistful of moss like a weapon.

"How long have you been up?" I whispered, like time even mattered in this place.

Sasha tilted her head toward the cave opening. "Probably about half an hour." She let the moss drop to the ground.

Blair stirred beside me, her eyes fluttering open as she rolled over to face us. "Is it…" Blair whispered, her voice barely audible, "...still out there?" She sat up as the thought formulated in her brain.

I nodded slowly. "Yeah. Listen."

We all did. All three of us held our breath, leaning toward that ragged rhythm. It was unmistakable and loud.

"It's asleep," I whispered, heart pounding.

Sasha's eyes narrowed. "Snoring."

A second passed. Then we moved—no words, just glances and tiny nods. I slung my pack over one shoulder and rose into a low crouch, my thighs trembling. The cave floor was uneven, slick with condensation, and scattered with moss, a few leaves, and various colors and sizes of rocks. Every tiny sound felt amplified—my breath, the soft brush of fabric, the click of Sasha's bracelets as she steadied herself and tied her rope bag around her waist.

We crept ever so silently toward the entrance. I could feel sweat dripping between my shoulder blades.

Closer.

And then... *closer still.*

There the strange creature was, slumped against the outside of the cave wall, massive and grotesque. Grayish skin stretched over a body that seemed stitched together from different animals—clawed feet, a hunched back, a face that looked almost human if you squinted, but distorted, a nightmare melting. Its mouth hung open, tongue twitching with each exhale. The stench was awful—wet fur, rotting meat, and something acidic.

I covered my nose with my hand, gasping quietly. Blair's blue eyes met mine. She looked like she might pass out. Sasha was already walking toward it.

We edged past it slowly, one at a time. Sasha first— graceful and silent. Then me, and finally Blair, who tiptoed like a ballerina over broken glass. Our escape was just a few paces away now, the light beyond pale and silvery.

We all managed to get past it, and my heart yelled, "We're free!"

Then a sound I would never forget permeated through the air, a gurgle trying to become a scream.

Suddenly, the snoring stopped, and I turned to look over my shoulder. The beast's several eyes were open, wide and blinking. Rage bled into its expression the way black ink spreads through water.

"Run," I hissed, grabbing Blair and Sasha's arms and yanking.

We bolted.

I didn't dare look back. I could hear it—snarling, scrambling to its feet with bone-cracking jerks. The sound of claws scraping stone chased us as we tore through the underbrush, ducking branches, leaping rocks, tripping over roots.

"This is bad! This is really bad!" Blair gasped behind me.

"It's gaining!" I shouted. "We need to find cover and fast!"

"But there's nowhere to go!" Sasha yelled.

I veered left, my lungs on fire. Then—like a gust of wind given wings—they came.

Dozens, maybe hundreds, of tiny creatures burst out from the silver trees around us like a river of light. At first, I thought they were birds. But as they swooped past us, I saw scales glinting, wings like mirror shards, and tails that coiled midair like whips.

They were lizard-like and flying, silver as moonlight. They attacked the beast in a frenzy from every angle—biting, slashing, and swarming it in a cloud of motion and light. The creature let out a guttural shriek and swatted at them, stumbling backward, blinded.

"Keep running!" I screamed, heart in my throat.

We ran and ran for what seemed like fifteen minutes or more.

We collapsed on a flat stretch of stone surrounded by towering silver trees. Exhaustion had pushed my chest open, and sweat plastered my shirt to my skin. I lay back and stared up through the branches, trying to breathe.

Blair was sitting cross-legged, her face pale, her hands shaking as she pulled her sketchbook out of her bag. Of course, she was sketching them while her memory was sharp.

"They saved us," Sasha said quietly.

I nodded. "I wonder why."

"This place sure is strange," Blair commented as she bit her lip and finished her sketch.

A strange rustling sound made me sit up. The flying lizards had returned. They were perched on branches, rocks, and one even sat on Sasha's outstretched arm. They weren't attacking. They were... watching. Hundreds of tiny, sharp faces stared at us with eyes like polished gems.

"Should we be worried?" Blair asked, not entirely joking.

Sasha didn't answer right away. Her gaze moved from creature to creature, calmly, almost reverently. Then she said, "I think they want us to follow them."

I blinked. "What makes you say that?"

"They saved us," Sasha said. "And now they came back. They seem to be waiting for us."

I looked in the direction the creatures were facing. It was away from the path we'd been taking. It was away from the mountains we'd been trying to reach.

"We don't even know where they're leading us," I said. "It could be into a trap."

Sasha shrugged. "Or they could be bringing us to safety."

"And if it's neither?" Blair asked apprehensively.

I sighed and wiped sweat from my neck. The truth was, nothing about this place made sense. The rules were wrong. Up felt like down half the time, and we were lucky to be alive at all. I glanced back at the path we'd been following. It led to a ridge we'd hoped would give us a better view of the terrain. But instinct—deep, primal instinct—told me that the answers weren't in that direction anymore. Maybe they never had been.

I looked at the creatures again. They hadn't moved. They were waiting ever so patiently for us to make up our minds. "Well," I said, hoisting my bag back onto my shoulder. "If I've learned anything in this *place*, it's that logic doesn't mean much. And at least these things seem to like us."

Sasha smiled softly. "Trusting intuition over reason, Alayna? I'm proud of you."

She was teasing, so I rolled my eyes. "Don't get used to it."

Blair stood too, brushing dust from her pants. "If they saved us once, maybe they'll do it again."

"Let's hope we don't need saving again," I said with a laugh.

Together, we stepped forward. The flying lizards took off like a single thought, glimmering silver streaks weaving through the trees, and then back again, so we wouldn't lose them. We followed, not because it made sense, but because if something else attacked us, we wanted to keep those small creatures close by.

After a few hours of walking, the terrain changed. One moment, we were weaving through trees heavy with silver-leafed branches, and the next, we stepped out into a clearing and saw an expansive basin that took my breath away.

It was massive, low, and wide, like a bowl cradled between jagged ridges. The ground beneath us shimmered black and gray, a mosaic of ancient stone veined with silver threads that caught the twilight like glass. My boots scraped against granite and gneiss, slick with frost and morning dew. The air was colder here and thinner, but it was still cleaner and fresher than any air I had ever breathed. Everything seemed to be still. Even the birds had gone quiet. This place felt older than time and somehow sacred. It was the kind of place that shouldn't be spoken of, or it might vanish altogether.

Blair let out a soft gasp beside me. "It's stunning," she whispered.

Sasha moved to the edge of a stone outcrop, peering down toward the heart of the basin. "There—do you see that?" She pointed to something in the distance.

I followed her line of sight. A lone figure was climbing the cliff-face opposite us, using ice picks and rope with the kind of casual grace that told me this wasn't his first climb. His silhouette moved rhythmically, as if the mountain were just an extension of his body. Twilight struck the crystalline cliff, scattering prismatic colors across the rock—and over him. For a heartbeat, it looked like the stone itself had decided to refract through him. He paused, glanced over his shoulder, and waved.

I blinked. "Did he just—?"

"Wave?" Blair said, squinting a bit. "Yep, he sure did."

"He saw us," Sasha said, smiling like she already knew something the rest of us didn't. "And he's making his way over to us."

"Do you think he's from here? Maybe he can help us get to a settlement, or even back home," I said hopefully.

We waited in wary silence as he traversed the cliff in our direction and then headed straight up toward us with practiced ease, muscles taut and deliberate. When he reached the top, he hauled himself onto the flat surface, twilight catching on his harness, gear, and even his cheekbones. It was ridiculous—no one should look that disarming while scaling a black stone cliff in the wilderness. Yet there he was, an easy grin blooming as he landed with a thud and a puff of dust a few yards from us.

"It's so good to see you," he said, sweeping a damp, black strand of hair from his forehead. His voice was smooth, but not rehearsed, honest, and warm. "Didn't expect to see anyone else out here."

"You're real?" I said before I could stop myself. "I mean— we've seen some weird things lately, and—"

"I'm real," he said, his grin spreading. "The name's Denali. Denali Kwaan. I'm from Juneau, Alaska. Or... that's where I was when I started this climb, anyway."

His words hit me like a stone dropped into still water. He wasn't from here either. He was from Earth. I glanced at Blair. Her brows furrowed as her hand drifted unconsciously to the red spiral birthmark on her arm. Sasha's tattoos flickered then shone brightly with brief pulses of light beneath her collarbone and over her shoulders. I touched my pendant. It was hot and humming.

Denali noticed. "I figured it was you three," he said, quiet now. "I saw your faces in the ice back home, inside the glacier just before I was sucked in and thrown out here, wherever *here* is."

I stared. "You what?"

He nodded, serious now. "I was on a solo climb deep into a new formation at Mendenhall glacier near Juneau. There's a tunnel that wasn't there the week before. Intrigued, I decided to follow it. That's when I saw the vortex—light spiraling like a ribbon of aurora. I touched it, and *POOF!*" He opened his hands like that was explanation enough.

"You landed here," Blair finished, her voice hushed.

"Yeah," he said. "Here at the bottom of this basin. I thought I was hallucinating, but then I started seeing things —flashes in the cliffside, like memories that weren't mine. And of course, your faces. Your voices, *and* some strange echoes."

Something in my chest tightened. "You saw us before now."

He nodded. "I sure did. I really thought I was cracking up."

He rolled up the sleeve of his jacket, and it opened. Around his neck hung a pendant—a black shimmering stone wrapped in delicate silver wire—almost identical in shape to mine. It caught the last traces of twilight, resting just above his heart, as if some quiet thread had always bound them. But his dark, nearly black eyes glowed with a faint blue tinge, like glacier light filtered through dark water.

Blair took a step forward. "Mine is red," she whispered as she pointed to his necklace. She showed him her red birthmark. "It showed up the night I... painted this place."

Denali's gaze snapped to hers. "You painted this?"

She nodded slowly. "Well, I painted what it looked like where I came through." She explained what it had looked like with red sand, obsidian spires, and those silver trees.

"That explains a lot," he said, almost reverent. "It felt like I was walking through a dream someone else left behind. Familiar, but… unfinished."

His words sent a chill down my spine. "You're saying you came here because you saw us?"

"I didn't have a choice," he admitted, as he started hauling on a rope and pulled his gear bag up. "It wasn't just curiosity. It felt like… a pull, from the moment I saw the swirling light."

I exhaled through my nose, glancing around. The basin sparkled beneath our feet, massive, ancient, and unmoved. Yet everything about this moment felt intentional—the synchronicity of the fated symbols and this man showing up out of nowhere echoed a dream none of us fully understood.

"I'm Alayna Archuleta. This is Sasha Kahn, and Blair Grindall," I told him.

"It's super nice meeting you all. I thought I was destined to be alone here with my hallucinations." Denali's expression softened. "I'm guessing we were all supposed to meet for some reason."

I wanted to argue. To rationalize this with science or field data or something that didn't involve prophetic ice visions. But I couldn't. Not after everything we'd seen. Not with the symbols glowing, and certainly not with Blair's paintings bleeding into life and Sasha's tattoos twitching with memory.

"I think you're right," I said finally. "I think we were meant to find each other."

Denali met my eyes then, silently, and I forgot where we were for a second. The exhaustion and impossible questions stacked up in my mind like archaeological layers. There was something steady in his gaze, anchored and kind. He quickly stashed his harness, a rope, and a few pieces of equipment into his bag and hoisted it over his shoulder.

He smiled again. "I'm just glad I'm not crazy."

"You still might be," I said, unable to hide my grin. "But at least you're in good company."

By the time we found a flat spot to stop, the horizon had deepened to a darker shade of purple. I hoped that didn't mean anything like it did back home, some sort of storm. A few bent trees formed a natural windbreak, and the stone shelf beneath us still radiated a ghost of heat. I dropped my bag with a grunt, muscles sore and aching in ways I hadn't felt since my first field expedition.

Denali knelt near a ring of old stones and began clearing out debris. Within minutes, he had coaxed a flame from nothing more than dry moss, bark shavings, and quiet intention. He barely spoke, but his movements were purposeful and confident. Stillness settled in with the kind of calm I used to find in ancient ruins—steady and unshakable.

Blair sat cross-legged, sketchbook in hand, humming softly. Sasha, always prepared, pulled out dried fruit, some kind of seeds she had been stripping from long grass-like plants, and her water flask. I offered my water bottle as well. "Dinner is served," she announced with a wink.

I took a piece of fruit, chewing slowly. The sweetness cut through the metallic taste that had crept into my mouth hours ago, probably due to nerves.

We passed the food around in silence for a few moments, each of us processing everything that had happened to us. The fire crackled gently, throwing warm light over the jagged stone walls and reflecting in Denali's black eyes like tiny comets.

"So," Blair said, her voice low but curious, "how did it happen for you? The vortex, I mean."

Denali poked the fire with a silver stick, then spoke for the first time since lighting it. "There was a storm," he said simply. "I was on a solo climb; it was the wrong time and ridge. No one had explored it before. I slipped when I saw the swirling light. I thought I was falling to my death. Next thing I knew, I was clinging to a ledge near the bottom of a basin that didn't exist before. No ice, just stone, and the visions."

I watched him as he said it, his voice quiet, words chosen with care. He didn't just speak—he *placed* his words, like stones in a river, intentionally and grounded.

As we settled in, Sasha reached for her flask and passed it around. She warned that we should just take a sip each time since we didn't know when we would be able to fill it up again. The water was warm but welcome. My throat felt less like sandpaper. We ate more, little by little. Nobody was rushing, and no one asked for more than they needed.

"So, what's the plan?" Blair asked. "When we wake up, I mean."

"We need to find some people. Hopefully, there are people, Sasha said hesitantly. "A village, outpost, or a temple —*anything.* "

I nodded. "Agreed. We need to understand where we are, why we're here, and how we will get home. Wandering around blind won't get us far. There has to be some kind of civilization here. Signs, tools, structures—something we can follow."

"Maybe even a map," Blair added, hopeful.

Denali didn't say anything right away. He just fed another branch into the fire, watching the flames rise like dancers in the wind. Then finally, he said, "If this place brought us here, maybe it'll show us where to go. Perhaps we just have to pay attention."

"Those little flying lizards brought us to you," Blair said quietly.

"That was strange. It was like they knew exactly what they were doing, but how?" Sasha asked.

"I'm not sure, but we need to find out," I said as I took a deep breath, held it, and released it slowly. It was my attempt to clear my brain so I could think clearly.

Everyone nodded and murmured agreement, and we each shifted into more relaxed positions. I leaned back against a rock, drawing my knees up. The fire cast flickering gold across everyone's faces, making me feel less alone.

Denali sat just across from me, arms folded, his gaze steady but not invasive. I found myself watching him more than I meant to. His presence wasn't loud. It didn't try to command anything, but anchored me like being tethered after too long a drift.

His black pendant caught the firelight as he moved, sending a chill down my spine. Were we all destined to find each other? Was something else at play here? Maybe it was just a coincidence. But in this place, I was starting to question coincidence altogether.

He caught me looking and didn't look away. He just offered a faint, knowing smile—not flirtatious or smug, just present.

I looked down, the edge of my own pendant warm against my collarbone. How could something so steady feel so unfamiliar and safe at the same time?

Sasha yawned, stretching. "We should rest. I'll take first watch."

"I'll take second," Denali offered.

Blair settled down, putting her bag under her head and adjusting it until it was somewhat comfortable. "Wake me for the third."

I didn't volunteer. I rarely slept deeply anyway. I could drift and still hear a hawk sneeze two valleys away. But more than that, I wanted the quiet.

As everyone settled, Denali leaned forward, feeding one last log into the fire. The flames flared, then settled, casting long shadows. He didn't say another word. He just sat there, hands loose, dark eyes watching us without judgment or assumption.

And I found myself thinking, *Maybe I don't have to carry this alone.*

6

THE SANDSTORM AND THE SWORD

I woke to the sound of wind humming across stone, low and steady like breath in a giant's chest. My back ached, my neck was stiff, and when I sat up, every muscle protested. It wasn't exactly ideal, but I'd slept worse on field gigs.

Sasha stood at the edge of our makeshift camp, arms crossed, looking out with a daydream expression that seemed like she thought it might change if she stared hard enough. Her silhouette was tall, thin, and still against the pale lavender sky.

"You're up," she said, without turning.

"Barely, you have run across any coffee bean trees, have you?" I whispered, not sure if everyone was up. I brushed grit from my cheek and stretched. "Where's Blair?"

"Sketching something by the rocks," Sasha replied. "Denali's cooking something on the fire. I figured we should all eat before heading out."

I nodded in agreement while staggering upright, the cool morning wind threading through my clothes. The air smelled like distant lightning and dry salt. It felt so clean and fresh as I sucked it in through a big yawn. Denali was crouched by a small fire, feeding it with dried moss. The flames danced golden-orange across his handsome face.

"Morning," he said, his voice smooth and low, like warmed honey.

Blair joined us and grimaced, "Do you know Denny wanted to cook one of the lizard bats? I told him it would be like eating a pet. Sasha forbade it even when he tried to convince her they were a source of protein."

Denali handed me a strip of fruit with a completely innocent look on his face. "We are going to need something more substantial at some point with all the miles we need to cover, but this will give us energy at least."

"Thanks." I took the fruit and chewed, watching as he worked efficiently and calmly. He moved with quiet confidence, the kind that comes from understanding the world better than most. I followed his gaze. In the distance, the three moons looked bruised, and it was a stunning sight.

Sasha approached, looking concerned. "I can feel a storm brewing behind us. We'll need to head out soon to keep in front of it."

We packed quickly. Sasha handed Blair a sip from her canteen, and I shared my water bottle with Denali. We had an unspoken agreement to keep walking and searching.

"We'll find something," Blair said, quiet but confident. "Civilization, or whatever passes for it here."

We crossed the plains under a dull sky as the wind picked up, tugging at our clothes and hair. The air remained dry, spiced faintly with something sharp and metallic, and the wind picked up with every step. I fell into step beside Denali for a while, trying hard to match his pace.

"I've seen this kind of terrain in dreams," Sasha murmured. "Before I ever stepped through the vortex."

I didn't ask what kind of dreams. Mine had always been filled with ruins and silence, too layered with symbols to explain.

We walked for what felt like hours. There were no trees or birds, not even our flying lizard friends, just endless rolling flats of pale stone. The wind howled like it was alive as we pressed forward across the vast, bone-colored plains. Dust stung my eyes and settled in my teeth. I kept my head low, the pendant around my neck pulsing faintly with a warning of something.

"I feel like we're walking into a bad dream," Blair shouted over the roar of angry air, shielding her sketchbook with her arm. Her red hair whipped around her face like wild threads of fire.

"I'd settle for any dream that doesn't involve my eyeballs being exfoliated," Sasha said, half-laughing and half-coughing as she adjusted the cloth she'd tied around her head.

Denali, walking just ahead of me now, turned slightly, his dark hair plastered to his face by grit and wind. "There's a canyon ahead," he called. "I saw it from the ridge. We'll need to cross it."

"Fantastic," Blair said under her breath. "Because this already wasn't enough of a nightmare."

When we reached the edge of the canyon, my breath caught in my throat.

It was enormous—jagged and yawning like the cracked shell of some ancient creature, carved deep into the ground. Not enormous like the Grand Canyon back home, but deep with sheer cliffs, and countless miles long. Wind whistled through it in ghostly howls, kicking up spirals of dust that danced like spirits. The rock shimmered with mineral streaks—silver and obsidian.

"Okay," I said, squinting at the narrow natural bridges that stretched between ledges like fractured ribs. "This looks complicated."

"We'll have to go one at a time," Denali said, calm but firm. "Sasha, can you use one of your tattoos? Something to watch our backs?"

Sasha blinked, caught off guard. "I—maybe?" She glanced at the raven inked on her shoulder, then back up, a half-shrug lifting her shoulder. "I've never actually tried."

Denali nodded, undeterred. "Then try now. Picture it not as a tattoo, but as something already alive and just resting on your skin. Imagine it lifting off and taking flight."

Sasha drew in a slow breath, furrowed her brow, and focused on the bird etched in ink. She whispered something under her breath, maybe a prayer, and held her breath as she willed it to move.

Nothing happened. She exhaled sharply, frustrated. "I don't think this is going to work."

"Try again," Denali suggested gently. "Don't force it. Just see it in your mind, flying. Feel the weight of it lifting off your skin."

Sasha closed her eyes, steadied her breath, and tried again. This time, a faint shimmer rippled through the ink. The tattoo twitched, then went still. Her fingers trembled, but she didn't stop. She took deep, meditative breaths. With a pulse of silver light, the raven stirred, then lifted, unfurling into a translucent shape. It hovered for a heartbeat before taking off in a swift arc, darting ahead and circling the ravine like a scout.

Everyone stared at her in shock until Blair let out a breathy laugh. "Okay, that was insane."

My mouth gaped open slightly. "I would never have believed that."

Sasha blinked like she couldn't quite believe it either. "Wow, I had no idea I could do *that*!"

The three of us turned to Denali in unison, eyes wide with the same question.

"How did you know that would work?" I asked, my voice edged in awe.

"Yeah," Blair added, squinting at him. "You said it like you were sure it would happen."

Sasha folded her arms, still watching the shimmering raven as it circled above. "Have you seen something like this before?"

Denali gave a slight, almost sheepish shrug, the corner of his mouth twitching. "Not exactly, but I've seen enough to trust that sometimes... things hidden inside us are just waiting for a moment like this to wake up." He met Sasha's eyes. "You looked like someone ready to fly."

Silence settled between us as we all digested this.

Blair stepped up beside me, drawing the small canvas from her tote. "If we need something more stable..." She didn't finish the thought. Just knelt quickly, pulled out her brush, and sketched a thin, pale stone arc between two points. The bridge she painted rippled and solidified, though it wavered slightly in the gusts.

"You're sure that'll hold?" I asked.

"No," she said, brushing hair from her face, "I made it out of instinct, not logic. It feels right."

That was becoming a theme here. "How does the raven fit into all of this?" I asked Denali.

"The bird will serve as a perimeter watch. While we cross, it will patrol the air above and behind us, crying out if something or someone approaches from the ravine or the trailing path. It can also circle back if the bridge falters or crumbles." He looked at Blair. "You have an incredible gift. Drawing this bridge is wild."

We crossed carefully, single file. My boots scuffed across Blair's painted stone as I followed Denali's sure steps. Halfway across, the wind shrieked louder, and the bridge trembled beneath us.

"Hurry!" Sasha shouted as she broke into a run. The raven flew beside us, gronking loudly, which helped us all to hurry even faster.

Blair's creation began to crack, pieces crumbling away behind us. We sprinted the last few feet, my heart hammering in my throat.

When we reached the other side, panting and dust-caked, I doubled over, hands on my knees, as the bridge ceased to exist. "That was entirely too close."

Sasha grinned at me. "You'll get used to it."

"No," I said. "I won't."

We found temporary shelter behind a cluster of stones, all of us catching our breath. The wind was shifting again, growing wilder.

"So," Blair said between gasps, "It's so bizarre because this just isn't Earth anymore, is it? I'm finding it hard to wrap my head around that, and I'm so worried about my home life. It's messing with my brain."

"It's not Earth unless Earth recently added two more moons, carnivorous vines, and massive monsters," I replied. "But on a serious note, I have the same issue." I looked at

Sasha and Denali. "I'm assuming we are all struggling with that."

We all laughed and then nodded in solemn agreement.

Denali glanced skyward, then looked at me. "Wherever this is, I don't think it wants us wandering blind. There's a path *if we pay attention.*"

"You sound like one of my exes," I said, flinching at the memories.

"Was he rugged and poetic too?" Sasha teased and then blushed when Denali winked at her.

For half a second, my chest tightened as I wondered if she would be pining away after him. I had to admit he had a certain sex appeal. "No, my ex, Vincent, was annoying. He had a way of blaming me for anything that went wrong because I clearly must not have been *paying attention.*" I mumbled before I could stop myself. A flicker of awkward silence followed. I tried to ignore it and change the mood by smiling widely.

Sasha reached over, her touch light on my arm. "You don't owe us your past, Alayna."

"I know," I said. "But it still wants to spill out sometimes."

The wind slammed down hard again, almost knocking us sideways.

"We need real shelter," Denali said. "Now."

We crested the next ridge and saw it, a crumbled structure, half-swallowed by sand and time. Pillars leaned at odd angles, and the roof was broken open to the storm-lit sky, but at least it would offer us some cover.

Inside, the air was cooler, the wind muted by ancient stone. My pendant buzzed softly at my chest, and I couldn't tell if it was a warning or recognition.

"This looks like an ancient temple," Blair whispered, stepping reverently over the threshold.

"Definitely ceremonial," I said quietly as I scanned the faded glyphs on the wall. I itched to study them but stopped when I caught movement at the far end of the hall.

A tall and solitary man stood in the center, moving through martial forms like a silent ritual. His body cut through the storm-dust in fluid arcs, every motion deliberate. He didn't seem to notice us, or he simply didn't care to break his focus.

"Whoa," Sasha breathed. "Who is he?"

He struck forward and pivoted, then dropped into a crouch before rising smoothly into a high spin. His silhouette looked carved from shadow and light, framed by a cracked archway. He moved with the stillness of someone who carried storms inside him but never let them loose.

I stepped forward, quietly.

He stopped and turned slowly. His gaze flicked toward us, stormy blue eyes sharp and calm, like rough water.

"You're not from here," he said, his voice like velvet.

"No," I replied. "Are you?" I crossed my fingers behind my back, hoping he was a native to these parts and would know how to get us home.

"My name's Elijah. Elijah Taylor. Or you can call me Eli," he said, his voice low and grounded, like it had traveled up through stone to reach us. "I came here through a dream."

We were still gathered inside the crumbling temple, our breath visible in the cold hush that followed the wind. Outside, the air shimmered with the last of the storm dust, but in here, everything stilled.

"Through a dream?" Blair repeated gently.

He nodded. "I was meditating near Uluru, Australia. I had a vision—a spiral carved in fire—so I followed it. Next thing I remember, I was standing in this ruin."

He turned his wrist toward us. A faint spiral etched in dark ink glowed just below the skin. It was the same shape as Sasha's tattoo and had the same eerie pulse.

Sasha's eyes widened, and for once, she didn't interrupt. She just… stared, listening intently to every word he said.

That alone made me sit up straighter. "I'm Alayna," I offered. "This is Blair, Sasha, and Denali. None of us is from here either. We don't know what this place is; we all came through different vortexes at different times and places."

Elijah nodded once. "Wow, that is wild. Perhaps we were meant to find each other."

Denali shifted beside me, arms crossed, but his posture wasn't defensive, just thoughtful. "If this is some kind of test," he said, "it'd be nice to know the rules."

"Or who's watching," Blair added, her voice barely louder than the wind.

Gradually, we all sat in something like a circle. I leaned forward, elbows on my knees, looking thoughtfully at the man. "Eli, do you remember anything else about the vision? Symbols, voices, anything that might be a clue to what's going on?"

"There were words," Elijah said slowly, closing his eyes like he could summon the memory. "Something like 'The spiral will gather its keepers. When the sky splits, follow the pulse.' It was a woman's voice, but not like any human voice. I got the feeling she was waiting for us. It was pretty bizarre."

"That's vague and kind of creepy," Blair said with a deep sigh.

"And exactly the sort of thing I'd find etched into temple ruins," I added, mostly to myself. "Though usually less poetic."

Elijah closed his eyes again for a moment and then opened them. "This land feels sacred to me, like everything in it has memory, even the wind."

Funny. I'd felt the same, but I hadn't said it aloud.

"So, what do we do now?" Sasha asked, finally breaking her silence. "We have barely enough food or water. And I don't know about you, but I'm not exactly equipped to survive in a magical alternate realm."

"I just remembered that I have granola," Blair offered, unzipping a pocket on the side of her tote bag. "She pulled out three bars."

Sasha laughed under her breath. "You've had that this entire time?"

Blair looked immediately apologetic. "I'm so sorry. I completely forgot about it until now."

"No worries, Blair," I said, mediating between them before a brawl broke out. "At least we have them now."

"You're in charge of rations from now on, Red," Sasha said quickly. I think she realized she sounded more upset than she should have. It had been an honest mistake.

Denali spoke up, changing the subject. "We could stay here tonight, I think. Forage for food and water first and then come back here for shelter." He looked at Elijah, probably relieved to have another man with us. "What do you think?"

Elijah nodded. "There's a ridge about ten minutes from here. I walked part of it yesterday—it overlooks what seemed to be a freshwater basin. I drank from a small spring, and the water seemed safe. I can guide you there before we get settled here. Water is of the utmost importance, even more so than food."

"I might even be able to find some more fruit or the roots we've tried," Sasha spoke up. "I'll go with you."

He met her eyes, calm and steady. "I would love the company. Would one more of you come so we can bring more water back?"

"I'll come," Blair offered. She looked at Denali. "You should probably stay here in case Alayna needs you."

Denali glanced at me and gave a lazy smile. "That works for me."

I wondered if Blair wanted to show that there were no hard feelings between her and Sasha after their brief exchange. I stood, brushing dust from my knees. "Let me give you my water bottle to fill, too." I reached into my day pack and retrieved it, handing it to Blair. "I was hoping to study these ruins, so I'm good with staying and keeping watch over anything you don't want to carry with you."

Blair took my bottle with a nod, tucking it into her tote before heading off with Elijah and Sasha. I watched the three of them disappear past the ridge line, their silhouettes shrinking against the hazy sky.

And just like that, it was quiet again.

Denali crouched beside a rock, fiddling with a piece of torn leather on one of his boots. I stood there momentarily, unsure what to do with the silence, until he glanced up at me with that easy smile.

"You want to sit?" he asked, nodding to a flat boulder nearby. "It's got a great view."

I let out a soft laugh. "Sold."

We sat side by side, with a comfortable space between us.

The wind had softened into a breeze, and I could hear myself think for once.

I stretched out my legs. "You know, I thought I'd be more panicked by now."

"Me too," Denali said. "But… I don't know. Something about this place's rhythm makes me feel at peace."

I hesitated, remembering some of the things we had come up against. "I don't know if I would go that far. Blair, Sasha, and I have had some close calls with several less-than-friendly creatures."

"That sounds intriguing. Care to elaborate?"

"I don't really want to bore you, but here's the short version." I briefly explained, and after I was finished, Denali laughed.

"Wow, I would have loved to see you three in action fighting the beasts and crazy vines. It sounds riveting." He joked.

"Very funny. It was terrifying, thank you very much."

We lapsed into silence again, watching the sky shift. The three moons started stretching long silver golden fingers across the ruin walls. I caught myself sneaking a look at Denali, at the way the light caught the planes of his face, and the gentle line of his mouth. I couldn't believe how smooth his skin was, and I tried to guess his age. Early to mid-thirties was my best guess.

He caught me looking at him, so I turned away quickly. Too quickly, perhaps.

"You've got something on your cheek," he said.

"Huh?" I turned back to him, but he went on before I could stop him.

"Hold still." He leaned in slightly, reaching out with one hand. His fingers brushed just beneath my eye, slow and careful. "Just a speck of black dust." I wasn't prepared for how his skin felt—warm and deliberate against mine. The spot tingled long after he'd taken his hand away, and just like that, I blushed.

I could feel it blooming up my neck, heat crawling across my cheeks. Denali pulled his hand back the second he noticed, and for a moment, neither of us said a word.

He cleared his throat. "Sorry. Didn't mean to—uh—"

"No, it's fine," I said quickly. "Just… dust. It's bound to happen here."

He gave a half-laugh and looked away, rubbing the back of his neck. "So. You're a professor, right?"

I jumped on the topic as if it were a lifeline. "Yes. Archaeology. University of Arizona. I lead field expeditions, primarily focusing on Mesoamerican sites. Petroglyphs, ancient pathways, that kind of thing."

"That sounds incredible."

"It's messy and exhausting and sometimes the bugs are smarter than the grad students, but… yeah. I love it."

He smiled again, more relaxed now. "I guide tourists through glacier caves. It's not quite the same level of discovery, but there's something sacred in the ice."

"You tell stories, right? Tlingit myths?"

"All the time," he said. "I can't believe you know that. People remember stories more than facts."

I nodded. "Same with symbols. We think we're chasing data, but what we really want is meaning."

I stood up then and wandered away from where Denali and I had been sitting, drawn toward the arching stone ruin half-buried in moss and shadow. Lichen crept along its fractured edges, and twisted vines curled around what might've once been pillars—symbols—etched deep into the stone and flecked with silver, bouncing faintly off the twilight. My fingers twitched with the instinct to grab my field journal, but of course, I didn't have it.

I crouched beside one of the larger stones, brushing away a thin layer of dirt and brittle leaf matter. The symbols weren't random. Instead, there were repeating patterns: a circular motif that reminded me of solar calendars, and something that looked like a maze.

"Looks like you've found your element," Denali said, his voice soft but close.

I didn't turn. "I can't help it. It's like my brain lights up when I see stuff like this." I glanced over my shoulder. He'd crouched beside me, arms resting casually on his knees. His presence was grounding in a way that surprised me.

"Do you think these are instructions or warnings?" He wondered.

I exhaled slowly. "Could be something like that, or a map, or even a story. That's the thing, symbols can mean one thing, or a dozen things, depending on the culture and the context."

He studied the stone with a furrowed brow. "That one," he pointed to a jagged mark at the top, "looks kind of like the Tlingit symbol for transformation. They carve it into masks, especially the ones that flip open to reveal another face inside."

I straightened a little. "That's fascinating. I've seen similar dual-layered imagery in Mayan iconography. It always has this sense of duality. You know, some hidden truth beneath the surface."

"Like this place," he commented.

I looked at him then. His profile was lit softly by the silvery glow bouncing off the stone. "You think we're meant to transform here?"

His steady gaze met mine. "I think we already are."

The air felt heavier between us, not ominous, just expectant.

"I used to think everything had to be explained," I said, returning my focus to the stone. "That if I could just label and translate everything, I'd be safe. But now…" I shook my head. "Now I'm not so sure. Some things are meant to be felt before they're understood."

He was quiet for a moment, then said, "My grandfather used to say stories are like rivers. You don't cross them by studying the current; you wade in and let the water teach you."

"That's beautiful," I whispered.

We stayed there, side by side, in silence for a moment. Then he stood and offered a hand. I hesitated only a second before taking it.

"Come on," he said. "Let's see what the rest of the ruins want to tell us."

We looked out again across the ridge.

For the first time since waking up in this strange, beautiful place, I felt alive inside with a glimmer of hope. I just wasn't clear what I was hoping for.

7

SAGE OF THE HIGHLANDS

A loud bang jolted me awake. My heart punched against my ribs as I sat up, hand instinctively gripping the spiral pendant at my chest. Beside me, Blair groaned and pushed herself upright, her red hair tangled around her porcelain face.

"What was that?" she mumbled before she yawned.

I heard Elijah's calm but mildly amused voice across the shallow campsite clearing. "You need to keep your balance lower, Denny. More bend in your knees."

Denali's voice followed, sheepish. "I *thought* I had it."

Sasha stood nearby, arms crossed, lips twitching in amusement. "Eli was trying to teach Denali a spin move, and Denali fell straight into that stone, which then fell off a bigger stone. It sounded awful, but it was actually pretty funny."

Denali stood and dusted himself off, his long dark hair sticking up at odd angles, an apologetic grin tugging at his mouth. "Sorry, I didn't mean to wake everyone."

"It was a graceful fall," Sasha said as she did some yoga stretches. "Truly Olympic-worthy."

He smirked, brushing debris off his pants. "Glad I could entertain you."

As we all stood and gathered our things, the air was crisp and different from the night before. The sky was a pale gray sheet with a hint of lavender, as if the realm had thrown a blanket over the moons.

Elijah handed me a strip of fruit and a handful of berries from his bag. "We should get moving. If there's anything like civilization here, we'll have better luck finding it while wide awake."

Sasha rolled up the shawl that she was using as a blanket. "Define 'civilization.' Because so far I've seen flying lizards, glowing moss, and a tree that growled at me."

Blair chuckled, adjusting her bag. "Don't forget the monster outside the cave."

"Why don't we follow the water for now?" I recommended. "I'm thinking any type of town would be located near fresh water."

"I agree," nodded Denali.

We packed quickly and set out in single file, boots crunching over slick pebbles and rock. Elijah didn't have a pack or a bag, just a small pouch at his waist, so he offered to carry the extra food we had gathered. About ten minutes later, we reached the stream that flowed slowly downhill, making no sound whatsoever.

"Anyone else starting to forget what day it is?" Sasha asked, trying to fill up the silence as we turned to parallel the water.

"I don't even know what *planet* it is," I muttered.

Blair shook her head. "If I wake up and this was all a dream, I'm never touching a paintbrush again."

"So, what do we think this is?" Sasha asked. "Cosmic accident? Trial by ancient spirits?"

"Aliens?" Blair interjected.

"If it's fate, it has a twisted sense of humor." Denali chimed in.

Elijah tilted his head. "Or maybe it's answering a question we haven't asked yet."

"I miss my yoga mat," Sasha said. "And the sound of Georgetown waking up." She looked up. "I miss the sun."

"I miss my studio," Blair chimed in. "The smell of paint and my weather-worn stone cottage, which is nestled at the edge of Fairy Glen."

"I love listening to your accent, Blair," I said with a smile. "And what exactly is a fairy glen?"

"It's the Fairy Glen of Skye, Scotland. It's believed to be the home of fairies, or "the little people." Blair giggled. "The grassy knolls are said to be a perfect place for fairies to dwell. On the Isle of Skye, which is further south, there are also Fairy Pools. There is a tale of the Clan MacLeod Chief who married a fairy. He was given a Fairy Flag, which is thought to have magical powers, and apparently, it gave him and his army good luck when they went to battle. It is said that the Chief and the fairy stayed together for one year and one day before the fairy had to return to her world. The Fairy Pools are said to be the entrance to the fairy realm," Blair explained.

"I wish we had Fairy Pools here so we could travel back home," I said, and we all laughed.

"I miss the Northern Lights, deep snow, and silence so perfect you can hear the ice hum," Denali said quietly.

"I miss my best friend Heidi," I said, feeling sadness set in. "We were planning a girls' trip. She would've freaked out over this place."

"Sounds like we're all missing something or someone," Denali said softly.

Our eyes met briefly, and something fluttered beneath my ribs, so I quickly turned away.

We kept walking. The path narrowed, forcing us closer. Sasha teased Elijah about being too stoic. Blair quipped about accidentally painting the beast when we had met. Even I found myself laughing, a real laugh.

Denali stayed close. Once, when I tripped over a tree root, his hand caught my elbow. It was so warm and soft. He steadied me, and my breath caught. All I could do was nod my thanks.

Later, as we passed a thicket of reeds, he reached out and gently brushed the reeds back so I could pass unscathed. As I walked past him, my body brushed against his. The touch was brief, but it lingered, and when our eyes met again, briefly, I shivered and then chastised myself for being so silly. This wasn't about attraction; it was about figuring out where we were and how to get out of this place.

Sasha cleared her throat and began talking about the ideal magical spa she'd build if we ever got back.

We rounded a bend, and Blair slowed. "Do you guys see that?

Sasha nodded and pulled her braid over her shoulder, pointing ahead. "That ridge over there is a little higher. Perhaps we could see further from on top of it."

I nodded, grateful for the suggestion. My legs ached, and the chill had started settling in my joints. Elijah moved ahead to scout the way, steady and sure, like the terrain itself responded to his steps. Denali walked beside me, not saying much, but his presence was grounding and electrifying all at once, like a fire you didn't have to sit next to in order to feel warm.

We reached the ridge in under ten minutes and collapsed onto a flat stretch of rock. From there, a lake spread out below us like molten slate, dark and vast.

Blair unhooked her bag and pulled out a folded cloth bundle. "Here's the rest of the granola bars." She divided it up between us.

"You're my favorite person right now," Sasha said as she snatched a piece.

Elijah smirked. "Interesting. I thought I was your favorite because I showed you where the water was yesterday."

"You were the favorite until about ten seconds ago. You brought zero snacks."

We all laughed, and it felt strange—but good—to laugh in a place where nothing made sense. There was still dirt on my palms from where I'd slipped earlier on the trail. My muscles were tight, and my stomach was still uneasy. But for a moment, it was just us—five strangers bound by chaos and spirals.

"Do you ever think about how weird this is?" I asked, popping a crumb into my mouth. "Like, none of us should even know each other. I live in the desert. Sasha on an island, Eli lives next to a giant sacred rock. Blair lives in what sounds like a literal fairy tale, and Denali lives underneath the Northern Lights and a whole lot of ice."

Blair gave a shy smile. "You'd love my fairy tale home. It's so pretty—full of strange hills and even stranger stories. Heather and moss surround my cottage, and there's always mist, even when the sky is clear."

"What do you miss most about it?" Sasha asked.

Blair paused. "The quiet. Not just silence, but that deep quiet that settles into your bones. And the way the wind whistles through the stones. I used to think they were trying to tell me something."

"Maybe they were," Elijah said. "Places like that, they remember."

Sasha leaned forward. "My home's loud. Georgetown isn't exactly peaceful. But I miss it all the same: the sea air, the aroma of my mom's herbal tea, and the plants in our courtyard. I used to lead sunrise yoga under a mango tree. It felt sacred."

"I miss the cold," Denali said quietly. "That deep, bone-scraping cold of glacier air. It hurts the lungs sometimes, but it's so clean and refreshing. And my cabin—it's small, tucked into the trees. There's a window above my bed where I can see the aurora if I'm lucky." His voice drifted off. I didn't realize I was staring until he turned to me.

"What about you, Alayna? What do you miss most?"

It caught me off guard. My fingers curled instinctively around the pendant at my neck. "The sky. That big, deep blue desert sky over Tucson. And then the brilliant orange sunsets. The way it burns like flame just before the sun dips below the mountaintops. I used to take my Jeep out for a sunset drive with no real plan, just watching the light and colors change."

For a moment, the only sound was the wind whispering through nearby reeds.

"I keep thinking," Sasha said, breaking the silence, "what if this place is a test? We're all pulled here because we're supposed to do something amazing."

Elijah stretched his legs out in front of him. "Or maybe we're all here because we were searching for something."

"I wasn't looking for anything," Blair blurted out. "I was painting and then suddenly, I was here."

"Okay, but what does it mean?" Sasha asked. "I keep wondering, why the five of us?"

Elijah nodded slowly. "Why not us?"

"I will let you know once we figure it out," I said, a frown appearing on my lips. I didn't say the rest: that I'd wanted an escape. That I'd been pushing myself deeper and deeper into my work, afraid of what I'd feel if I ever stopped moving. That part of me had hoped Sonora would give me answers not just about ancient civilizations, but about myself.

"Maybe this realm is listening to us right now," Denali said, his voice quiet and steady.

"Well, that's not creepy at all," Sasha said, rolling her eyes.

We sat there a while longer, passing food, sharing stories. At one point, Sasha coaxed a tiny painted bird from her tattooed forearm. It fluttered around like a dragonfly and landed in Denali's open palm. His smile when it happened was pure, boyish wonder.

Then—

"Do you hear that?" Elijah asked, frowning.

A hum. It was low, rhythmic, and almost like chanting— except no voice spoke.

I turned, and down across the lake, something shimmered in the gloom.

Our eyes fixed on a faint glow rising above the waterline as we stood.

We stared, frozen.

Elijah exhaled. "Well, I wasn't expecting this."

We ambled down the slope and stood on the edge of the lake that looked carved from obsidian. Its surface flickered with shards of black against black forks of light.

But that wasn't what stole our breaths.

It was the floating dolmen. Three stone slabs, monolithic and impossibly suspended in the air, hovered with eerie stillness above a man sitting cross-legged on a wide, flat rock. Symbols spiraled out around him, etched deep into the ground, glowing faintly. They looked like the kind of markings I had only ever found buried under centuries of sediment—symbols that whispered more than they told.

"He looks human," Blair said softly, her voice half-awe, half-resignation.

Sasha tilted her head, curls bouncing, eyes narrowed. "He's meditating with floating rocks. This has to be a dream, right?"

"No way," Elijah said, his arms folded across his chest. "Dreams don't have this much reality." His shirt whipped at his torso as a large gust of wind swept across the lakeshore, and I wrapped my arms tighter around myself, teeth chattering even though I'd hiked in colder weather.

Denali stood beside me, dark eyes fixed on the dolmen, his expression unreadable. Something about his stillness mirrored the man beneath the stones, like he was listening... not to us, but to the world.

"I've never seen anything like this," I whispered as I looked at the dolmen. "On my first day in this realm, I saw floating river stones. I didn't believe it then. But it was nothing like this."

Denali nodded, barely. "Neither have I. It's astounding, really."

We lingered at the edge for a while, none of us quite ready to move forward, like crossing some invisible threshold would break a spell. Eventually, we dropped to sit on a curve of stone a safe distance from the glowing runes. The five of us huddled close as wind stirred the trees behind us, and the lake hissed quietly under the electric sky.

Blair dug around in her bag and pulled out a cloth-wrapped bundle. "I've got more dried fruit if anyone wants it."

"I will never say no to food in this realm," Sasha said, taking a handful and offering some to me with a wink.

I smiled faintly and said, "No, thank you."

Elijah chuckled. "I think we should wait until he's finished. I don't want to disturb him."

"Good idea," Sasha said as she moved to sit beside him. "The view is better from here." She smiled as she peered ahead.

"Careful," Elijah said, his grin flashing. "I might take that as a compliment."

Sasha smacked his arm lightly and laughed.

I smoothed my lips together and thought, *uh-oh, she's smitten.*

We settled into an easy rhythm, the tension ebbing slightly now that we'd all survived a few near-death experiences. It was strange how quickly we'd adapted to danger, and it was even stranger how familiar everyone was starting to feel.

"So," Sasha started. "While waiting for him to finish meditating, does anyone else miss their bed so much it hurts?"

"Mine has a view of the Glen," Blair said wistfully. "There's moss outside my bedroom window that glows after it rains. And my little wood stove makes these tiny ticking sounds when it cools down for the night."

I turned to her, curious. "That still sounds like a fairytale."

She smiled shyly. "It sort of is."

"What about you, Eli?" Denali asked.

Elijah leaned back on his palms, gazing out across the lake. "I have a very comfortable bed. I lie on it to enjoy the sunrise at Uluru."

I swallowed. "That sounds incredible."

He nodded. "I didn't realize how much it meant to me until it was gone."

Sasha's eyes softened. "I feel that way about my bed too. It's funny how one single item could transform our time here."

Denali turned to me then. "What about you, Alayna?"

"I'm rarely in my bed," I said at last. "I'm always either on a dig, away at some kind of conference, visiting Heidi or my parents, or just out camping. It's always something. When I do finally crash, I'm so exhausted I don't even recognize that it's a bed I'm sleeping on."

"Sounds awful," Denali said. "I miss my bed, that's for sure, and waking up with snow caked on the windows and the forest breathing outside." His voice was low and warm; for a moment, I found myself looking at him instead of the lake. A small smile tugged at his lips. I couldn't look away.

"I don't want to stay here," I said. "Not forever. But I need to stay long enough to know why we're here."

Everyone was quiet for a moment, likely thinking the same thing.

"I feel that too," Sasha finally said. "These tattoos move a lot now. They're alive and shifting right under my skin, but it doesn't scare me. It feels like I was meant to be here. I just don't understand why I feel that way."

Blair nodded. "Same. My art moves and comes alive."

"I find that so amazingly strange," Elijah said, brows raised.

"I know," Blair said. "But I wasn't trying to do anything like that the first time it happened. It was like I had no control over it."

Denali looked at me again. "Has anything changed for you?"

I hesitated. "Not like that. But I feel like I've stepped into one of my own field journals. Every stone or symbol—it's like I can almost read them. Not with words but with instinct."

He smiled. "That's something."

Our eyes lingered a second too long. My stomach flipped, and I looked away again, focusing too hard on the lake.

"Anyway," I said, "if this is some kind of ancient realm, I'd like to file a formal complaint about the weather and lack of inhabitants."

Sasha laughed. "Right?"

Denali leaned closer, just enough that his arm brushed mine. "It's nice, though," he said. "All of us, here. I mean, not the terrifying unknown part. But this, talking, laughing, and sharing stories. It reminds me of how quickly the guides bond with a group of tourists who come to explore the glacier. It's hard for me to say goodbye every single time."

Something in his voice made my pulse stutter. His hand lingered near mine, not quite touching. Then he reached out and brushed a strand of hair away from my cheek. The touch was gentle, unthinking, but I felt it everywhere. I sucked in a breath and felt heat rushing to my face. I knew I was blushing. He froze, noticing, and our eyes locked.

Denali chuckled softly, backing off with a sheepish look. "Right. Yes, let's focus on important things, like mysterious floating stones."

My face was still burning. I prayed no one would tease me about it—Sasha was already smirking like a cat who'd cornered a bird.

And then something shifted.

The air around the dolmen thickened, vibrating like the pause before thunder. The man beneath it opened his piercing blue eyes—and I swear a flash of lightning paused mid-fork, caught between sky and stone.

He stood slowly, but not threateningly. He wore a long, loose-fitting gray shirt and pants of a drapey fabric that gave the impression of ancient robes, weathered and sun-bleached. His presence was vast.

Elijah stood first. "Who is he?"

"I don't know," I whispered. "But he's intense."

The figure stepped from the center of the circle, and the dolmen sank a few inches, still floating and humming.

He looked at us and smiled faintly. "You've come far." His voice was calm and grounded, like roots in deep soil.

"Who are you? What's your name?" Denali asked.

The man stepped closer, stopping just outside the edge of the symbols.

"My name is Parker, Parker Stonehouse."

8

WINGS OF THE DEVOURERS

The man let the silence settle for a moment, then gave a slight nod, not in greeting, but as if assessing a puzzle. "Nice to see you here," he said, voice even. "I didn't expect company, but you don't look like threats."

"Do you live here?" Elijah asked cautiously, but I could see his light blue eyes were full of hope.

"No one lives here," Parker replied, then smirked. "Not really. I arrived a few days ago—woke up beneath that dolmen, and I've been trying to understand it ever since."

Sasha tilted her head. "So, you're lost too."

"Depends on how you define lost," he said. "I was hiking near Mount Shasta, then all of a sudden I wasn't. This place doesn't follow the rules that I know."

Blair took a step closer. "I'm Blair, and this is Alayna, Sasha, Elijah, and Denali. We're happy to run into you. You've been alone this whole time?"

"Nice to meet you all. I've met no one until now." He looked at each of us, eyes sharp. "And yet, here you all are. That doesn't feel accidental at all."

Denali's brow furrowed. "We don't know why we're here either."

"Then we have something in common," Parker said. "I don't know who you are, or why this place brought us together, but I'm willing to find out. Are you?"

We all nodded, and he waved us over to where he was meditating. "Come rest."

The six of us sat in a loose circle beneath the hovering dolmen, its massive stones outlined in soft lavender light. I watched Parker out of the corner of my eye, assessing him. Tall and quietly magnetic, Parker had a spiky crown of blond hair and intense green-blue eyes, like the sea, that seemed to hold the weight of unspoken truths. He was unbelievably good-looking, his closely shaven goatee giving him the air of a thoughtful traveler, and a calm, introspective energy softened his muscular frame. He looked like someone who spent his life walking sacred paths. There was a stillness about him, not the kind that comes from silence, but from understanding.

Parker passed around a cluster of pale golden orbs, each the size of a walnut. "You'll find these delightful." Their skin was slightly translucent, and when bitten into, they burst with a cool, citrusy nectar that tingled at the back of the throat.

Sasha's eyes widened as she chewed. "Do you think these are fruit or fungus? Either way, they are oddly refreshing."

"Fruit," Elijah guessed.

"I'm not sure what they are. I found them on the side of one of those silver trees." Parker emphasized. "Don't worry, they are safe to eat. I've had many."

"They're quite delicious," I commented as I took another one.

Above us, the three moons drifted silently across the sky, glowing in the ever-present twilight. There was no day or night in this realm—just this lavender haze that seemed ever-existent.

"They move with intent," Parker said, noticing my gaze, his voice low and reverent.

I blinked. "What?"

He looked up. "The moons here, they're clearly not orbiting, they're responding. I don't think we're entirely in charge of where we go next."

Denali tilted his head, intrigued. "You think we're being guided?"

Parker nodded. "There are celestial rhythms at play here —subtle energies and mythic echoes. I've discovered this realm has intention, intelligence, and sadness too."

Blair leaned forward. "Sadness?"

Parker placed his hand on the mossy ground. "It feels like the land is waiting for something. I think it's mourning. This twilight we keep finding ourselves in is not natural. It feels suspended, like this world is caught between inhale and exhale."

I rubbed my pendant between my fingers. "Who are you exactly?"

He laughed and said gently, "I'm a Geomythic Interpreter."

Sasha gave a half-smile. "That sounds made up."

Parker laughed again, deep and genuine. "It does, doesn't it? It's a real field, though very niche. I study geography, but not just the maps and mountains. I explore the myths encoded in landscapes. Sacred places and hidden stories in stone and soil. I teach people to read land like scripture."

"So, you're saying the land speaks?" Elijah asked, arms crossed.

"Not in words," Parker said. "But yes, through patterns, energy, and rhythm. This place thrums with old magic, and not just elemental—emotional. There's grief here and longing."

Denali exhaled slowly. "Can you interpret what it wants?"

"No," Parker said. "But I feel someone who does. Someone ancient is mourning. I feel this presence. It's powerful but restrained."

Blair, Sasha, and Elijah stood, brushing off their legs.

"We're going to look for more food and water," Blair said. "Denali, Alayna, are you coming?"

Denali hesitated, looked at me, then nodded. "Yeah."

Soon, it was just me and Parker under the dolmen. I sat near the edge of the symbol field, where the ground was etched with swirling glyphs and sigils—spirals within spirals with cross-hatched lines that reminded me of ancient petroglyphs.

"What do you make of these?" I asked.

Parker traced a line with his finger. "Some of these resemble solstice markers. Others are more abstract— emotion-maps, perhaps. Something trapped and needing a way out of the spiral maze, perhaps. I can feel grief and hope. You feel that too, don't you?"

I nodded, my voice quiet. "Yeah. Like this place has a veil over it, or it's frozen in time." It was strong, and although it didn't scare me, it did make me a bit uneasy.

He smiled. "Exactly. You're attuned to it, but not everyone is."

"I teach archaeology," I said. "Mostly Mesoamerican. But I've always believed symbols are more than just records. They're intentions left behind."

He looked at me with genuine interest. "Then you understand. These are not just markings. They are echoes. The land here is layered with myth, like sediment. The farther we walk, the more we'll feel it."

I liked how spiritual Parker was. I could tell we had a lot of similarities. I touched the edge of a spiral etched into stone. It pulsed faintly under my fingers—not with heat, but resonance, like touching a bell just after it's rung.

Parker watched me. "You have a lovely pendant. What is it?"

I held it up. "My mom gave it to me. She said it was made in Sedona and has vortex energy." I laughed. "At the time, I rolled my eyes, but now, well, I have more faith in it."

"I have a spiral as well." He lifted his shirt, and I leaned closer. Just below his sternum was a large spiral mass of scar tissue. It was pale, the way healed scars never take on color. "I don't know how I got this. I've had it as long as I can remember. No one in my family ever talked about it. Perhaps I was injured as a child. I used to hide it, but it's a part of me."

I almost reached out and touched his torso but restrained the urge. Something about it felt ancient, older than this world, certainly older than Parker, who was probably in his mid-thirties. I guessed he was only a year or two older than I was.

"It's very interesting," I told him, not knowing what else to say.

Parker let his shirt settle against his chest again. "I don't know why I showed you that."

"The lines around the scar," I said, "they almost looked like they were moving."

He gave a small, almost embarrassed laugh. "Yeah. I thought I was imagining that at first. When I was a kid, I used to trace them with my finger and swear they changed positions overnight."

"Did they?" I asked.

"I think so," he said, a little more serious now. "There were times I'd wake up and the tissue, the shape, it would be warm—like it had been holding onto something. Energy, maybe. Memory? I don't know. But lately it's been reacting more. Especially in this realm. It hums when I'm near certain places, and sometimes it feels like it's pulling me somewhere."

"Pulling you where?" I asked, narrowing my eyes.

He shrugged, but his expression darkened with thought. "Nowhere specific—just forward. Like I'm supposed to keep moving, keep going, even if I don't know why yet." He paused, then added quietly, "It feels like it knows the way even if I don't. And yet something kept me returning here each day after my wandering. I didn't know I was waiting for you. Each of you."

We sat in silence for a moment, a light wind ruffling my hair. "Do you think we'll get home?" I asked.

Parker didn't answer right away. "I think wherever we're going next, it's not random. I think we're all part of something bigger than ourselves. I don't know what yet, but it's big, old, and broken."

I swallowed the lump in my throat. "What if we can't leave until we fix it?"

He looked at me, his ocean-colored eyes steady. "Then I guess we figure out what 'it' is."

In the distance, a warm light flickered—Denali's fire starter, no doubt. I could hear Sasha laughing, the sound light against the heavy hush of twilight.

But I stayed where I was, my hand on the stone, and my heart beating to a rhythm I couldn't explain. I didn't know what was guiding us, but I was starting to believe Parker was right.

We were not alone. And this realm, whatever it truly was, was waiting for something. Maybe that something was us.

The terrain sloped unevenly beneath our feet, its surface veined with glowing silver fissures like ancient scars pulsing faintly beneath the lavender sky. I walked close to Denali— partly because he made me feel steadier, and partly because my legs were starting to hate me. I was exhausted after walking for several hours, and if I slipped, at least he would be there to catch me.

We hadn't seen a single sign of civilization: no smoke, ruins, or even a trail.

Elijah slowed beside Parker, his brow drawn. "Have you seen any settlements or villages?"

Parker shook his head. His blond hair, stiff with humidity, was swept back in small, spiked waves. "Nothing. No architecture, cultivated land, or people."

"Great," Blair mumbled from behind me. Her voice was tight but clipped. "So, we're just wandering aimlessly."

"This realm responds to intention. Do you want to move forward or take a rest?" Parker asked calmly.

"Let's walk for a little bit longer," I answered, even though my feet were starting to feel heavy.

"I agree with Alayna," Sasha said. "We'll take a break in half an hour if everyone's good with that."

No one contested her suggestion, so we pressed on.

The light didn't shift here, so there was no real sense of day or night, but the air did. It grew colder as it became what I thought was dusk. My breath began to fog, and a prickling sensation gathered at the base of my neck, like static before a lightning strike.

Denali's hand brushed my lower back, steadying me as I stumbled slightly on a jagged rock.

"Are you okay?" he asked quietly.

"Yeah, just a little unsteady."

"You're not the only one," Sasha agreed. Her voice trembled, and I turned to see her tattoos—usually still unless summoned—rippling faintly along her skin.

"Something's wrong," I said, stopping mid-step.

The wind had changed. It whispered past my ear with a sound like silk tearing.

That was when I saw them.

Dark shapes emerged from the sky—gliding and dipping, silent at first, then swarming. Dozens—no—*hundreds*. Like bats, but wrong, with translucent wings stretched too broad and far too thin. Their bodies shimmered with decay, flickering in and out of visibility like dying memories.

"Oh hell," Elijah snarled. "What are those now?"

Parker backed up and momentarily closed his eyes as if trying to connect with them. "They want to prey on us but not for food, for something else, but I can't get a clear reading on what."

One swooped far too close to my head, and the tip of its wing brushed my shoulder. Instantly, a wave of cold confusion crashed through me—I couldn't remember my last name. I blinked hard, heart pounding. "Alayna," I whispered aloud, just to anchor myself. "My name is Alayna. What is my last name?"

Denali grabbed my arm. "They touch you and you forget?"

"I think so."

Another wing grazed Sasha's thigh, and she staggered, eyes unfocused. "I—I was just about to say something… but I've forgotten what it was."

"I think they're Lunaraiths," Parker said, breath short. "I read about them in an inscription back at the dolmen, and I saw drawings of them. They consume identities and hunt in swarms."

Blair shrieked. Her brush was in her hand, sketching of its own accord across her canvas. Tendrils of paint came alive—lashing and twisting—one of them nearly caught Elijah.

"Blair, stop!" Elijah shouted, dodging the spectral vine as it whipped past his head.

"I'm trying!" she cried, backing up as her art spiraled out of control. "It's painting itself and I can't stop it!"

"Retreat!" Denali called, placing himself between Sasha and the nearest swooping creature. "Back to the rocks! Move!"

Sasha's voice cut through the din. "Everyone, circle up! I think I can shield us with a ward, but only temporarily!"

She dropped to one knee, hands glowing, tattoos along her chest and arms sparking with violet and green light. A pulse echoed out from her like a heartbeat. A transparent dome snapped into place, shimmering with symbols—birds, stars, and spirals.

The Lunaraiths slammed into the shield, recoiling with shrill screeches. I dropped beside Sasha and grabbed her shoulder.

"You good?"

She nodded through gritted teeth. "Not for long. This is draining me fast. We need to figure out how we're going to fight these things before I can no longer shield us."

Blair's canvas flared again, her brush skittering across it like a possessed spider. Spectral shapes burst forth, writhing in panic. One tentacle nearly wrapped around my ankle.

"Blair! Focus!" I shouted.

"I—I can't—it's fear-painting! It's reacting to them!"

Parker crouched beside her, voice calm. "Then paint your way out of it. Command it. You're the artist, not them. Calm and steady. Relax and breathe in and out really slowly."

She inhaled sharply, her eyes wide, but she nodded. She dragged the brush through the center of the painting with a defiant stroke, and the flailing tendrils stilled, melting into swirls of fog and then vanishing.

"We can't hold here," Denali said. "Alayna, climb!"

"What?"

He threw me a rope. "That spire, now!"

I looked up and saw a jagged stone pillar jutting from the ridge about thirty feet away. It was the only high ground. I nodded and took off running, the rope in one hand, my other gripping the pendant at my neck.

The wind screamed louder, and I had to cover my ears with my hands. The Lunaraiths dove lower, their wings brushing the ward, crackling at the edges.

My boots scraped against rough stone as I climbed, and I felt every tendon in my legs strain, but I pushed on. At the top, I braced myself and unclasped the pendant from around my neck.

"C'mon," I whispered to it. "*Do* something."

I held it high and focused all my energy into it.

The spiral began to glow, silver, then turquoise, and then blinding white. I watched as the light pulsed outward in rings. The ripple against the sky was mesmerizing. The Lunaraiths froze midair, then they twitched, shrieked, and scattered, disoriented.

"Now!" I yelled down. "Run!"

The other five bolted toward me and the rocks.

Denali hauled an exhausted Sasha up and over his shoulder, as if she weighed nothing. Elijah grabbed Blair's canvas while Parker supported her. We fled across the rocks, the wind chasing us like breath from an unseen beast.

When we finally collapsed underneath a massive canopy of silver trees, our hearts were hammering, but the swarm was gone.

The sky above us returned to soft lavender. The air warmed slightly, and the silence that followed rang in my ears like an aftershock.

Denali eased Sasha down gently, and she slumped against a boulder, her tattoos flickering dimly. "What is with this place and little creatures with wings?" He exhaled.

He looked from Sasha to me and said softly, "You both did well."

"Thank you," I replied with a slight smile, but Sasha merely closed her eyes, heaving.

"I forgot my own name," Blair whispered, trembling. "It came back, but it felt like it was being pulled out of me."

Parker sat cross-legged in the dirt, eyes closed. "They tested the threads that bind us to who we are. That was no accident."

"Do you think they'll come back?" Elijah asked, his voice still taut with battle tension, as he remained standing guard.

"Undoubtedly."

I stared at the pendant in my hand. The spiral still glowed faintly, pulsing in rhythm with my heart.

I crouched beside Sasha, who looked incredibly pale. "Are you alright?"

She nodded. "That took a lot out of me. I had no idea I could do that."

"It was very cool," Blair said, rubbing her shoulder. "You just rest."

Denali sat beside me. "That was a close call. How are you doing?"

I looked at him. His black eyes were full of concern but not fear. His hand hovered near mine, not quite touching. "Okay, just shaken and exhausted."

"You and Sasha saved us," he said.

"No, we *all* did that." I nodded. "Thanks for the rope. I actually didn't use it, but it made me feel like we had a lifeline."

I glanced around at our makeshift crew—a martial artist, a sage, a healer, an artist, a glacier guide, and me, an archaeologist with a pendant that glows when it feels like it.

Somehow, we'd made it out together.

But I had a feeling this was just the beginning.

We didn't speak for a while.

The six of us sat in a crooked semicircle, our bodies trembling in the aftermath, our minds worn thin like river stones. The cold was enveloping us again, and our breath clouded in the air. Sasha wrapped herself in her shawl, her skin pale beneath the glow of her flickering tattoos. Blair rubbed at her elbow, her thumb brushing the birthmark.

"Are you okay, Blair?" I asked.

She shrugged. "Yeah, my birthmark is burning a bit."

"I get that too," Sasha murmured wearily.

"I think they scraped the edges of us," Parker said. He sat with his knees drawn up, one arm resting over them, his eyes distant. "They were after our memories."

I looked at my hands and flexed my fingers. I was relieved my name had returned, but in those few seconds of forgetting, I'd felt unmoored, like a soul without a tether.

"So, what now?" Elijah asked. He stood still, arms crossed, muscles taut beneath the fabric of his shirt. He looked like he was guarding the perimeter, even though nothing stirred beyond the stone ridge.

"We think," Parker answered calmly. "We reflect."

Blair glanced up. "On what?"

"On why we're here, and more specifically, what this land wants from us."

That word again, *want*. This place didn't feel like it just *was*. It *wanted* something. I shivered at the thought.

Denali added a few dry twigs to the growing fire. "And what can we offer it?"

"Nothing," I said too fast and sharply. Then, quieter, "At least, not yet."

Parker's piercing eyes glowed in the firelight. "It's chosen us for a reason."

I stared at him. "You think we were chosen?"

"Yes," he said simply. "We were not summoned by accident. Each of us carries something—knowledge, power, memory, maybe just potential. This place has a consciousness."

That settled heavily in the silence.

Blair added, "Then what does it want from an artist?"

"What does it want from a martial arts teacher?" Elijah said. "Or a tour guide?"

Denali didn't flinch. "It probably wants some sort of connection."

Sasha gave a soft, thoughtful hum. "I think it wants healing, or maybe it wants to show us what's broken."

The fire crackled and popped. I leaned back against a rock, wrapping my arms around my knees. My pendant was warm again, resting just below my collarbone. That had to mean something.

"I think it wants truth," I whispered. "And it knows we're the only ones reckless enough to go digging for it."

Parker gave a quiet laugh. "Spoken like an archaeologist."

I scrunched my face. "Very funny."

The flames danced between us, throwing shadows like moving glyphs across the dirt. Denali, who had been mostly quiet, picked up a smooth stone and rolled it between his palms. Then, without warning, he began to hum.

It was low, melodic, and familiar in a way that made my skin rise.

And then… he sang.

> *Where trees do cry and stones do sing,*
> *The Stag still waits with a broken wing.*
> *It wept for us, we laughed in vain,*
> *And turned its joy into ancient pain.*
> *Now those who feel may find the gate,*
> *But none may pass who carry hate.*

I didn't know the words. None of us did. But I found them in my throat anyway. Sasha's voice wove in—rich and low, like temple bells in mist. Blair followed, soft and breathy. I joined, too, although I don't sing. *Ever.*

The melody wound around the fire, rising and falling like tidewater. None of us looked at each other. It wasn't awkward or dramatic. It just was.

It ended as softly as it began. No one said a word. None of us asked where the song came from. Instead, we just inched closer. The fire was small, but it felt bigger than us. Like it had witnessed something.

"I only sing in the shower," Blair whispered after a while.

"I don't even *like* music with lyrics," I admitted.

Sasha smiled without turning her head. "It wasn't just music. It was memory."

Parker stared into the flames. "Or prophecy."

We fell quiet again. But this time it wasn't heavy. It was still. Full and satisfying.

Denali finally stood and walked toward the other side of the ridge, Elijah trailing behind him. Parker followed after a moment, and I noticed they were giving us space. I hadn't realized how much I needed that.

The guys made camp about a hundred yards off, their silhouettes softened by the distant shimmer of firelight.

Blair stretched her legs and lay on her side, propping her head on her palm. "So… which one of them is going to end up breaking our hearts?"

I laughed, too tired to pretend I wasn't thinking the same thing.

Sasha rolled her eyes. "Don't start with that."

"I'm not saying I *want* anything to happen," Blair said. "Just, haven't you noticed? There's a pull. Like magnets we didn't ask for."

Sasha sighed. "Yes, and it's unsettling."

I added, "And confusing, but also... "

"Right," Blair finished for me. "Which makes no sense at all."

Sasha lay back to stare up at the violet sky. "Maybe it's not about attraction, maybe it's recognition, like we knew them from before."

"In another life?" I asked.

"In this one," she said. "But maybe we just forgot."

The idea sent a shiver of quiet dread through me.

We finally settled under the odd, never-dark sky, wrapped in borrowed warmth and unspoken questions. We didn't talk about what the Lunaraiths had taken, not yet; that wound still felt too raw.

But as we drifted toward sleep, my thoughts circled the same question over and over: Why us? Why us six? And why did it feel like we'd already been through something far more profound than we could remember?

9

THE HEXAD'S TEMPLE

The warm scent of stone and the hush of twilight greeted me when I woke in stillness. The others were still curled in sleep, scattered in their makeshift bedrolls. A soft whir of wind moved across the plateau, stirring my hair and sending a chill down my arms.

Sasha was already up, sitting cross-legged near a cluster of silvery rocks, her eyes closed, breathing slowly. I moved toward her, quietly, and sank down beside her.

"Couldn't sleep?" I asked.

She cracked one eye open and smiled. "Not really. I have too many questions."

"Same." I tugged my sleeves down and exhaled slowly. "I keep thinking something is guiding this, like we're not just lost travelers anymore."

She tilted her head. "We're not. I think we're being called. You feel it too, don't you?"

I nodded just as Blair's footsteps shuffled toward us. Her red hair was a tangled mess, barely held back by a loose tie, and her eyes were still heavy with sleep. She hadn't said a word yet—just blinked at us blearily like her mind hadn't fully caught up to her body.

"You both look like you're plotting something," she said softly.

"Just processing," Sasha corrected.

"Plotting sounds like more fun." I said as Blair sat with us and drew her knees to her chest.

"Did either of you notice the mountain to the east? It's glowing red like it wants us to notice it," Sasha said, still admiring it.

I turned, following her gaze. The mountain loomed like a flame-etched monolith, its edges tinted with rust and ruby, even under the lavender sky. I was shocked that I hadn't noticed it, but I had just woken up and I'm not sure how long it had been since I had any coffee.

"Hmm, it could either be calling to us or trying to trap us so it can harm us," Blair responded thoughtfully.

"Sheesh, I sure hope it's not the latter!" Sasha said as she eyed it suspiciously. "It's pretty stunning regardless."

In the men's camp, Denali stirred, then Elijah, and Parker like they were dominoes. One by one, they joined us, quiet and alert, like soldiers sensing the tide of something sacred.

"We should go soon," Parker said, already shouldering his bag.

"Without breakfast?" Elijah arched a brow. "I think we need a minute to get our wits about us."

"And the sleep out of our eyes," Blair added after a big yawn. She stretched her arms high and took in a breath, holding it, then releasing.

"I agree with Parker," I said, surprising myself. "Something about that mountain, just like Sasha said, wants to pull us in for some reason. I'm curious to know what's there."

No one argued with me. We moved quickly, packing our few supplies and tying up what served as blankets. My pendant felt unusually warm against my chest, but I didn't mention it to the group. I wondered if it was reacting to that mountain, which made me even more anxious to get to it.

The red mountain dominated our view as we approached, throwing strange shadows that danced and shimmered even though the sky remained unchanged. The air shifted—thicker, charged, and almost reverent. Beneath our feet, the soil gave way to smooth stone etched with faint patterns, like ancient script scoured by the wind.

We were halfway up the slope when Denali slowed, one hand raised like he'd caught scent of something on the wind. I paused behind him, catching my breath, while the others came to a halt too, boots crunching softly on the stone.

"Hold up," he murmured, crouching near a cluster of low shrubs that had managed to root themselves in a narrow crack beside the path. The leaves were dark silver and waxy, curling slightly at the edges, and nestled beneath them were clusters of berries the color of ash—dusty, gray-black, with a strange silver shimmer.

"They look dead," Sasha said, wrinkling her nose. "Like shriveled grapes left in a fireplace."

Denali grinned without looking up. "They're not dead. I think they're *ashberries*. I used to forage for something really close to these back home near the glacier ridges. Not identical, but close enough. I'm hoping these are harmless." He winked at us, which made us all laugh nervously.

I knelt beside him, brushing my fingers lightly over the nearest cluster. They felt cool, almost cold, and the silvery coating stuck faintly to my fingertips like powdered frost. "They look… cursed," I said honestly.

He snorted. "Only if you count delicious as cursed." And without hesitation, he plucked one from the branch, crushed it gently between his fingers, and held it up. The skin broke open to reveal a shock of vivid red, like the inside of a pomegranate, and juice glistened along his fingertips.

Before I could say a word, he popped it into his mouth and chewed. For a second, he said nothing—just closed his eyes, brow furrowed.

"Denali?" Sasha asked cautiously.

He suddenly clutched his throat and fell over onto his back, rolling around.

"Denali!" I shrieked, rushing to his side. "Denali, are you alright? Talk to me!" Panic surged through me, and my heart rate accelerated quickly.

He pulled his hands away from his throat and began laughing. I smacked him, although lightly. "That was not cool. You had me really worried."

He sat up and grinned. "I couldn't resist." He closed his eyes as he chewed a bunch. His eyes snapped open. "Okay, no joke, that's *insanely* good. Tart, sweet, and a little zingy—like cranberry had a love child with blood orange." He grabbed another, holding it up for the group to see. "Go on. You'll thank me."

Parker raised an eyebrow. "You're assuming we'll survive the hour."

"I'm not saying you *won't* go blind," Denali said, teasing. "But if you do, you'll be the happiest blind person in this realm."

Sasha rolled her eyes, but she was already crouching. "If I die, I'm haunting your glacier."

One by one, we gave in. I picked the smallest one I could find, cracked the skin, and hesitated—then slipped it past my lips. A rush of tartness hit first, sharp enough to make my mouth water, followed by a deep, almost wine-like sweetness. My fatigue faded slightly, the ache in my legs softening, and I couldn't help the slight noise I made—half surprise, half delight. "Oh my *god*," I breathed.

"Right?" Denali said, already popping more into his mouth. "Sometimes you just have to trust the wilderness."

We sat there for a few minutes, passing the berries around and licking the juice from our fingers, the silence between us easier now, lighter. The red mountain loomed ahead, but for that moment, we weren't lost strangers anymore—we were something closer to a team. Even Parker ate a few bunches.

About two hours later, we rounded a ledge, and there the mountain was. There was a massive door carved into its side, framed by twin stone columns and flanked by a squat block of dark granite. The block shimmered faintly.

We all stopped and stared in awe.

Parker stepped forward first, fingers brushing reverently across the stone. "There are etchings," he looked at me specifically. "Some kind of proto-symbolic language… but it's not any one script I've ever seen."

I crouched beside him. "Some of these resemble Mayan glyphs. And these spirals—they're similar to the ones I've seen in petroglyphs across the Southwest."

Blair knelt, whispering, "It's almost as if this mountain gathered stories from different places."

Parker nodded and began to translate slowly. "Temple of the Six," he recited. "The Hexad's Temple."

We all stilled.

I turned, meeting their eyes. Denali's expression tightened. Elijah folded his arms. Blair's lips parted slightly in awe. Sasha just whispered, "Hexad?"

Parker stood. "A Hexad is a sacred group of six. Each person embodies a distinct aspect of balance—an archetype, if you will. Together, they create wholeness."

"Us?" I asked, already knowing.

He didn't answer. He didn't need to.

I turned back to the stone and read the next part aloud. "Together, they form a mystical union chosen by the realm… to awaken forgotten truths… and face the trials of a fractured world."

"Forgotten truths?" Sasha echoed. "Like history that's been erased?"

"Or truths about ourselves," Blair wondered quietly.

"And trials," Elijah said. "What kind of trials?"

Parker exhaled. "In most mythic traditions, trials are challenges—tests of strength, skill, heart, or spirit. They force transformation. They're not meant to punish. They're meant to reveal."

I ran my fingers along another line. "It says: 'A symbol will awaken the passage, 'The Spira.'" I frowned. "Spira. That's Latin for 'coil' or 'spiral.'"

At once, all of us looked down. We didn't have to say it—we knew.

Each of us exposed our spirals. Sasha's tattoo over her heart. Blair's birthmark near her elbow. Denali's carved necklace. Elijah's inked on his wrist. Parker's branded in pale scar tissue across his ribs. And me, the pendant my mother had given me, still warm and glowing faintly.

We almost laughed nervously and stepped in closer, spirals held between us like secret keys, but nothing happened.

"Well," Elijah muttered, "that was anticlimactic."

Parker pressed his hands to the door, searching for a handle, but there wasn't one. "There's no way to open this door."

"It has to be more than just a handle," Sasha said. "Maybe intent or energy?"

Blair stepped forward and laid her palm flat against the stone. "Hello?" she said gently. "We're here."

Still nothing.

Then Denali looked at me. "Come with me." He extended his hand, so I took it. As we stepped forward together, something shifted.

A low rumble echoed beneath our feet. My pendant flared—a coil of silver and turquoise light swirling inside it like a storm. The spiral began to turn. The door groaned—stone grated against stone, splitting slowly down the center with a sound like thunder cracking underwater. A wave of warmth burst outward, washing over us like sunlight. It felt like we were being accepted.

None of us spoke; we were all too mesmerized by what was happening.

I stepped forward, hand pressed to my pendant, chest tight with so many emotions I couldn't decipher any of them. The doorway now yawned open before us, revealing a shadowed interior.

"It feels... " I began, then stopped. The words caught in my throat.

Denali touched my shoulder. "What?"

"It feels like home," I whispered.

No one questioned my words because I knew they all felt it too.

———

We stepped into the mountain together, the six of us moving as one body, one breath, drawn into the dim corridor as if the walls themselves had exhaled and invited us in. The air was warm—almost too warm—and dry like old parchment, laced with a faint scent of copper and something floral, like dried petals crushed into stone.

The moment we crossed the threshold, the walls came *alive*.

Light began to ripple across the stones. Glyphs bloomed into view, not etched, but growing like moss, slithering across the surface in fiery silver and indigo threads. The lines curved and danced, forming shapes, symbols, and then entire stories. They pulsed like living fire, flickering with intelligence.

"Holy shit!" Sasha cried, stepping closer, her dark brown eyes reflecting the glow of ae lantern. "They're not just carvings… they're *alive*. How is that even possible?"

"I've never seen anything like this," Parker said softly beside me, awe leaking into his voice. "It's not just light or illusion. I actually think it's memory."

"Or prophecy," Elijah added.

The glyphs twisted, converged, then parted again, this time forming a breathtaking vision. Six figures spun across the walls, celestial bodies silhouetted in cosmic light. Stars wept down around them. Then came a goddess—silver-skinned, crowned in flame, eyes like twin eclipses—being torn apart by an invisible force. Her body split into six radiant pieces, each shooting like a comet into separate corners of the realm.

I swallowed hard, my fingers tightening around the pendant at my throat. It was glowing brightly, but it wasn't hot; it was pretty cool.

"Did we just watch a goddess get fractured?" Blair asked, her voice barely audible.

"Fragments, I think," Parker breathed, his voice cracking.

"And we're those mortals," Denali said quietly, almost rhythmically. "Aren't we?"

The image shifted again. The six fragments—now flickering with hints of our silhouettes—stood at the edge of a battlefield. Blades of light crashed overhead. Shadows like serpents encircled them. But together, they began to glow, merging into a spiral of radiance that shattered the darkness.

The walls pulsed with heat.

"It's telling our story," I whispered. "Or the one we're meant to live." My heart kicked to life, thundering in my chest at the thought.

More glyphs poured across the far wall, forming trails and constellations that looped through landscapes—mountains, forests, lakes, all shaped like the ones we'd passed through. One section formed what looked eerily like the crystalline basin where we first found Denali.

"There's my glacier caves," he noted, pointing. "Even the curve of the ice… It's *exact*."

"And the floating dolmen," Blair said. "That's the field where we met Parker."

My heart thudded. "It knew we were coming. It's always known." I felt dizzy, sick, and weak. I wasn't sure if it was from excitement or dread.

The image changed yet again.

Now we stood in a circle. A vortex of energy—spiral-shaped, of course—opened beneath us, lifting us upward in columns of color, each hue echoing our energies. I saw golden orange and knew it was mine. Purple arched toward Sasha. A sapphire blue glowed near Denali. Emerald green bloomed at Blair's feet. A bold crimson swirled around Elijah, and finally, a sleek silver spiral enveloped Parker, glinting like moonlight on water.

"It's beautiful," Blair whispered, eyes wide. "But it's terrifying."

I nodded, the truth settled in like a weight on my chest. "We're not just here to explore. We're here to restore something ancient or divine."

"Balance," Parker said, voice deep and even. "The word keeps showing up in symbols. That, and… " He paused. "Justice."

The glyphs intensified, sparking and flashing as a single phrase looped again and again in sharp, jagged lines. Parker stepped forward, his fingers tracing it in the air.

"To mend the fractured world, the six must do the unthinkable," he read aloud.

"Um, the unthinkable?" Sasha repeated, unease threading through her tone.

"Guys, this is a little scary, right?" Blair asked, her voice wavering and shaky.

I didn't have an answer. My mind was spinning with symbols, half-translated meanings, and something more profound than words—a knowing in my bones.

We all fell silent, *really* silent.

Each of the six walls now depicted a different scene. And strangely, each one reflected something personal. One showed a woman climbing a steep canyon wall, alone, clutching a pendant with a spiral maze. I recognized myself instantly. How was it possible that she looked exactly like me?

Sasha stood rooted before a wall where tattoos peeled off a woman's skin and flew like birds toward a storm. Her eyes widened. "Oh, my god! That's me."

Denali's breath caught as he stepped to another—an ice cave, lit by pale blue fire, where a man faced a beast made of shadow and memory. "That's my dream," he cried out.

Parker stared at a wall depicting a great tree growing through a circle of stones, each ring inscribed with glyphs. "Mount Shasta," he whispered.

"I think mine is here," Blair said softly, pointing to a mist-shrouded glen where paint bled from the sky into living creatures that walked out of a canvas.

Elijah stepped up to an image of a man meditating beneath a blood-red moon as a firestorm raged around him. "I saw that years ago, but I thought it was just a dream."

We stood for what felt like hours. The room was quiet, except for the soft buzz of the glyphs —a lullaby sung in flame and silence.

Eventually, Sasha turned to us. "So… what do we do with this? I feel like we're in some kind of fantasy movie."

I felt the answer before I spoke it. "We keep going."

"But toward what?" Denali asked.

"We need to explore," Parker said, quiet and steady. "I can feel that something or someone is waiting for us."

"Wait," Blair said, eyes narrowing. "What if this place only awakened because we were all here? All six."

"The Hexad," Elijah said, the word now heavy with meaning. "We must be the Hexad."

I looked around at all of them—these strangers who felt like echoes of something I'd lost or maybe always known. I didn't wholly understand what bound us, but I felt it really strongly now, almost like a bond between siblings.

A pulse from the ground traveled through my boots, through my spine, through the pendant at my chest. I felt warmth and belonging. "I know I should be frightened, but instead I feel oddly soothed by this place."

We all turned to look at the final glyph—one that glowed brighter than the rest.

A spiral of fire, cradled by six hands.

"I don't know how," I said. "But I think it might have something to do with her."

Sasha raised her brow and pointed to the wall. "Her?"

"She looks like a goddess," I whispered, and deciphered the symbol. "I think her name is *Calista*."

As soon as I said the name, something in the walls moved like lungs—glyphs undulating across obsidian surfaces, glowing faintly with silver-blue light. We were still inside the Temple of the Hexad, standing on smooth black stone warmed from within, as if the temple's very heart beat beneath our feet. High above, the vaulted ceiling curved like the inside of a geode, refracting the glow of ancient runes in ripples that shimmered like water. The space thrummed with sacred resonance.

That was when the mist gathered.

It spilled from the arches like fog from a dream, curling low and thick, blurring the light. The glyphs dimmed, and the sound shifted—no longer just a hum, but a whisper. A figure emerged, tall and deliberate, as if she'd stepped from the oldest part of the realm's memory.

She was draped in layered robes the color of dusk—plum, shadow, and glinting threads of silver light. Her hair, white with pale blue strands, drifted as though caught in unseen tides. But it was her eyes that held us: silver, still, and depthless. Looking into them felt like falling inward.

"Be still," she said, and the room obeyed. Her voice was as smooth as flowing water, low and melodic, like a lullaby, soothing in a way that bypassed thought and settled directly into the bones.

Denali moved subtly closer to me. His presence was solid and anchoring. Blair slipped her hand into Sasha's. Elijah had instinctively lowered his head while Parker narrowed his eyes, absorbing.

"You have crossed threshold and thread, storm and echo," the woman said. "I am Zanira, a Spirit Whisperer and Shaman Guide. I am the Daughter of the Moonveil, and Keeper of what the living forget."

There was a reverence in her tone, not arrogance, like someone who carried a burden too sacred to name.

I took a breath. "We don't know where we are or how we got here."

Zanira glided forward—there's no other word for it—and looked directly into me, not *at* me, *into* me.

"You are in the Realm of Aztalun," she said. "This is the realm between realms. Here, memory breathes. Here, spirit and stone speak."

My spiral pendant pulsed again, glowing softly. Her gaze dropped to it, then back to my face. "The spiral calls only to those who are ready to return to truth," she said as she moved toward me in an instant, defying all laws of speed. Her hand rose, and when her fingers brushed my chest to pick up the pendant in her hands, warmth surged through me like fire.

"You are the Seeker, the one who journeys inward through outward paths. You are the Explorer."

I swallowed at how right she was. "Why us?"

Zanira's voice became a breathy wind. "Because you are the Six. The Hexad. Called not by chance, but by need. Each of you is a fragment of the balance that once kept this realm whole."

She walked among us, her silver eyes flicking up and down our bodies, then settling on our faces.

To Sasha: "You are the healer of the inward flame. You have skin that remembers, and your magic is inked in rebellion. You are Form, wild and rising." Sasha's chest tattoo flickered with subtle light as she talked about them.

To Blair: "Ah, you are the Creator. You breathe the unseen into shape. Your brush is your vision and also a doorway. You are the Dream." Blair lowered her eyes, cheeks flushed.

To Denali: "Lover of stories, you ache for connection. You are the heart that remembers. You are Emotion." Denali's hand clenched briefly, then released.

To Elijah: "Hero carved by fire and silence. You move not to conquer, but to protect. You are Will." He gave a solemn nod.

To Parker: "Sage of place and myth. Your maps lead to meaning. You are Thought." Parker's lips moved silently, as if recording her words.

Then, returning to me, she whispered, "And you, who chase shadows in stone—Memory is yours to bear."

She returned to the center of the room. Her presence filled the space, made it feel smaller, and more intimate. "Calista, the imprisoned goddess of balance and knowledge, has chosen each of you. She sleeps within the Obsidian Fortress. She is held by bonds not of metal, but of forgetting."

A flicker of pain crossed her face. "Varek stands watch. But he is not friendly, and you must beware."

The name 'Calista' stirred something inside me. Not recognition, but yearning.

Zanira lifted her arms. "To awaken her, you must embrace the Temples and conquer the five trials."

"Temples?" Blair asked quietly.

She spoke, voice echoing through the chamber. "Each of you represents one of the temples. Temple of Thought: A fortress above the storm, where riddles weigh more than walls, for the Sage. Temple of Emotion: A glade of weeping stone trees, where memories sing in grief, for the Lover. Temple of Will: A black mountain that burns with every step, for the Hero. Temple of Memory: Where forgotten truths linger, beneath petrified roots and fossilized time, for the Explorer. Temple of Dream: A skywalk only art can reach, for the Creator. Temple of Form; a desert of shifting ink and burning tattoos, for the Magician."

She continued, "But before the temples, you must face the trials and walk the Spiral."

Each word struck like a drum.

I knew exactly what she was saying lay ahead for us. We would have to pass some challenges. *Wonderful!* "What happens if we fail?" I asked.

Zanira's silver gaze pierced through me. "Then the balance collapses, Calista fades, Varek consumes himself, and Aztalun becomes ash in twilight."

No one moved or spoke.

Then she stepped close once more and placed her hand over my heart again. Her voice softened. "The spiral does not choose lightly. You are not here to be lost from your Earth. You are here to fight for your destiny."

She turned, the mist swirling around her like a curtain. As she vanished into the sacred fog, her final whisper curled through the glowing air: "Six shall walk, where one once stood. Through grief and flame, memory and storm. What is hidden must be seen. What is fractured must be felt."

And then we were alone, in the still breath of the temple, holding the truth in our hands like flame.

I was the first to speak. "Well," I said, trying to steady my voice, "at least now we know why everything here feels like it's watching us."

"Yeah," Sasha murmured. "And why my tattoos haven't stopped buzzing since we arrived."

Blair looked at her hands. "I think… I've been dreaming about that temple in the sky for years. I just didn't know it was real."

Denali let out a slow exhale. "So, we each have a trial? That's pretty heavy. But maybe it's what we were made for."

"Chosen," Elijah corrected. "Either way, we can't back down."

Parker, thoughtful as always, looked up at the glowing room. "It makes sense of everything we've been experiencing."

I nodded slowly, heart thudding. "She could have given us more information."

"I'm sure she will in time," Parker reassured me.

"I hope you're right, Parker. I really do." I had so many emotions inside me that I didn't know what to think, and that was a bit scary.

10

FRAGMENTS OF DESTINY

We had settled into a loose circle around the chamber, some sitting, some standing or pacing. No one spoke much. Blair was sketching something in the dirt with her fingertip, absently, almost like she didn't realize she was doing it. Denali sat cross-legged, rolling a small stone between his palms. Elijah stood near one of the walls, studying the shifting symbols like they might rearrange into answers if he stared long enough.

Sasha glanced at me. "Do you think she's watching us?"

"I don't know," I admitted. "But I feel like this room is."

Then the air shifted again, like someone turning a page inside the bones of the room.

We turned as one, and she reappeared.

Zanira stepped forward from nothing, as if space had folded open to let her through. "Forgive my absence," she said gently. "I had to tend to a... disturbance nearby."

My skin prickled at her mysteriousness. *That* didn't sound promising. It made me wonder where she went and what she meant.

The chamber was dim, but not dark. Light pulsed gently from the center like breath—alive, ancient, and waiting. Zanira stood at the heart of it, her silver eyes half-lidded, long white hair veiling her shoulders like moonlight draped in silk. Around her, everything in the room seemed to shimmer and shift. If I had been alone, I would have taken several hours to go over every inch. It was enchanting and inviting. Instead, I turned my attention to the ethereal being waiting to talk with us again.

She raised one hand, slowly. The floor beneath her responded, and a spiral of light uncoiled outward from her bare feet, glowing with threads of silver and indigo. It spilled in curves and lines across the stone, mapping itself into rivers and staircases, forests and fire. It looked like a living map, if you could even call it that. It pulsed in rhythm with the six pendants, tattoos, and marks that we bore on our bodies.

"This," Zanira said, her voice a wind echoing through the room, "is the Maze of Shadows."

We all stood frozen, holding our breath. I heard Blair exhale softly beside me, the sound thin and shaken, like she'd forgotten air could move.

Zanira's hands moved again, fingers sweeping gracefully over the glowing image. Each section of the map shifted beneath her touch—liquid terrain reforming with every pass: forests of woven memory, towers of mirrored light, and cracks in the world bleeding fire. The air itself began to pulse, faint at first, then louder.

"The maze was born from betrayal," Zanira said, "a realm forged to imprison not flesh, but essence. Calista, once the guiding flame of knowledge and balance, now dreams within the Obsidian Fortress at its center. She is not dead, but she is also not conscious. She is only still."

No one spoke. Even Parker, who typically held himself with such confident stillness, looked rattled, his broad shoulders tight, his eyes locked on the moving flames near the bottom left of the map.

"Five trials guard the path to her prison," Zanira continued. "Each one is a gate, a mirror, a wound. They will test you, not your strength, but your essence. Each of you carries a fragment of Calista's soul, whether you remember it or not. These fragments—your powers and truths—were scattered across Earth long ago. The six of you were never destined to meet on Earth."

We looked at each other when she made that statement. I knew I was feeling lucky to have met them, so her words hit deeply. The look in their eyes reflected my thoughts, making my heart smile.

Sasha took a small step forward. The shifting map illuminated her dark skin in lavender and silver. The tattoos on her chest shimmered faintly, responding like tuning wires. "So, we're not just chosen," she said quietly. "We're pieces."

Zanira nodded. "You are echoes of a goddess fractured by divine fear. Your bond is not random."

I felt my breath catch.

It sounded like we were fragments of this woman named Calista. Was that why I felt this impossible connection to the others? To Denali, Sasha, Elijah, Blair, and even Parker, with his cryptic calm? We were all strangers, yet something about them felt almost familiar. I'd noticed it when I met them, but figured it was just me being relieved not to be alone anymore.

Zanira's hand hovered over the map again. Five sections now pulsed brighter than the rest. She pointed.

"The Trial of Fire—where your rage will either burn through illusion or consume you. The Trial of Light—where you must walk a staircase made of memory and not fall into your own past. The Trial of Song—where silence is sacred and speaking the wrong word can shatter your voice. The Trial of Reflection—where each of you will see the truth you deny. And the Trial of Stillness—where time collapses and you must remember who you are when all else is stripped away."

The names alone made my skin crawl. And yet, I wanted to know, *needed* to know. My eyes drifted to the forest etched into the map—its branches curled like fingers, its trees impossibly tall. I wondered what it would ask of me, and what it already *knew*.

Denali stepped closer, his dark eyes glinting with unease. "And if we fail?"

Zanira's gaze slid to him, and her voice softened, like mist clinging to vines. "Then you will forget who you are, perhaps forever. The maze does not kill, it unravels. It will not be easy, but you six must decide if the goddess is worth laying your lives down for. I promise you, if you succeed, there will be great gifts given to you, ones that you could never imagine."

A quiet hiss of breath came from Blair. Her fingers had gone white around the strap of her bag.

"But why?" Parker's voice was steady and low. "Why imprison a goddess of balance?"

Zanira turned toward him slowly. Her silver eyes fixed on his with something close to sorrow.

"Because knowledge is not always gentle, Sage. Balance does not always bend toward mercy. Calista weighed too much. She stripped minds of memory to preserve order. She pulled truths from futures not yet born. She decided which secrets could be revealed and which must remain hidden. She called it mercy, but others called it tyranny."

A heavy silence fell.

Elijah crossed his arms, brow furrowed. "She was trying to help, wasn't she?" I knew he was trying to understand this, as we all were.

"She was," Zanira whispered. "But help without consent is not harmony. The other gods grew afraid, not just of what she did, but of what she might do next. And so, they lured her into the maze. They forged the Obsidian Fortress not of walls, but of paradox, into a place where no truth holds. A prison only you six mortals can unlock, for no god may unchain another."

Sasha whispered, "But we're not gods."

"No," Zanira said. "You are much more dangerous. You are Calista's scattered essence—human, imperfect, and free."

The map flared again, its light brushing against each of us like a breeze made of stardust. I felt it hit my pendant and burn through me in waves. I didn't realize I'd grabbed Denali's arm until he looked down, startled. I let go quickly, mumbling something that probably wasn't a real word.

"She's calling us," Blair said with a heavy sigh. "I can *feel* her. In my art and my dreams. I thought I was going mad."

"You are not," Zanira said gently. "You are remembering."

Blair's lips parted, but no sound came.

I turned my attention back to the map, willing myself to focus. There had to be a way through, some sort of pattern. I studied the curves of the labyrinth thoughtfully. My archaeologist's brain kicked into gear: symbols, markers, and meaning. Except this wasn't clay or stone, this was soul. I was used to dead civilizations, but certainly not living gods. Gods? It felt so weird to think it was true.

Denali's voice was low beside me. "Are we ready for this?"

I looked at him, but his expression was unguarded—just raw, honest fear. I didn't know if I was ready; I only knew I had to try. I wasn't sure if it was Alayna Archuleta thinking my thoughts, or this fragment of Calista I held within, but I couldn't ignore it.

"I'm not sure we get a choice," I said quietly. "But maybe that's the point. We all have to choose this or deny it. It can't be only some of us. I don't think any of us could do this without all of us."

Sasha stepped forward again, standing shoulder to shoulder with me. Her tattoos sparked faintly, curling with magic. "Then let's make it count. If we're fragments of her, maybe we're meant to show her what she forgot, and what it means to be whole again."

Elijah gave a firm nod, fists clenched at his sides. "We've fought monsters already. We can fight whatever this is."

Blair remained quiet, but her fingers began sketching something in the air, shapes I didn't recognize, but it made the glowing map ripple in response.

Parker simply said, "Balance isn't stasis, it's movement. Perhaps we're the motion she needs."

Zanira's eyes gleamed with a strange light. "You speak well, Sage. But remember, balance demands cost. The maze will take what you do not want to readily give."

We all looked at each other then, obviously a little spooked.

Elijah, the protector; Blair, the quiet storm; Denali, the heart; Sasha, the healer; Parker, the seer; Me? I was the restless one, always searching.

Zanira stepped back from the map. "The path lies ahead. But first, you must enter willingly. The maze does not open to force; it only opens to intent."

She looked at me, and then *through* me.

"And you, Explorer. You must take the first step. The pendant you wear remembers the way, and you will find it is the key, more times than you will understand."

My heart thudded in my ribs.

I stepped forward, feeling the purr of the map rise beneath my boots like a tremor. I looked at the others, then back at Zanira. "I'm scared," I admitted. "But I *have* to know."

Zanira's smile was small, but full of light. "Then you are ready."

One by one, Denali, Sasha, Elijah, Blair, and Parker stepped forward, and we all held hands in unison. Our decision was made without words.

The map shifted once more, forming a spiral of stairs ascending into the unknown.

Zanira's gaze swept over us—gentle, but with weight behind it. We stood still, each of us pinned in place by the quiet power in her silver eyes.

"These trials," she began, her voice smooth and low, "will demand more than courage. You will face moments that require trust, transformation, and sometimes sacrifice."

My fingers curled around the edge of my pendant, the cool spiral pressing into my palm. *Sacrifice* wasn't a word I liked. It meant giving something up, and lately, I'd fought hard to keep what little I had left of myself.

"You will not walk this maze alone," Zanira continued, stepping toward a corridor that glimmered into being behind her. "But you must be prepared to lose what no longer serves you."

Uh-oh, I didn't like the sound of that!

Blair shifted beside me, her red hair catching the silver-blue light like a flicker of flame. Denali's jaw was tight, his dark eyes fixed on Zanira as if trying to read the truth beneath her calm.

She turned, robes swishing. "Come. You'll rest here tonight."

We followed her down a long corridor, our footsteps echoing across the carved white floor. The air smelled of some strange spice I couldn't name. It reminded me of rituals I'd studied in Mesoamerican temples, offerings burned at altars.

The hallway opened into a vast chamber lit by glowing vines that spiraled up the walls like veins of light. Six beds—low and carved from the stone itself—formed a rough circle around a small hearth where a fire was already lit. A thick, padded material covered each bed, and what looked like plush blankets were folded neatly on each one, in deep purple and gray, embroidered with symbols that shimmered faintly when touched. Lush pillows were at one end. Gorgeous flora lined the outer edge, and a waterfall was located on one wall. It was beautiful.

Zanira turned to face us again. "I could separate you into private quarters, but I believe you'll benefit more from staying together tonight. There are things you must say to one another, questions that must be asked, and fears that must be voiced. You will, no doubt, be discussing your plan."

She paused. "I will return once you have rested."

And with that, she vanished with no sound. Just gone, like smoke pulled through a keyhole.

We stood in stunned silence for far too long. Then Elijah cleared his throat. "Well… that was ominous."

"Sacrifice," Sasha echoed under her breath, sitting carefully on the edge of her bed. "She really had to tell us that, huh?"

Denali dropped his bag to the floor and sat with a grunt, elbows on his knees. "She could've told us *what kind* of sacrifice. That might've been helpful."

I exhaled and moved to the bed farthest from the door, setting down my pack and letting the pendant fall back against my chest. The spiral glinted briefly, catching the light. I didn't want to talk yet. My thoughts were a knot of questions I couldn't untangle.

Blair paced slowly, running her fingers along the grooves of the stone wall. "Do you think the map she showed us was literal or a metaphor?"

"Both," Parker said, stretching out on his selected bed with one arm behind his head. "That spiral didn't just *represent* the maze. It *was* the maze. And the markings responded to us almost as if from a memory."

"That's not creepy at all," I sighed as I stretched my arms behind my back and yawned.

We fell quiet again, each of us watching the fire that crackled softly at the center of the room, throwing shifting shadows across our faces. For a long while, nobody said a word. Each of us had seen something in that map, something we didn't yet understand. I stared into the flames and tried to picture what I might lose in there. What part of me wouldn't make it out?

Elijah finally broke the silence. "So, how are we supposed to get through this?"

Sasha's eyes met his. "By actually *being* together. I don't think that means just walking side-by-side, but trusting each other, and letting our inner selves be seen."

"That's a tall order," I said before I could stop myself.

Denali looked over at me, his expression softening. "Maybe. But we've all been pulled here for a reason. We didn't come through by accident, so something must be tethering us together, and we'll likely need to learn how that works."

"True," I agreed. "But I don't know if that makes me feel better or worse."

Blair perched at the foot of her bed, sketchbook open in her lap. "Do you think Zanira's holding back on purpose?"

"Yes," Parker said, without hesitation. "I think she *has* to. I don't think this works if she tells us everything. Just a hunch."

Sasha tilted her head. "Why?"

"Because the maze doesn't want a rehearsed version of us. It wants who we *are*: our flaws and inner truths. If we go in too prepared, we might lose the very thing that could help us defeat it."

Blair rubbed her thumb along the spiral birthmark on her arm. "So we're supposed to just stumble through and hope we don't die?"

Elijah smirked. "Sounds about right, but I think we're going to come out of this stronger than we went in."

"Maybe she's giving us a chance to figure it out ourselves," I said, still watching Blair. "Like any real teacher would."

Denali leaned back on his elbows. "I hate to admit it, but that makes sense. I've led people through caves before, and the ones who only follow instructions never really *see* what's in front of them. They don't remember the feel of the ice or the way their breath sounds in the silence. They're just checking off a list."

"And we're not here to check boxes," I said slowly, the thought unraveling as I spoke. "We're here to become something else."

The words hung there, too heavy to ignore.

I looked around at the others—at Parker's faraway stare, Sasha's quiet strength, Elijah's steady presence, Blair's focused intensity, and Denali's open warmth. Each of them had something I didn't. Each of them *was* something I wasn't. I felt a sudden pang of inadequacy, sharp and unwelcome.

What if the maze stripped me down and found nothing worth keeping? "I don't know what I'm supposed to become," I admitted, voice low. "But I'm scared of what I might lose along the way."

Blair met my gaze, her clear blue eyes steady. "We're all scared, Alayna."

"Good," Elijah said, rising to toss another log on the fire. "Fear means we know this matters."

"And that we're alive," Denali added with a small smile.

The fire flared up, throwing golden light across the chamber. It flickered over the spiral tattoos, pendants, and marks each of us bore—six pieces of some greater whole. We didn't feel like heroes. We felt like people trying to understand what the hell was happening.

But still, we were there together, instead of running away, terrified. Perhaps we should have been horrified.

I lay back on the stone bed, which was unbelievably comfortable, thanks to its thick padding, and pulled the embroidered blanket over me. It was surprisingly soft and smelled faintly of juniper, with a hint of something older. I stared at the ceiling, which was carved with the same spiral patterns we'd seen on the map. Slowly, they began to pulse, ever so faintly, in time with the beat of my heart. I wasn't sure if it was the firelight or something else entirely.

"We'll get through this," Parker said quietly, as if reading my thoughts. "One step at a time."

I wanted to believe him, I really did. But as sleep crept toward me, curling around the edges of my mind, I couldn't shake the question that kept circling like a hawk above the ruins of my thoughts: *What part of me will I have to give up to find the truth?* And would I still recognize myself when it was all over?

11

TRIAL OF THE FIRE OF ILLUSION

I woke to the smell of something clean and herbal, like sage and morning frost. Zanira's voice was soft but commanding as she stood by the door, her indigo robes pooling around her bare feet like smoke.

"It is time," she said, her silver-gray eyes sweeping over us.

I sat up groggily on the thick blanket and rubbed my eyes. Around me, the others stirred. Blair, clutching the edge of her blanket like she'd been dreaming something too vivid to let go of, Sasha already half-seated and alert, her eyes watchful beneath her halo of dark curls. Denali stretched like a wolf, his long limbs graceful and his long, straight hair spilling over his shoulder. Elijah pushed up with a soldier's efficiency, and Parker blinked behind a veil of quiet thought, his blond hair tousled like he'd fallen asleep reading something ancient.

I was honestly surprised by how rested I felt, almost like I'd just had the best sleep of my life. When I glanced down at the bedding, I blinked in disbelief. It looked like something that should've been lumpy and hard, but somehow it had cradled me like clouds. How was that even possible?

Zanira stepped forward, her hands cupped together. "Each of you, take one."

She opened her palms to reveal six rings—silver and obsidian bands, each etched with a spiral symbol I swore matched the one on my pendant.

"These are protection rings," she said. "They will allow you to create a portal in times of desperation. But hear me clearly—it will not take you where you want to go, only where the realm sees fit. It may be better, or it may be far worse."

"Worse?" Sasha echoed, arching a brow as she took one, rolling it between her fingers.

Zanira nodded. "Use it only if there is no other way. Speak the word 'Virena' and press your palm to any surface. A portal will open, but it will choose the path."

I turned mine over in my hand. The metal felt light. It was cold at first, and then it turned warm, almost pulsing in sync with my heartbeat.

"Try it," she said. "But only open, do not pass through the portal."

We stood in a circle. Blair hesitated, but Denali offered a gentle nod. She pressed her palm to the floor and whispered, "Virena." A circular shimmer like moonlight on water rippled beneath her hand, and then vanished. We each did the same.

"Good," Zanira said. "They are now bonded to you."

She stepped back, folding her arms. "Each of you has something unique. You must remember that. You, Alayna— The Explorer. You are the seeker of truth and meaning. You walk toward mystery when others retreat. Your courage will keep your group alive."

I felt my throat tighten. No one had ever summed me up so cleanly.

"Sasha, The Magician and Healer," she continued, "you challenge the order of things. You hold raw, untamed power. It wants shaping but not caging. You will be able to trick your opponents. Remember that."

Sasha gave a slow nod, her expression determined.

"Blair, The Creator. You give magic form. Beauty flows through your hands with worlds born in color and shadow. Embrace it and use it to your advantage. Your gift is most powerful in combat."

Blair flushed, looking down, the tips of her ears pink.

"Denali, The Lover," Zanira said warmly. "You are the heartbeat of this Hexad. You carry devotion, story, and the steady ground of emotion. You will keep the Hexad bonded."

Denali's eyes softened, though his jaw tightened like he wasn't sure how to receive it.

"Elijah, The Hero. Strength and protection live in you, but so does the burden of always standing guard. You act, but you must also learn when not to. Discipline and strength are yours to bear."

Elijah gave a respectful bow of his head, arms crossed over his chest.

"And Parker, The Sage. You see through illusion. You hold knowledge not just in the mind, but in the spirit. You remember what others forget. Let it guide you."

Parker didn't speak, but his eyes flicked up to hers in silent understanding.

Zanira's voice dropped lower. "You must work together. Your powers will not bloom in isolation. They are tied, woven, and interdependent."

"How do we learn to use them?" I asked.

Her lips curved, not unkindly. "You already are. But I cannot tell you how. Each must walk their own spiral."

Blair whispered, "That's terrifying."

"It's meant to be," Zanira said, then gestured toward the far doors. "Come, you will need strength."

She led us into a vaulted room filled with warm light and flickering lanterns. A feast stretched across a long stone table—roasted root vegetables drizzled in honey, lavender fruit compotes, braids of golden bread, and earthenware bowls of spiced grains. Steam curled from wooden cups, I sure hoped they were filled with something like coffee; and there were a lot of other foods we couldn't name.

My stomach growled loud enough for Denali to laugh softly beside me. "Guess that settles it."

"Eat well," Zanira warned, "but not to excess. The trials are near, and you must be alert and ready."

We dug in quietly at first, the sounds of utensils and muted chewing the only music. The food tasted unreal, like it was magical, and maybe it was. Even Parker, ever the composed one, closed his eyes after a bite of something I had never seen before.

I found myself watching them, my strange, powerful companions—Sasha and Blair trading quiet conversation. Elijah was chewing thoughtfully, always alert. Denali was cracking a joke that actually made Parker smirk. And me, sitting among them, the girl who once thought ancient civilizations were the greatest mystery she'd ever face.

After the meal, Zanira returned. "You have a little time before we begin. Clean up. Prepare. Say what needs saying."

We stood slowly. My hand brushed the ring. Its weight reminded me we weren't just guests in this realm; we were marked by it now. And what waited ahead wouldn't just test us, it would reveal us.

The staircase ended where the world unraveled. Beyond it, sand stretched in every direction—an endless ocean of heat and silence. No horizon, just haze. The light wasn't from the moons, but from somewhere deeper, almost beneath the sky. Zanira raised her hand. "This is the Illusion Desert. What you see may not be real, but what you feel will be. Stay aware."

I nodded, jaw tight, even as the wind pushed against us with a sound like distant weeping. The others walked forward together—Parker silent, Elijah with stormy eyes constantly scanning, Sasha composed, Denali close by, Blair pale but determined. I followed, boots crunching against sand that felt strangely warm, as if it were a living thing.

Then it hit me.

The wind changed, laced with something I recognized: the scent of sage smoke and sun-warmed leather, reminiscent of my parents' home in Albuquerque. But it was too late; I realized what it meant.

I looked down.

My hands were bloody and shaking. I blinked and wiped them on my shirt, but the stains deepened, seeping into the fabric like ink. My bag hung at my side, torn open. Inside were my field notes, smudged and unreadable. The photographs I kept of my family were crumpled and torn. Vincent's voice crept in, uninvited.

"You think you're strong? Nobody can see you here."

"No," I told myself. "This is not real."

But then they appeared, ghostly outlines of people I'd let down, mentors I'd disappointed, students who dropped out, a professor from UCLA whose approval I'd chased for years, my own sister, Julia, her face pinched. "You weren't there when I needed you!"

Each whisper felt like a blade, cutting through my ribs. I turned in a circle, heart racing, vision blurring. I didn't know if I was breathing.

My pendant—my anchor—hung cold against my chest. The turquoise in the center of the spiral dimmed to gray. I sank to my knees in the sand and wept uncontrollably while I watched everyone I had disappointed turn and walk away from me.

"I don't belong here," I whispered. "I'm an imposter, a fake, a failure."

"Hey." Sasha's voice cut through the storm. "Look at me."

I lifted my eyes to hers, dark, steady, and alive. She knelt, pressing a firm hand to my chest, right over the pendant.

"Fear is a liar," she said. "And you don't have to fight it alone. You have saved us all, and we are all here for you."

Blair came next, sliding her hand into mine. Her touch was featherlight, but grounding. Denali wrapped his arms around me and hummed. Parker took my other hand, while Elijah said, "We will protect you and keep you safe."

I breathed—one heartbeat at a time, and then another. The whispers faded, and when I stood, the sand no longer clung, and I could breathe easier.

I could hear an echo on the wind and recognized Zanira's voice. "You have defeated your fear, Alayna. Keep walking ahead."

The moment the wind shifted, I felt the change in Denali's posture. His broad shoulders tensed, his breath caught, and he stopped walking.

"No… " he mumbled, voice already cracked. "Raven, my love?"

He moved ahead of us without explanation, feet dragging like he was underwater. The dunes around him shimmered and twisted. I broke into a jog to catch up.

And then I saw her. It must have been this woman named Raven who haunted him. She wasn't a mirage, but a memory dressed in flesh. And she was stunning.

Raven stood just ahead, her back turned. Long, black hair tousled in that effortless way Denali always described. Her blue parka rustled in the hot wind, though it shouldn't have existed here.

He called out her name again, louder this time. She didn't turn; she just walked on.

I reached him as he started after her, sand slipping beneath his boots.

"Denali, it's not real."

He didn't hear me or didn't care. His hands trembled. "I should've gone with her."

"No, you shouldn't have," I said.

"But what if I'd tried harder? What if—"

She turned then, the illusion of Raven, and I saw her face, beautiful but cruel. Her lips curled with venomous calm.

"You held me back," she said. "Your love felt like a weight dragging me down."

He flinched. "That's not what you said."

"It's what I meant."

The wind howled, throwing sand into his face. The world swam around us. He dropped to his knees as a pool of icy blue light expanded beneath him, flickering with memories. I saw him holding her hand in Alaska, cooking breakfast in a cabin, carving driftwood gifts, and then all of it shattered.

I knelt beside him. "She left, Denali. That's real. But you didn't deserve it."

"I'm always the one who holds on too long," he whispered. "People leave, and I just… stay. I'm paralyzed and can't leave my homeland."

Sasha appeared beside us, calm but fierce. "You stay because you love deeply, that's not weakness."

Blair stepped forward and painted a silvery streak through the mirage with her fingertip. The Raven illusion cracked. Still, Denali didn't move.

"You were too much," the mirage hissed. "Too intense. Too emotional."

His whole body caved inward, like he was bracing for that old wound to split wide open again.

I leaned in. "You are intense, and it's beautiful. Your depth is the reason I trust you. It's why we all do."

His eyes finally met mine, red, wet, and desperate for truth.

"You don't have to let go of how much you loved her," I said. "But you don't have to stay trapped in her departure forever."

"I broke her heart." He reached for my hand, fingers digging in like he was anchoring himself to something solid. His grip was desperate.

"I didn't want to be found," he whispered. "That's why I came here."

The illusion flickered again. The image of Raven shattered into a burst of icy wind, then nothing. The sand beneath him stilled. The spiral on his ring flared faintly.

Behind us, Elijah stood guard, and Parker raised a hand in solemn silence. No one offered platitudes, and no one rushed him.

Denali let his forehead rest against my shoulder. I felt his tears seep through the fabric of my shirt, but I didn't pull away.

"I feel hollow," he said.

"You need to release your guilt, Denali," I told him. "You need to let it go."

And slowly—very slowly—he got to his feet. He took my hand and didn't let go.

The others gathered around us without a word. Our presence was enough. Denali looked out across the dunes. The wind had calmed, the illusion burned away, but he seemed different now, still carrying the ache, but no longer letting it carry him. He took a breath like it hurt to fill his lungs, then turned to us. "Let's keep going."

No one argued, and we fell into step around him, shoulder to shoulder. The desert wasn't done with us yet, but neither were we.

Sasha walked a little ahead, her spine rigid, the wind tugging at the sleeves of her woven wrap. Her hair whipped around her face, but she didn't seem to notice.

Then she stopped.

She was staring at something none of us could see yet, her shoulders rising with shallow breaths. Her tattoos—the ones that always pulsed like silent chants—flickered erratically beneath her sleeves.

"Do you hear that?" she asked.

We caught up, and that's when I heard it too.

Voices.

Not loud, but layered, like echoes crawling out of a canyon. "It's my best friend, Natalia," Sasha said, but then she began to cry.

Natalia materialized and said, "You help others, so you don't have to heal yourself."

Another voice: "You pretend to be whole, but you're not."

A ring of glowing figures emerged from the sand around her: clients, family, friends, and lovers. Their faces were hollow and blurred, but their tone was unmistakable.

"You failed me."

"You were no help."

"You let me drown in my own pain."

Sasha stepped backward, shaking her head. "No. This isn't real. I won't listen to this."

"You abandoned me," said her mother's voice. "You didn't come home when I was sick."

"You let me fall in love with you, and then you disappeared," said Leroy's voice, sharp as glass.

Her breath hitched. "I had to protect myself."

Then came the cruelest blow: a warped version of herself appeared in the middle of the circle, small and hunched, eyes wide with fear beneath ceremonial robes.

"You use us to feel worthy," it whispered. "Your healing is just smoke and mirrors. Your rituals are a mask for what you are afraid to reveal."

Sasha's legs buckled, and she dropped to her knees in the sand. Her spiral tattoo above her heart dimmed, the lines pulsing erratically.

"I tried," she gasped. "I tried to be enough for all of you."

Sasha's body started convulsing.

"We need to do something," I said quickly.

I took a step forward, but Sasha's body stilled and flinched away as if burned. "Don't." Her eyes opened, and she glared at us.

"Sasha—" I said, as I reached out to her.

"They're right," she said. "I can't let anyone really see me. If I do, they'll leave. Nobody can see who I am inside."

Blair moved quietly beside her. "We're a part of you. Let us see you. Choose to let us see you, and I promise we will stay here with you."

Elijah crossed the circle without hesitation and crouched beside her. "You don't need to carry everyone, Sasha. That's not love, that's self-destruction."

Her tattoos flared slightly.

I knelt across from her. "You don't have to prove anything to us, or to any of them."

The hollow version of herself bared its teeth and she screamed, stood, and began to run. We ran after her, but she yelled at us to leave her alone.

"We will not leave you, Sasha," I yelled after her. Finally, Elijah reached her and embraced her. Her arms were flailing about as she fought him.

"No more," he said. "We are here, Sasha. Even when we see inside your soul we will stay."

Sasha's body thrashed again and then went limp in Elijah's arms. He laid her body on the sand as we all knelt beside her. The figures danced all around, and the voices got louder and louder, until Sasha wept.

The tattoos on her arms lit up in waves of color—violet, gold, crimson. A delicate hummingbird, inked near her ankle, came to life and took flight. It zipped between the illusionary figures, dissolving them one by one. The voices died in the wind, their accusations falling to dust.

But Sasha hadn't risen yet. She sat in the sand, breath ragged, palms pressed to the ground like she needed to feel something solid.

"I was terrified," she whispered. "That if I stopped being the healer, I'd be nothing."

"You were never just that," I said. "You're a whole person, brave, wounded, and worthy."

Blair offered a hand but didn't rush her. Sasha looked up, tears streaking her cheeks. "I don't know how to let people help."

"You just did," Blair replied.

Sasha reached out not just to Blair, but to all of us.

We helped her stand, and she smiled, a tired yet genuine smile.

"I'm going to need reminding," she said.

"Then we'll remind you whenever you need us to," Elijah said.

As we continued walking, she stayed in the center of the group this time, not ahead or behind. And for the first time, I saw the healer let herself be held.

Elijah never showed fear. He walked like a fortress, tall, silent, and reliable, with a warrior's calm and a monk's presence. But as the desert deepened, I noticed his hand flexing at his side, a slight tension in his jaw. His eyes narrowed, tracking something only he could see.

Then, without a word, he stepped into the fire. Flames erupted around him in a sudden, terrible circle—alive, crackling, and licking the sky. They moved like sentient beings, shifting to form images within the heat.

We all yelled his name, but he didn't look back.

"Elijah!" I screamed, my boots skidding through hot sand.

Inside the ring, the flames twisted into memories: a dojo engulfed in smoke, children crying. One small figure—maybe a student?—lay motionless on the floor. Another image emerged—he yelled out his sister Grace's name—she was wide-eyed and reaching for him just before she vanished in ash.

He turned in place, fists clenched. "I couldn't stop it. I wasn't fast enough."

The scene shifted again. A woman kissed him and told him she loved him, but then she turned her back to him as she walked away without a word.

"I stayed for everyone else, for the cause, the students, and the order," Elijah said hoarsely. "But no one ever stayed for me."

He fell to his knees. The fire flared higher. The heat singed my skin even from a distance of yards.

"Elijah!" Denali shouted, trying to run in, but the fire stopped him like a wall.

Parker tried and was able to step right through, calm and confident. The flames didn't scorch his skin. He walked right up to Elijah.

"This is fear," Parker said. "Not truth."

"I should've done more," Elijah cried. "I should have held the building longer. Maybe they wouldn't have died."

I stepped into the fire beside Parker. It didn't burn me because I knew it wasn't real. "You did everything you could," I said. "And they knew that. You're still here because of your strength. But it's okay to let it break sometimes."

Elijah turned toward me, face streaked with soot and sweat. "If I break, who carries the rest of you?"

"We all do," Sasha said gently, stepping past the flames without flinching. "That's the point."

Elijah's hands dropped from his face. He looked at each of us—me, Parker, Sasha, along with Denali and Blair, who waited just outside the circle, eyes wide with silent worry.

His breath came shallow, a single tremble in his chest. "I've never been able to let it go. Her name was Maya, she was six, and she was burned alive because I couldn't get to her."

"Then let her go now," I said. "She's ready for you to let her go."

"What about your sister?" Sasha asked quietly. Elijah looked up at her and smiled faintly. "I could only save one of them, and I chose my sister." Tears slid down his cheek. "I tried to go back inside again, but it was too late."

"It's alright, Elijah. You could only save one, and you chose someone you loved. That doesn't mean you chose wrong," Denali told him.

Elijah slumped forward, and Parker caught him, solid and quiet.

The fire flickered, dimmed, and then died away.

But it wasn't just the flames that faded. It was the weight in Elijah's shoulders and the tension in his jaw. His mask cracked open, and it didn't break him. He let out a deep breath and opened his eyes.

He turned to Blair, who walked forward now, her palm outstretched.

"You're so much stronger than you think," she said.

He took her hand, rough fingers curling around hers.

"I felt like a failure," he admitted, voice rough. "I've been trying to make up for it ever since."

"You're not," I said. "You're worthy of love just like all of us. You're important."

He stood then, shakily but on his own. Not perfect or invincible. And for the first time since we met him, Elijah didn't walk at the edge of the group. He walked in the middle.

We walked on, knowing it was the only way to get to the next scene.

Blair stopped cold.

At first, I thought she saw something in the distance, another illusion. But then I saw her face. Her whole body had gone still, her mouth slightly open, and her eyes locked on something floating in the air before her.

It was a painting. Not just any painting, one of hers. But it was all wrong.

The canvas hovered a few feet above the ground, twisting gently in the hot wind like it weighed nothing. Colors pulsed across its surface—angry reds, charcoals, rusted oranges. Creatures writhed at the edges, half-formed things with eyes that blinked open and shut without rhythm. One of them snarled and began to crawl free from the brushstrokes.

Blair took a shaky step back.

"I didn't paint this," she cried. "I mean, I did, but not like this. I never meant for it to hurt anyone."

The creature slithered down from the canvas—part wolf, part wasp, and part nightmare. It snarled at her with a wet, gurgling sound.

"This is from my sketchbook," she choked out. "It was just a concept I abandoned years ago. It was just supposed to be for a book cover."

"You didn't bring this to life," Parker said, stepping beside her. "Your fear did."

Blair's eyes flicked to him, then back to the canvas. Another figure began to form, something humanoid and faceless, its skin stretched thin like damp paper. It staggered forward, arms reaching, and broke free from the canvas with a sickening tear.

The thing landed in the sand with a wet thud. It rose, twitching, head tilted as if sniffing. It had no eyes or mouth, just a smooth blankness where a face should be, and then it lunged.

Blair cried out and stumbled back. Elijah was the first to react, his body moving in a blur, intercepting the creature mid-leap and driving it into the sand. It shrieked like a hundred people crying at once.

Sasha threw her hands forward, summoning a ring of blue flame that circled the creature, holding it in place, but it writhed, gnashing its arms like teeth.

Denali grabbed a nearby obsidian shard and used it like a blade, slashing through one of its limbs. Black paint splattered across the sand.

Parker traced a symbol into the air, and a sudden tremor rippled through the earth beneath the creature's feet, momentarily unbalancing it.

"Blair!" I shouted. "Now!"

She stood tall, breath heaving, and raised her hand. She took the painting and ripped it to shreds, and the creature disintegrated instantly.

Blair fell to her knees and sobbed. "I keep everything inside," Blair whispered. "Every idea and every fear. I lock them in my art, and I thought that was control. But it wasn't, it was just containment, and now they're being unleashed through my paintings."

"You're not dangerous," I said softly.

"But what if I am?" she asked, tears spilling over. "What if I create something I can't undo? What if one day I hurt someone or kill them?"

Her hands were trembling.

"I wanted to share beauty," she went on, "but the shadows come too. I've spent years hiding the darker side of my art and of me."

Sasha knelt beside her. "Darkness isn't the enemy, Blair, denying it is."

Denali stepped forward slowly, as if approaching a wounded animal. "You've never used your gift to harm. Even your nightmares have purpose. They show us what we need to face."

Elijah added, "The fear doesn't make you dangerous. Fear without support does."

Another creature leaped off the next page. It was a large black dragon with red eyes that breathed fire at all of us. Blair held up her hand. A swirl of color bloomed in her palm, cool blue and soft lavender.

"I see you," she whispered. "You're part of me, but you don't control me."

The creature paused.

And with a slow, deliberate gesture, Blair drew a spiral in the air, then flicked her wrist. A burst of silver light shot from her fingertips and struck the dragon. It buckled, howled, and then folded in on itself like crumpled foil, vanishing into dust while the creation faded with a whisper.

"I've been terrified of what's inside me," she said, voice hoarse. "Not the beauty, but the chaos, the parts I don't show."

I knelt beside her. "But you just showed us, and we're still with you."

She looked up at me, then to the others gathered close. "I thought if people saw what I keep inside, they'd be horrified."

"We're not going anywhere," Elijah said, kneeling to pull her gently into a hug.

Blair's head dropped to his shoulder, tears soaking into his shirt.

"You're not a danger," Parker said. "You're a mirror. You show truth, and that's why your art breathes into reality."

Blair gave a weak laugh. "That's a terrifying compliment."

We all chuckled softly. But none of us looked away from her. Because finally, Blair had let herself be seen.

We all forged ahead, knowing Parker was next. He had been quiet for a while, too quiet, even for him. He'd walked a little ahead of us since Blair's trial, shoulders squared, lips pressed tight, eyes scanning the horizon like he expected the sand to rearrange itself into something readable.

And then he stopped.

A flicker of movement caught my eye, shadows rising from the dunes, coalescing into the shape of a house, but not just any house. It was a modest, ivy-choked brick home with peeling shutters and a sunken garden in the back.

"My house," Parker said slowly. "But why?"

But now, the garden was dying, and the ivy shriveled. The windows were black, and in the center stood a single figure, a young boy.

At first, the boy just stared at Parker, but then his expression twisted.

"You left me," he said.

"Aris, my baby brother. I didn't leave you. I had to go."

"You were supposed to help her," Aris continued. "When Dad started drinking again and hitting her. I called you, but you didn't answer."

"I didn't know," Parker said hoarsely. "I didn't know it was that bad."

"You were chasing stories, dust, and runes and ancient myths, while we were falling apart."

"I was trying to find meaning," Parker whispered. "Something to explain why things break."

Aris shook his head. "You missed everything. You weren't there. That's why we broke."

The house began to sink into the sand. The sky above it turned gray, warped with guilt. The spiral on Parker's ring dimmed to almost nothing.

I stepped forward, but he didn't see me.

His hand shook as he reached for the mirage, as if trying to stop time. "I had no idea that he had begun to hit her."

"You never came back for us," the illusion said.

Parker dropped to his knees, the desert swallowing him in stillness.

"I should have been there," he cried. "I made knowledge more important than love."

Denali crouched beside him. "You followed what called to you. That doesn't make you selfish, and you didn't know."

Blair stepped in close. "You've helped all of us understand this place. You've carried us with your maps and metaphors. You didn't abandon your family, you just didn't know they needed you."

Sasha knelt beside him. "And it's not too late, Aris isn't gone. Your family still exists, and you're allowed to make mistakes. You can still reach out to them and make it up."

Parker lifted his head slightly, tears brimming. "But what if I don't know how to go back?"

I crouched in front of him. "Then start with this: come back with us."

He looked at each of us in turn, as if waking from a dream, and then he stood.

The illusion of the house flickered, and Aris vanished. The dead garden bloomed briefly, just long enough for Parker to notice.

"I still don't know how to fix things. I don't know what to do," he said quietly.

"You will. We will help you," I said. "You're the one who helped us see this place for what it is."

He nodded slowly, more to himself than us. Then he reached into his coat and pulled out a folded page from one of his journals. It had a sketch of a spiral temple on one side, and on the back was a note to Aris he'd never sent. He let the wind take it. And as it sailed away, the sand beneath us settled.

1 2

TRIAL OF THE LIGHT OF MEMORY

The path narrowed as we moved through the canyon, the sandstone walls rising so high they blocked the light of all three moons. The air turned gritty, thick with the scent of iron and something mustier—moss, dust, and the faintest trace of smoke. Each step we took seemed to echo too loudly.

"I hate it already," Blair mumbled, hugging her tote bag to her chest. Her boots scuffed the gravel with each reluctant step.

"You hate everything ominous," Parker replied, his eyes scanning the carved symbols on the rock face beside us. "Which is unfortunate, given where we are."

"I'm not scared," Sasha said, pushing ahead. "I'm just annoyed we couldn't take a portal closer or just float there. Or, I don't know, not walking through a literal death canyon."

"We needed to come on foot," Elijah said quietly from behind me. "I believe the trial watches how we approach, not just how we endure."

"Great," Denali said under his breath. "It's judging us already."

Suddenly, the wind shifted. It wasn't a breeze anymore. It slithered through the canyon, a breath through clenched teeth. A groan echoed through the rock around us, low and mournful, as if the canyon had exhaled something long dead. Blair pulled her hoodie up and mumbled something I didn't catch. Parker slowed beside me, his eyes narrowing at the sigils etched into the stone, their curves older than any language I knew. Sasha, uncharacteristically quiet, moved ahead without a complaint. The temperature dropped so fast my skin prickled, and a low moan rose from somewhere deep in the stone. The rocks themselves seemed to be warning us to run. Ahead, the canyon narrowed into a jagged slit of darkness, and the light dimmed.

We didn't speak. Then came the vibration. It was subtle at first, just a tremble in the sole of my boots. Then it came stronger. The ground beneath us thudded once. I glanced at Elijah, who'd gone still, hand hovering near the small pouch at his belt like he was readying himself for almost anything.

A few more tentative steps, and we were around a bend where the canyon spat us out suddenly into a basin of cracked stone and more shadows. There were no longer any trees or sound. The silence pressed dense against my eardrums. I felt the pulse before I saw it, A hum of grief echoing up beneath the surface.

The tomb rose ahead, carved into the cliffside itself, its entrance a mouth of jagged archways and glyphs that pulsed faintly as we neared. The door stood open, yawning wide with darkness.

"This must be the tomb," I said, though the words caught in my throat.

No one replied. We just stood there, all six of us, caught in the hush.

Then Elijah stepped forward without a word, and one by one, we followed, drawn not by courage, but by something heavier—duty or maybe even fate. There was a thread of something we couldn't see. Whatever it was, it pulled us into the dark. At least we were together.

I didn't like the way the ground sounded when we stepped inside.

Each footfall echoed like we didn't belong. The air was dry and stale, filled with a sour scent of something trapped too long. The walls stretched out like ribs in the dark, carved with sigils older than memory. Something about this place felt wrong in my bones. It was too quiet and far too still.

"Anyone else feel like we just walked into the lungs of a corpse?" Sasha whispered.

"I was going to say something slightly more poetic," Parker answered, "but yes."

A whisper drifted past my ear, not the wind but a word. *It was my name.*

I froze. "Did you hear that?"

"More than hear it," Elijah said. His shoulders tensed, "I felt it."

The whisper came again, but this time it was layered, like voices speaking through one another. I recognized one of them, it was my mother, not her voice exactly, but a twisted echo of it.

"This isn't what I raised you to do."

My breath caught in my throat.

To my left, Sasha flinched and murmured, "No. No, don't say that—"

Denali turned sharply. "What's wrong?"

"They're in our heads," Sasha said, her voice barely above a whisper. "It's my dad. I think it's him, but then it's not. I can't explain it."

"This place is feeding on our memories," Elijah said quietly. "Emotion and especially guilt."

"We need to anchor ourselves, or it could devour us," Parker warned.

"Oh, good," Blair said from behind me. "Friendly *and* ominous. What a great combination."

Then the tomb *moved*.

The floor trembled beneath our feet. Faint blue light crawled from the carvings along the walls, and the whispers sharpened into screams. Cracks appeared and something heavy breathed behind the stone.

"Back!" Elijah shouted, pushing Sasha behind him just as skeletal arms clawed out of the nearest crypt.

Dozens of them, figures wrapped in decaying burial cloth, bone-white and snarling without mouths. They poured out like smoke and bone, faster than I expected the dead to move.

"Scatter!" Denali barked. He slammed his palms into the floor. A fissure exploded out from beneath him, and the ground between us and the swarm split open like a jagged grin. Bones tumbled into the crevice with a sickening crunch.

Sasha grabbed my hand and yanked me left as one of the skeletal figures lunged. She raised her palm and blasted it with a flash of violet energy—raw, crackling, and chaotic. The creature shattered into bone dust.

"I am so done with creepy dead things," she panted.

"You say that like it's not our first encounter," I said, ducking under a swipe of claws.

A shriek tore through the air—inky and colorless—and I turned just in time to see Blair drop to her knees, papers spilling from her bag.

"No, no, no," she gasped. "Not here—please—"

Her unfinished sketches were scattered across the stone, and one began to *move*. Ink bled out across the ground, pooling and twisting upward into a writhing shape— humanoid, faceless, pulsing with color and shadow. It stepped off the page.

"Eli!" I yelled.

He was already moving. He spun, swept low, and kicked the creature backward. It staggered, then howled with a mouth it didn't have. Elijah flowed into a wide stance, hands raised, breath steady. "Blair, pull it back!"

"I'm trying!"

She reached for the sketch, fingers shaking.

The creature lashed out. Elijah caught the strike with his forearm, flipped backward, and struck it midair with a sharp palm to the chest. "Parker! Help her!"

Parker stepped into the chaos with unnerving calm. His voice rose above the cacophony—an incantation smooth and rhythmic, like water cutting stone. The ink-creature stuttered. Parker kept speaking, each syllable pulling the monster's limbs taut like marionette strings.

Blair squeezed her eyes shut, whispering apologies to the parchment. She dragged a line of charcoal through the creature's chest in midair—just *willed* it—and the thing began to unravel, pulling itself back into the sketch with a groan of tearing canvas.

When it vanished, Blair dropped the paper, panting hard. "That was not supposed to happen."

"We'll debrief later," I said. "We're not done."

With a flick of Elijah's wrist, he sent another one hurling into a cluster of risen dead, and the explosion knocked them into the air like broken marionettes.

"Eli!" Denali shouted. "On your left!"

Too late—a spectral child stepped from the shadows behind him. Her eyes were hollow, and her tiny hands reached for his chest.

Elijah faltered. His breathing hitched.

"What's wrong?" I shouted.

"I know her," he said hoarsely. "Myah. I didn't save her."

The shadow-girl drifted closer. Elijah didn't move or fight.

"Elijah!" I grabbed his arm and shook him hard. "This isn't real. You did nothing wrong."

He blinked once, then twice. Then his eyes hardened, and he nodded. "Right."

He turned and faced the girl, then bowed, not out of fear, but reverence. When he straightened, she was gone.

The tomb began to shift again. The walls moaned, and the whispers twisted into accusations—louder now, and much more vicious. My mother's voice returned. *"You let your sister down. You left everything behind. You never returned."*

I wanted to scream. I tried to run. But my legs wouldn't move. Instead, I turned to the nearest sarcophagus. Glyphs danced along its side, familiar and ancient. I dropped to my knees, tracing the sigils with shaking fingers.

"Alayna, what are you doing?" Sasha called.

"This is the way through. I'm sure of it."

The symbols warmed under my touch. The whispers quieted, only slightly, but it was enough. I kept tracing, faster now. I recognized them from a dig site in Belize, buried under volcanic ash. Protective runes, and not meant to lock evil in, but grief.

"This place isn't attacking us," I said aloud. "It's *mourning*."

Behind us, the others formed a circle, shoulders touching, backs to each other. Denali kept the ground solid beneath us, arms raised, face streaked with dirt. Sasha hurled arcane bolts like wild comets. Parker stood at the center, voice resonating through the stones as he chanted. Elijah flowed like water, guarding the perimeter, not just with strength, but with calm. Blair clutched her sketchbook and drew a seal midair, paint forming directly from her bare fingers, the ink glowing gold. Sasha sent arcs of fire along the floor, forming a protective perimeter around us. And Parker whispered names—real ones, ancient ones—and the spirits paused, as if finally being heard.

Then I found the final glyph. I pressed it with both palms. The floor shuddered. A low, keening sound echoed from the tombs—a *release*. One by one, the figures stopped moving, and the whispers dimmed into a hum. The cold loosened its grip.

I didn't realize I was crying until I tasted salt on my lips.

Silence fell.

I sat back on my heels, heart thudding like it was trying to escape my chest. "Is it over?"

Blair collapsed next to me, her breathing shallow. "God, I hope so."

"That was... " Sasha trailed off, rubbing her arms. "Crazy!"

"Are you alright?" Denali asked, stepping over carefully, his voice low and concerned.

I gave him a tired smile. "I think I left half my soul back there, but yeah. I'm good."

Elijah sat cross-legged on the ground, head tilted back, eyes closed. "That was a test."

Denali stood at the edge of the fading fire line, eyes scanning the room. "I think we passed."

"Barely," Parker added, helping Blair to her feet. "But yes."

Sasha pressed her fingers to the tomb wall. "This place is resting for now."

"I'm not," Blair muttered. "My hands are still shaking."

"Better than not feeling anything," Denali said. He lowered himself to the stone beside her, offering his canteen. Looking up he caught Sasha's eye. "You were incredible in there, Magician."

Sasha looked away, cheeks flushed. "We were all incredible."

"Yes, we were." I breathed.

Parker brushed soot from his cloak, looking far too composed. "Next time, I'd like to request a trial that doesn't involve psychic torment and physical dismemberment."

Blair let out a weak laugh. "I second that."

I looked around at all of them—these people who were strangers not long ago, now marked with the same scars, holding the same secrets. Something had changed. We'd all seen parts of ourselves we'd tried to bury. But we were still here.

"Hey," I said softly, feeling weak. "We did it. That's something to be proud of."

Sasha raised her hand. "Still voting 'never again,' for the record."

"Duly noted," I said.

But deep down, I knew this was only the beginning.

We stayed there for a long while, recuperating and just taking a breath.

Blair finally opened her eyes and stood, her face pale but resolute. She looked older, somehow, or maybe just more worn down by something we couldn't see.

"This tomb was part of the original sanctum," Blair said, her voice barely more than a breath. "A resting place for those who tried to restore balance once before they failed."

"Failed?" Sasha asked, blinking. "You mean there were others like us?"

Blair nodded slowly. "I think so."

That hit harder than it should have. I looked around at all of us, so different in strengths, in our pain, and in our past. Were we stronger, or just lucky?

"I have the sense that we're running on borrowed time," Blair said, lowering herself onto a fallen slab. Her hands still shook. She started sketching absently, thin lines forming a circle that spiraled inward.

Denali stood near the edge of the dark, his eyes narrowed. "We aren't those people. We've made it further already."

"Only just," Parker muttered. "Next time, I'd prefer to be emotionally eviscerated *after* breakfast."

Elijah chuckled, low and brief, but real. "That would be nice."

He looked different now, lighter, still intense and deliberate in his body language, but something about his shoulders had relaxed. Confronting that ghost-child had unknotted a part of him he'd carried too long.

"Are you alright?" I asked.

Elijah nodded, gaze still on the floor. "It's strange. I thought the worst part would be the guilt. But it wasn't. It was the idea that maybe that moment was all I'd ever be."

I nodded slowly. "Yeah. I get that."

Sasha plopped down beside Elijah and leaned into his side without asking. "I vote we nap here. Just for, like, a year."

"I'm not against it," Elijah said, draping an arm around her shoulder.

She smiled, eyes closing for a second, like she might actually fall asleep. For all her spark and sass, Sasha was still just a girl who'd lost her dad, faced her fear, and stood her ground.

"I need to paint," Blair said suddenly. "Something gentle that isn't trying to eat me."

"Could you paint us a hot spring?" Denali asked. "Maybe one that hums lullabies and serves tea."

"No promises," Blair said, then paused. "But I could try."

I sat down next to her, wrapping my arms around my knees. "Did you guys feel it too? At the end, that sense that the tomb was finally at peace?"

Parker nodded. "It's quiet now, like a story was finally allowed to end."

"And we're still in ours," I whispered.

A long silence followed. But this one wasn't heavy. It was filled with relief, and a sense of belonging. We didn't know what came next. But after today, I knew we'd face it together.

Later, as I stood apart from the others, trying to pretend the trembling in my hands was just adrenaline. The tomb behind us had fallen silent, but its weight lingered like ashes in my lungs. My muscles ached from tension, and I closed my eyes, just for a second.

I didn't hear Denali approach, but I felt him. He didn't speak, just came to stand beside me, close enough that I could feel the heat radiating off his body. His presence wasn't overwhelming; it was calm and steady, like the slow rhythm of a heartbeat against a cold wall.

"You were amazing in there," he told me, voice low and rough at the edges.

I gave a breathless laugh. "I don't feel amazing. I feel sick and weak."

He didn't answer. Instead, his hand found my shoulder, warm and careful, his thumb brushing just slightly across the curve of my collarbone. The contact sent a slight jolt through me, something electric and embarrassingly welcome. I didn't move away. Instead, I leaned into it—just a little. I must have needed the connection.

The world around us didn't fall away, but it softened. My pulse slowed. Denali's touch was a tether, holding me still in a space that had tried so hard to pull me apart. I let my shoulder rest against his chest, just for a heartbeat longer than necessary. I felt him exhale.

When I looked up, he was watching me with those dark eyes, which were so full of silence and stories I hadn't asked to hear yet. But I wanted to. God, I wanted to get to know him better.

Our eyes held for a long moment, neither of us blinking, like something was unfolding wordlessly between us, something quiet and real. Denali leaned his face closer to mine, and I could feel his warm breath so close to my lips. It wasn't a kiss or a confession. But it *was* the beginning of something dangerous, possibly even worth trusting.

The memory of the tomb faded behind us as we walked out of its shadow, the towering spires shrinking with every step we took. It still glowed faintly, like embers banked under ash, but the deeper into the forest we went, the quieter everything became. Even the air felt hushed and reverent.

We walked in silence, each of us wrapped in whatever we'd just seen. My legs ached, and the magic buzzing beneath my skin felt raw, like a sunburn on my soul.

"There," Denali said, pointing toward a sloped ridge dappled in moss-like flora.

Tucked between two jutting boulders was a narrow cave. Elijah stepped forward without a word, ducking into its mouth. A few minutes later, his voice echoed back to us. "It's deep, dry, and feels safe to me."

That was enough for me. I slid my pack off with a groan. "Let's stop here."

Inside it was much cooler, metallic scented, and still. Parker brushed his fingers along the cave wall, his expression changing as interest grew, whispering something I didn't catch. Elijah lingered near the entrance, eyes scanning the surrounding area in case creatures were lurking about.

Sasha crouched to build a fire. "The energy here is different. It's very grounded."

Denali laid his coat out for Blair to sit on. "We need our rest."

We spread out our makeshift blankets in a quiet ring, back against the stone. No one said much; we were too exhausted. The cave welcomed us.

Outside, the sky deepened slightly, and far off, the tomb's glow dimmed to a mere memory.

13

TRIAL OF THE SONG OF ECHOES

I woke to the faint sound of dripping water echoing from somewhere deep inside the cave. My back ached from sleeping on stone, and the fire we'd built the night before had long since burned to ash. Around me, the others stirred—Sasha stretching like a cat, Blair blinking slowly, still wrapped in her blanket. Elijah sat near the cave's mouth with Parker and Denali, the three of them silhouetted against the soft lavender light leaking in.

"Morning," Elijah said, voice gravelly.

"Barely," I said, rubbing grit from my eyes. "Did you sleep at all?"

Elijah shrugged. "I didn't want to miss the sky changing since it rarely does."

Blair joined us, hugging her knees. "The air feels different today."

"It seems more charged," Sasha added, running her fingers over the spiral tattoo on her chest.

Parker turned to us, his tone hushed. "We're near something ancient. I felt it all night."

We gathered our things quietly. No one needed to say it; we all felt the same pull.

Outside, the jungle revealed itself. The trees glowed from within. Luminescent vines cascaded from branches like falling stars, and the air shimmered with floating flecks of golden light, beautiful, ethereal, and otherworldly.

"Found it," Elijah called out in a low but certain voice.

We all hurried toward him, and there it was, just beyond a dense curtain of hanging vines. The glowing jungle opened like a dream made real, bathed in light that couldn't have come from the sun, since there were only moons. The surrounding trees glistened with bioluminescent bark, their canopies pulsing. This wasn't just a forest; it was our next destination. The subsequent trial awaited us, the next unknown. I braced myself

The jungle pulsed around us as we entered it, not with danger, but with an ancient rhythm that felt like it remembered us. Vines glowed faintly, curling like question marks. The trees arched high, their silver leaves glowing, as though lit from within. I stepped over a root that seemed to twitch, making me jump back, and cast a glance back at the others. Blair caught my eye and offered a small, uncertain smile, one hand clutching the strap of her bag like it was a talisman.

"Still no signposts," Denali said, just behind me. "But, somehow, I think we're going the right way."

"Don't jinx it," I told him, brushing a damp fern out of my face. "Whatever is guiding us, I'd like it to keep doing that."

"It's instinct," Sasha said from the middle of the group, her eyes scanning the trees. "We all feel it, right? It's like gravity, except it's sideways."

"She's right," Elijah said. His voice was steady, grounded. "Every time we veer off even a little, something in my chest tightens. I think the land wants us to find this place."

"Or something *else* wants us to find it," Parker added quietly. "We should be cautious."

He always spoke like that, softly, with meaning folded under meaning. I appreciated it, even when it unsettled me.

I stepped around a slick, mossy rock and nearly slipped, catching myself with one hand on a tree. It hummed beneath my palm, *literally*. A low vibration, like a cello string plucked in another realm. I looked up, and golden pollen drifted through the air like fireflies underwater.

"Did anyone else feel that?" I asked.

"The hum?" Blair said. "Yes. I thought it was just me."

Denali moved beside me, brows drawn. "It's strongest right here, almost like the trees are echoing something."

Sasha touched her spiral tattoo through her shirt. "They're responding to our energy. I think we're really close."

We pressed on. It got hotter, the air syrupy with moisture and the scent of crushed leaves. My shirt clung to my back and sweat dripped into my eyes. But I couldn't stop, none of us could. There was a pull, as if our bones remembered a story the rest of us had forgotten.

"We're all okay, right?" I asked suddenly, not because I needed to know—we were clearly not okay—but because I wanted to hear the answer.

Elijah, at the back, nodded. "We're here, and that's enough for now."

I met his gaze briefly. His light blue eyes were calm, like still water. I found it oddly reassuring.

"Can't lie," Blair said softly, "part of me feels like I've dreamed this before."

"You might have," Parker said, not unkindly. "Aztalun bends time, making memories bleed backward."

"Great," I muttered. "So, I can blame this place for all my weird recurring dreams?"

Denali chuckled. "Only if they involve glowing vines and ghosts."

"Ghosts?" Blair asked, stopping mid-step.

He gave her a crooked smile. "Sorry—just a feeling."

I turned and raised an eyebrow. "What kind of feeling?"

"The kind that says don't turn back." He nodded, but his typical smile was missing.

We emerged into a clearing, and every sound dropped away. No birds or wind, just silence.

And then we saw it. The cavern mouth yawned open at the base of a craggy rock wall, jagged with broken obsidian. Vines draped its entrance like curtains of green fire. Pale mist spilled from within, curling around our ankles as we approached.

Sasha went first. "This must be it," she said, voice hushed. "It seems to be a lake of some sort."

We followed her down a narrow slope. My boots scraped stone slick with dew, and the air grew colder with every step. The glow above dimmed, and the path leveled into a vast underground chamber.

I stopped breathing as I saw it.

The cavern lake stretched out before us, silent and smooth as black glass. It reflected not just our bodies and the shadows behind our movements, but also faint flickers of color in the dark.

Stalactites hung like icicles from the ceiling, dripping silver water into the stillness. Glowing fungi dotted the stone walls, throwing an eerie teal light that painted everything in underwater tones.

And there—on the far side—were jaguars. Three of them. They didn't move. They just stood there, half-light and half-shadow. It was enough to make every cell in my body go rigid.

Their eyes blazed like moons. Not white or yellow, but something spectral, piercing, and ancient. They were magnificent, and their eyes were mesmerizing.

I didn't realize I'd taken a step backward until Denali caught my arm gently. "Alayna," he said, low. "Look away."

I did. It took effort, like pulling myself out of wet sand.

Blair's breath hitched behind me. "They're so beautiful."

"And lethal," Elijah said. "That stare drains your energy. Don't look into their eyes. I did and felt them unravel me from within."

"They're not attacking," Sasha whispered.

"They don't have to. They're guarding," Parker said, awe in his voice. "I think they are spirit sentinels."

"What is that?" Blair asked, blinking.

"Sentinels are part spirit, part shadow, and part memory. The fact that we can see them means we've seen them before," Parker informed us.

"So, we're not meant to fight them?" I asked, the realization settling into my bones. "We're meant to understand them, or be seen by them?"

"I don't think they attack unless provoked." Parker murmured. "I think they are guarding the lake itself as it must hold deep spiritual power."

"Wow, this is surreal," I said, looking into the water.

"Will there be beasts in that water?" Sasha asked, alarmed.

"They aren't just animals; they are guardians of something older than language. They measure the weight of your soul before letting you pass. We have to walk over to them. I think we need to be able to get past them to survive the trial," Parker explained.

Denali was still holding my arm. I glanced down at his hand, warm and steady against my skin. I didn't move away.

For a long moment, no one spoke.

Then Sasha asked, "Can anyone else feel time slowing?"

"Yes," Elijah said, eyes still locked on the lake. "It's like the air's thick with memory."

I felt it too. My thoughts dragged. My limbs felt heavy, as if I were moving underwater. But deeper than that, something inside me stirred. The pendant at my neck buzzed faintly, matching the hum of the jungle above.

"We're in a liminal space," Parker explained. "Between what was and what could be."

The jaguars stared at us unmoving and unchanging. I felt seen. Not as I presented myself, but all of me: ambition, fear, heartbreak, and even the ache I never talked about. Heidi would have understood. She always did. I could almost hear her voice, teasing me to stop trying to outthink the world.

Denali let go of my arm but stayed close.

Sasha knelt and dipped her fingers into the water. "It's warm."

Parker tilted his head. "That's impossible."

"Why?" Blair asked.

"Because we're too far underground for it to be warm," Denali answered slowly.

"This whole place seems impossible," I said, my voice barely above a whisper. "But here we are. Impossible or not, if it's warm, then it is warm."

The spectral jaguars didn't blink. And I knew we were being tested, not just for strength or magic, but for the truths we carried within us. Maybe this was a mirror.

"We need to cross this lake," Elijah said as he drew in a deep breath.

"We don't know what kind of creatures may be in there," Blair said, her eyes growing wider the more she thought about what might be lurking under the surface.

I knew crossing the lake was the only way forward. "Maybe if we swim across it super-fast, whatever is in there won't have a chance to catch us."

"I think we should all go at the same time," Sasha suggested. "If we all dive as far out as possible, swim the fastest we have ever swum, and then help each other get out on the other side, we might be able to get across before whatever's in there even realizes we're there." She looked so hopeful.

"Here's a question," Blair said. "What do we do about those jaguars once we get up on the other side. I mean, they're right there. Won't they attack us as we climb out of the water?"

I was thinking the same thing, and I could feel my knees shaking.

"Hmm," Parker said. "I'm positive they won't attack."

"Positive as in one hundred percent, or somewhere in the seventies?" I asked, a little freaked out.

"Let's go with ninety," Parker decided. We all looked at him with our eyebrows raised, then turned back to the lake.

We stood at the edge, all six of us, staring out at the smooth, dark water. The spectral jaguars waited on the far bank, still and watchful, their twin-moon eyes burning with intelligence that made my skin crawl. They didn't move, growl, or even blink; they just watched.

"Parker," Elijah said, "I think it would be best if you climbed out of the water first."

Parker chuckled and stepped forward. "They're waiting to see who we are beneath our surface, judgment through reflection. I think they're watching to see how we decide to do this."

I exhaled through my nose. "Of course it's metaphorical."

Denali took off his jacket and stuffed into his gear bag, eyes on the water. "Or maybe it's literal. Either way, we have to cross."

The water shimmered—black silk touched by mystery— and I hated how much it taunted me.

"I'll go first," Elijah said, stepping into the lake. He moved like he was wading through molasses. "It's thick."

Sasha was next. Then Denali. Then Blair.

Parker hesitated. I reached out and touched his arm. "We'll stay close." I promised.

We slipped in. The water clung to me and held me. Every movement was a negotiation. My pendant pulsed against my chest, as if trying to anchor me.

Halfway across, I heard Parker's sharp gasp. He faltered, his body jerking sideways.

"Parker!" I surged toward him without thinking.

His eyes were glassy, and his limbs were slow. The water wasn't just draining his energy; it was showing him something. Fears, maybe? The past? I didn't know. I just knew he was sinking.

I finally reached him and grabbed his shoulder, and the weight of the water wrapped around me like a living thing, dragging me away from him. The water was like shadowed silk and clawing its way into my lungs.

"Alayna!" someone shouted.

I barely heard it. My limbs burned, and my breath vanished. Parker's hand slipped from mine.

And then Denali was there. His arms caught me like a current, strong and sure, and he whispered my name over and over. "Alayna. Alayna, look at me."

The panic in his voice grew. I tried to speak but couldn't. My body felt like it was dissolving, and it felt like my lungs were filling up with mud.

"Stay with me," he said, cradling me against his chest. "I've got you."

He kicked powerfully, dragging us toward the surface. His warmth wrapped around me, defying the cold pull of the water. We broke the surface together.

I gasped, lungs finally finding air, and Denali held me tighter. "I've got you," he repeated, softer this time. "You're safe, Alayna."

"Where's Parker?" I gasped, my fingers gripping Denali's arm.

"He's safe. Eli's got him." Denali breathed as I let him carry me the rest of the way to shore.

Blair had reached the shore first, pale and trembling. Her bag clung to her like a soaked husk. Her eyes darted between the jaguars and those of us slowly climbing to the rocky beach.

"I can't paint," she breathed. "Everything's damaged."

Sasha turned sharply, "Then don't create, redirect."

"What?"

Sasha's voice dropped into command. "You don't need pigment to shape what's already here. You're a visual interpreter. Sculpt the light. Use your magic and hands to paint what we need."

Blair blinked and then looked up. The cave ceiling shimmered with reflected moonlight from the jaguars' eyes. She reached out—fingers twitching—and concentrated. Her breath slowed.

"I need motion and contrast," she whispered.

Blair moved like she was sketching in the air, manipulating shadow with instinct rather than tools. The light refracted, curved, and then took on a distinct shape.

A flickering mirage appeared across the water. A blurred human outline, dancing along the edge of the lake. It shimmered like smoke on glass, unreal, but real enough.

The jaguars shifted, intrigued.

Sasha stepped forward, hands glowing. Her voice was steady. "I'll distract the jaguars."

She moved toward the water again. Her spiral tattoo ignited with purple fire, and the lake answered. Ripples formed a spiral around her feet. The jaguars prowled closer.

"Now," Sasha whispered.

Elijah grabbed Parker's arm and hauled him up the rocks.

I tried to rise, but my legs gave out. The water had taken too much.

"I've got her," Denali said, voice low and steady. He scooped me into his arms again, muscles trembling beneath the weight, but he didn't stop.

The jaguars hesitated, their eyes still burning, but they focused on the illusion Blair had shaped from moonlight and desperation.

The six of us staggered into a narrow tunnel beyond the lake. The moment we crossed the threshold, the air changed —cooler, sharper, laced with stone and breath.

Sasha stayed back until the rest of us had entered the tunnel. As soon as she entered, the illusion fractured—a flash and then silence. The jaguars turned their heads toward us, but they were too late. We collapsed inside the tunnel, gasping.

Elijah dropped to one knee. "Everyone okay?"

"No," Blair rasped. "But not dead."

Sasha sank to the floor, her hands shaking. "They weren't just watching us, they were listening. Do you think they would have attacked us if Blair hadn't given them that illusion?"

Denali answered, "I think they would have given us a hard time, yes, but I don't think they would have attacked us."

I was still in Denali's arms. He sat down but didn't let go of me.

"You can set me down," I whispered.

"I know," he said. But he didn't move.

Our eyes met. Denali's were dark, warm, and impossibly present. I expected concern. But what I saw rooted me; there was an ache that mirrored mine, a type of longing. He finally set me down gently, brushing soaked strands from my face.

"Thank you," I murmured. "You didn't have to—"

"Yes, I did," he said, voice thick. "Every single time."

I turned away before the heat in my chest became too obvious.

Blair broke the silence. "Maybe they judged us not on strength, but on how far we'd go for each other."

Sasha nodded. "Vulnerability as currency."

Elijah looked at Parker. "What did you see out there?"

Parker hesitated, his gaze dropping to the ground, and for a moment, I thought he might dodge the question, but then he spoke.

"I saw my father," he said quietly. "Drunk, angry, and telling me I'd never be anything but a disappointment. I was six years old." His voice didn't waver, but something in it frayed around the edges. "Then I saw myself, grown and giving lectures, writing books, pretending I didn't care that he never came to a single thing I built. I pretended I didn't still want him to look at me and say he was proud."

Silence felt like a stone wall.

"I thought I'd buried that," he added, softer now. "But the water wouldn't let me suppress it. It pulled it straight out of me."

I swallowed hard. My throat felt thick. I didn't know Parker well, but I knew that kind of ache. The kind that lingers even after you've rewritten your whole life around it.

Denali shifted beside me, his hand brushing mine. He offered no words, just presence. "What did you see, Alayna?"

"What I saw back there was myself, fighting everything alone, never letting anyone else in, and almost drowning for it." I turned to Denali. "But you didn't leave me alone or let me drown. You saved me." He was watching me, and suddenly, I wasn't afraid of being seen, not by him, not anymore.

Parker lifted his head again. "The jaguars didn't flinch when we got past them or try to lunge at us. They just watched it all, and I think how we came together, that was enough."

None of us argued because obviously, it was.

We found a hollow beside a phosphorescent wall. The ground was uneven, but dry, and none of us cared.

Sasha was the first to curl up, her long braids draped over her arm like dark silk. Blair leaned against the cavern wall, legs pulled up, eyes already shut. Elijah stripped off his wet shirt, steam rising from his skin as he mumbled something about the warmth being an illusion. Parker lay with his back to the wall, head tilted up, eyes vacant, still caught in the memory the lake had dredged up.

I lowered myself beside Denali, who was lying on his back. He didn't say anything, just looked at me with a small smile, and opened up his arm.

I didn't even hesitate. I let myself lean into his side, head on his bare shoulder, the heat warming me instantly. He wrapped his arm gently around my shoulder. His thumb traced small, absent-minded circles on my upper arm, and I didn't stop him.

None of us spoke. I was sure everyone was asleep, except maybe Parker and Denali. The hum of the phosphorescence, the distant trickle of unseen water, and our shared breath filled the silence. I finally closed my eyes. I didn't think I could sleep, not after everything that had happened, but I had to try. Who knew what we would be up against the next day? I shuddered at the thought, and Denali squeezed me for a moment, and then we both fell under the spell of sleep.

14

TRIAL OF REFLECTION AND RELEASE

The wall glowed faintly, soft and steady, phosphorescent veins of turquoise and green running through it like living moss. I didn't remember falling asleep. One moment I'd been leaning against Denali, and the next I was waking up alone. My cheek was warm where it had rested on his shoulder. I didn't move.

Around me, the others stirred. Sasha blinked slowly, curled like a cat near the wall. Blair stretched and winced, mumbling something about her hip. Elijah was already sitting up, running a hand through his tangled hair. Parker moved stiffly, his eyes shadowed but alert.

"No dream this time," Blair whispered, as if surprised.

We gathered our things, which were no longer soaked, and stared into the corridor ahead. There was no clear path, just a low arch of stone and darkness swallowing the way forward.

"I don't like this," Sasha said slowly.

Then, just as I was about to say we should go left, I heard it.

Go right.

It was a whisper, barely audible, female, like the brush of wind over still water.

"Guys. I just heard a female voice whisper that we should go right," I said as my heart rate kicked up.

"I'll bet that was Zanira guiding us," Parker guessed.

"You're probably right," I said. "Yes, I think it was her voice now that I think about it."

The tunnel curved and narrowed, then opened into a great stone amphitheater. Moss and mushrooms covered its steps, and carved pillars rimmed the space like sentries. At its center lay a six-pointed court, patterned with jagged lines and symbols.

My breath caught. "Parker, the glyphs. Let's go see if we can figure out what it says."

He was already beside me, crouched near a carved wall slick with moisture.

"Twin deities," I deciphered. "I think they're Mayan. It says here that they'll challenge us, not physically but spiritually."

"It says it's a game of soul forfeit," Parker sighed.

My spine tightened. "What does that mean?"

He glanced at me, eyes unreadable. "Each of us has to give up something personal that costs us."

Denali stepped closer behind me, quiet and solid. "Like what?"

Parker didn't have a chance to answer. The stone beneath our feet pulsed and grumbled.

I knew we stood at the edge of something ancient and sacred. I could feel it in my bones.

Around me, the others fell silent, the weight of it settling over us all. We were awake, and this was real. There was no escape, no way we could bypass this, and no shortcut to get out quicker. The game had already begun. And the only way forward was through.

The arena pulsed with golden runes beneath our feet, ancient lines weaving like constellations across the floor. The moment we stepped onto the court, the air shifted. It was thicker and sacred. The gods' voices echoed above us, resonant and layered, like wind through bone and thunder through canyon.

"Offer what binds you or be bound forever." The voice was male and deep. I looked around, but saw no one other than ourselves. I also didn't see any cameras or anything to make me think someone was there.

My breath caught. I looked at Denali beside me, his dark eyes scanning the perimeter as well, his broad shoulders squared and steady.

The court lit up with orange and blue light beneath our feet, urging us forward.

"What do they mean, offer what binds us?" I whispered.

Denali looked thoughtful, and there was a strange sort of knowing in his eyes. "Whatever we're still holding onto. It's that 'something personal' we were speaking of before."

My heart thudded. Of course, it would be that. I didn't like the idea of sacrificing any part of me.

A vine began to grow from the floor, twisting and curling toward me. It glowed faintly, green with gold edges. I froze. I knew this shape. It was too familiar.

The thorned vine coiled around my chest, not genuine in the way vines are real, but metaphorically and emotionally honest. It pulsed with fear, my fear. The fear of commitment

I had dragged through every relationship since I'd learned to doubt myself. The vine grew tighter, pressing into my ribs.

I clenched my fists. "This is mine," I said. "It's been mine for years!"

Denali stepped closer but didn't touch me. "You don't have to fight it alone."

But that was the point. I always fought things alone, never letting anyone get close enough to hurt me ever again.

Tears prickled behind my eyes, and my voice cracked. "I'm afraid that giving this up means I'll get trapped again, and I'll lose myself like I did before."

"Then maybe the vine is lying to you," he said gently.

The words shattered something. I gritted my teeth and reached for the vine. Its thorns cut into my palms, but I held it anyway. I peeled it away, inch by inch, from around my chest, feeling it resist, tightening and clinging. Every tug felt like ripping open old wounds, but I kept going. When it was finally released, I stumbled back. The vine dropped to the court, shriveled into ash.

I felt raw and exposed, but something in my chest fluttered—air and lightness.

Then Denali inhaled sharply. Mist was curling off his shoulders. A memory made physical. A woman's silhouette, long hair, eyes full of knowing, lifted from him like steam. I knew it was Raven. I didn't even need to ask. The way he looked at her said everything.

He dropped to one knee, breath unsteady. "I loved her," he said softly. "And I held on long after she left. I was so full of guilt."

The mist coiled, wrapping around his chest like a scarf, then began to lift. It resisted, like mine had, but Denali closed his eyes, and I saw it: he let it go, not with anger, denial, or sadness, but with grace. When the mist vanished, the court glowed between us. I looked at him, and he looked at me.

There was no need for words, just the hum of something new and fragile. It was an understanding and recognition. Commitment didn't have to be a prison; it could be trust and freedom. The gods said nothing, but their silence rang with approval.

The lights on the court changed to glow purple and red. Sasha and Elijah stepped forward as Denali and I retreated to the edge of the court. My chest still ached from what I'd released, but watching the two of them, a different kind of tension built like a gathering storm that had no thunder yet, only pressure.

Elijah moved like a man made of marble, controlled and carved from purpose, but I could feel the fracture lines running beneath. His steps were steady, but his jaw was clenched like a locked door. Sasha walked beside him, tall and fluid, but her eyes flicked toward him now and then, worry just barely veiled behind curiosity. She knew energy better than anyone. She could probably feel the quake under his surface.

The runes beneath their feet flared brighter, light twisting in circular patterns, almost like chakra wheels. The court was responding to them differently than it had to us. Less aggressive, more discerning. It was asking them to look inward rather than confront something external.

Elijah stopped. The light beneath him condensed into something massive. A stone shield erupted from the ground behind him, taller than he was, strapped to his back by ethereal chains. It shimmered with scars and inscriptions I couldn't read, but I could feel them. They were memories, burdens, and proof.

He dropped to one knee, his breath a sharp drag through his teeth.

"What is it?" Sasha asked, her voice low and reverent.

"I've worn this my whole life," he said, not looking up. "It's not real. It's just what I thought I had to be." He ran a hand along the edge of the shield. "I made myself into a protector, a warrior, someone who doesn't bend, because bending meant breaking."

The chains around the shield glowed as they tightened further.

"My father used to tell me that strength is what separates the living from the dead. But he never told me how lonely it would be."

Sasha took a half-step forward. "So, take it off."

His laugh was bitter and low. "It's not that easy."

"Try."

He did. He reached up, grasping the chains, muscles straining. But the shield didn't budge. His arms trembled with effort, the veins in his arms popping. His eyes clenched shut.

"I can't—It's part of me now."

"Yes," she interrupted, firm. "You can. But not with muscle, with permission."

He opened his eyes, staring into hers.

"Tell yourself it's okay to be scared."

His lips parted. The words didn't come easily, but I heard them—barely more than a whisper. "I'm allowed to be afraid."

"Repeat it, Elijah, but louder. You have to mean it when you say it," Sasha coached him firmly.

"I am allowed to be afraid."

Nothing happened.

"Again," Sasha encouraged.

Sweat poured off Elijah as tears rolled down his cheeks. "I am allowed to be afraid."

"Say it again with every feeling in your heart. Believe it," Sasha said, her voice full of support.

"I am allowed to be afraid. I am allowed to live," he said and then breathed out a big sigh like he was pushing doubt out of his soul.

A shudder moved through the court. The shield cracked, fractures racing through its surface like lightning in stone.

Elijah stood slowly. As he rose, the shield fell away—not shattering, but gently breaking apart, like a husk shedding from his back.

His breath came easier.

But Sasha had started trembling.

The court had turned to her now. Her tattoos were glowing, vibrant, living things. A bird on her collarbone took flight, wings of flame beating the air, while vines twined down her arms, pulsing like veins.

She dropped to a crouch, clutching her chest.

"My power," she said. "It doesn't want to be tamed anymore."

"What are you afraid of?" Elijah asked softly.

She looked up at him. "Of becoming too much or too strong, of letting it out and never finding my way back to myself."

The court darkened around her, shadows curling like ink spilled in water.

"I've always held it in check. I always used just enough of my strength to help others but never enough to lose myself."

Another tattoo flared—an orchid twisting open across her neck.

"What if I stop holding back and I disappear into it?"

Elijah crouched beside her, not touching, just steady. "Then we'll come find you and pull you back."

She shook her head. "No, that's not your job. I have to take care of myself. I can't put that burden on you." Tears were streaming down her face.

"You're right," he agreed. "It is yours, but we're here for you. That's the difference now. We're here to help you when and if you fall or fail. You have great power for good. It is time it were unleashed. Your goodness will direct it and guide it."

A long silence passed between them.

Then Sasha took a deep breath. Her eyes fluttered closed, and I could tell that she let go.

The bird burst into complete form, flying high above her, calling into the air. The vines receded into her skin. The court flared in response, not with chaos, but with harmony. Every rune in the arena pulsed once, like a heartbeat.

Her hands dropped to her sides, open. "I don't feel like hiding anymore," she said quietly. "I know it's time to trust myself."

The magic didn't retreat; it settled, and so did she.

Elijah stood beside her, his expression unreadable for a moment. Then, slowly, he reached for her hand. She took it and let him pull her up to her feet.

They didn't smile. It wasn't a triumphant moment; it was merely a release.

They had met their gods, not through conquest, but through clarity of vision. And that kind of victory echoed even louder than the battle.

The court accepted their offerings. A quiet wind rippled through the arena, scattering golden dust like blessings. We had all seen the heart of them now, and it was beautiful. The lights shifted to green and silver.

Blair and Parker stepped into the center of the court as the rest of us moved back, the six-pointed symbol beneath our feet dimming until only theirs remained alight.

I wrapped my arms around myself. The energy had changed again, gone soft and strange, almost like the hush before snowfall. The gods were watching, and this time I could feel it.

Blair's fingers twitched at her sides, her palms flecked with faint streaks of paint that hadn't been there moments ago. Her red hair was tucked behind her ears, her gaze low. She looked like she wanted to disappear into the stones. Parker stood straighter, taller, collected, and almost scholarly, but I could see how tightly he was holding his breath. His whole posture felt like a wall.

The court shifted, glowing bone-pale, stark, and honest. A single object rose from the ground between them. It was a mask, silver, smooth, and nearly featureless except for the faintest suggestion of Parker's own face. His reflection warped across its surface.

He didn't move at first, just stared.

"That's mine," he finally said.

Blair tilted her head. "What do you mean?"

"I made this," he said. "Not literally, but spiritually. I've worn a version of it my whole life. It helps people to see what they want, but not what's real."

He stepped forward, slow and hesitant, like the mask might bite him. "I thought if I shaped myself just right, always listening and never pushing, I'd be accepted, maybe even loved, but all I ever did was vanish inside myself."

I felt that in my chest. Too much of myself knew what that tasted like.

Blair observed him. "What happens if you take it off?"

Parker laughed once, brittle and hollow. "Then I have to hope what's underneath is enough. I'm not sure there will be anything."

"Parker, take it off. Believe that it's okay to remove it," Blair guided him.

His fingers wrapped around the edges of the mask, but it fought him—*literally* fought him. The metal bent, screaming in protest, writhing like a thing alive. His face strained.

"Let it see you," Blair said. "Let us see you."

He growled and yanked harder, but it seemed the more he pulled at it, the more it grabbed onto his face.

"Try again," Blair encouraged him. "You have to want us to see the real you deep inside. You have to believe that it's safe, that you'll be there."

Parker tried again, but this time he took a deep breath first and very gently reached up to remove it. The mask cracked. The sound split the air like glass breaking underwater, deep, distant, and final.

When it crumbled to dust in his hands, I saw Parker exhale, just once, like he hadn't realized he'd been choking. He inhaled and exhaled over and over again until the breaths didn't need to be forced. He looked different, not physically, but spiritually—more *him*, less mirror, and more presence. I saw tears glistening in his eyes but not falling.

Then the court turned to Blair, and something began to burn.

A paintbrush rose in front of her. The bristles dripped with red, not paint or blood, but something older. It floated into her palm and immediately glowed white-hot, searing her skin. She screamed and we all tried to run to her, but our feet were frozen to the ground. The more she screamed, the more we tried to get to her, but invisible chains held us back.

"She has to do it by herself," Elijah said, a single tear sliding down his cheek as he watched her writhe in pain.

She finally stopped crying out, and her whole body went limp. "I know pain. I always thought pain made my work real," she said, voice trembling. "Like if I wasn't hurting, it wasn't worth anything."

The brush hissed in her grip, smoke curling around her fingers as the bristles rounded out and grew longer and longer until they melded with her hair. Blair screamed again, but it was quicker this time.

Blair heaved a breath and closed her eyes. "I've always believed that suffering was the only thing deep enough to pull something beautiful from. And maybe I've been creating my own suffering all along. I don't know who I am without it."

Parker was finally able to step closer, but none of us could. "I know who you are. You're someone who creates magic, Blair. Not because of the pain, despite it."

She shook her head. "What if I lose that edge? What if I can't paint anymore without the ache?"

"You'll find new colors," he said. "Ones you've never dared to mix."

Her blue eyes flicked to his, and then back to the brush.

"I don't know how to create from joy. I don't trust it to last."

Parker gave a soft smile. "Then start small. Create from this moment and this choice."

"I can't. I'm afraid."

"Is that why all of your paintings are menacing creatures that come alive?"

Blair nodded and put her head in her hands. "I don't know if there is any beauty within my soul, so I can't connect with it by brush and paint."

"There's a universe of beauty in your soul. Reach inward and find it," Parker said gently. "Think of what makes you happy and allow yourself to bask in it. You need to reach down deep and find it, Blair."

Blair stared at the burning brush a second longer. Then, slowly, deliberately, she opened her hand, and the brush dropped. It hit the ground and exploded into color, not flame or destruction, but pigment and light, swirling into shapes—warm, lush, and free.

The court responded immediately. A canvas rolled itself open beneath her feet, filling with the hues of sunrise—mauve and coral, pale gold and soft teal, like dawn after too many sleepless nights.

Blair knelt and pressed one paint-smeared hand into the blank center. "I want to create from healing," she whispered. "Not just heartbreak."

The air shimmered around her like magic, responding to that vow. And then—gods, it was subtle—her spiral birthmark near the inside of her elbow flared just slightly, almost pulsing in time with Parker's steps as he crossed to kneel beside her.

He reached out, not to touch her hand, but to place his over the canvas too. Light threaded from her palm to his and back again, and for a brief moment, I could see it, not just them, but the idea of them.

Creation and clarity. Magic and myth. Wound and wisdom.

The gods didn't speak, but we didn't need them to as the court quieted. The runes faded, for they'd seen what they needed to see, and it was enough.

We were still in the middle of the glowing court, half afraid to move, when it happened.

A low rumble sounded beneath us, more vibration than noise, and one of the far stone walls shimmered. The runes lining it flared every color of the rainbow, and then peeled open like petals, revealing a doorway where there had been only smooth stone moments before.

None of us moved at first. Then Blair stood, slow and wide-eyed, paint-stained fingers brushing her thigh.

"Is that real," she asked, "or am I so delirious that I'm dreaming?"

"If you're dreaming, then I'm inside your dream," Elijah said, his voice hoarse but steady.

We drifted toward the doorway like moths toward a warm flame. Inside, the room didn't look like anything we'd seen in this realm before.

It was stunning. Not in the way the court had been, all power and symbolism and divine resonance. This was softer, more human, and comforting.

Six real beds, each tucked into arched alcoves carved with ancient spiral motifs, glowed under soft moon-colored light. There were pillows stuffed with something lavender-scented, blankets woven from thick wool in desert and sea tones, and the floors were made of smooth, white stone, polished but warm underfoot.

And in the center of it all was a table covered in food.

I mean, actual food, not spirit-essence or mystical herbs. There were roasted vegetables drizzled with honey glaze, wild rice, and fruit compote, baked bread still steaming, a dark stew in obsidian bowls, and jugs of water infused with citrus and violet leaves.

Denali blinked hard, like he thought it might disappear if he focused too long.

Sasha moved first, running her fingers over a goblet, then picking it up slowly and taking a sip.

She closed her eyes.

"Oh my god, it's wine," she whispered. "Real red wine."

That was all the permission we needed.

We collapsed into the meal, half-grateful, half-delirious. None of us talked much, but we were close: elbows brushed, shoulders leaned, and we passed things wordlessly. It wasn't just the taste; it was the grounding of it. Food that reminded us we were alive, that we had bodies and needs and bellies that could be full again.

Blair barely spoke, but she ate three rolls in a row and curled her toes when she bit into a lemon tart.

Parker poured himself water with shaking hands and stared at the flickering lanterns like they were old friends.

Sasha spooned stew into her mouth like she hadn't eaten in days. Elijah nudged her shoulder when she dropped a piece of bread into her bowl by accident. She smiled faintly.

And Denali sat across from me, silent, watching everyone with soft eyes. He looked full of quiet relief.

I couldn't finish everything on my plate. I kept looking around at the others, this ragtag group of strange souls drawn together by fate and gods and something else.

"I was just thinking," Denali ventured. "We're all vegetarians here, right?"

"I am," declared Parker.

"I am," said Sasha. "Except I eat nonfat yogurt."

"I am," I shared. "Except I eat eggs and dairy."

"I am," said Blair, smiling coyly. "Except I eat fish and fowl."

"Fish and fowl?" I smirked. "That sounds like the name of a pub."

She laughed. "It does indeed, or a cozy tavern."

"I am," said Elijah, solemnly. "Except after piling my plate high with vegetables, I leave just a little bit of space for a grilled ribeye."

Sasha snorted, and we all chuckled.

Parker raised an eyebrow and stared at Denali without blinking. "And, what about you, Denny? Are you a vegetarian?"

"I am," nodded Denali, straight-faced and somber. "Except I eat fish and fowl. And rabbit. And pork. And beef. And venison. And bison. And elk. And chocolate."

We all burst into laughter. The kind of laughter that leaves you gasping for breath. The kind of laughter that makes your eyes water. The kind of laughter that leaves your cheeks sore from smiling too much. The kind of laughter that washes away fear and pain. It was glorious.

Afterward, one by one, we peeled away.

Blair was the first to retreat to a bed, curling onto her side in the carved-out alcove nearest the corner. Her red hair fanned over the pillow like paint spilling across parchment, and within seconds, her breathing had slowed into sleep.

Parker followed soon after, choosing the alcove across from her. He didn't say anything, just pulled the thick blanket over his chest with the weary precision of someone who hadn't rested in years. His eyes closed before his head even touched the pillow.

Sasha moved next, scanning the room like she wasn't sure she'd earned the right to stop moving. She paused near Blair's alcove, as if checking in, then brushed her fingers along the wall and turned toward the opposite side of the room. She slid into the third bed, on the far side, sitting upright for a long moment before finally lying down, one hand resting on her chest like she was anchoring herself to her own heartbeat.

Elijah lingered near the feast table for a while longer, silent. Then he walked to the alcove closest to the door, glancing once toward Sasha before lying down on his back, arms crossed loosely over his chest. He didn't curl or fold, just let the silence wrap around him like armor he didn't need anymore.

That left two alcoves. And two of us still sitting side by side.

I didn't move, not yet. Denali hadn't either.

We sat side by side on the edge of the fountain that trickled from one corner of the room. Denali turned his head and looked at me. I didn't breathe. Then, he took my hand, just like that, and everything in me coiled. Not in fear of him, but in fear of what this might become, of what I might become. But I still didn't pull away. His fingers wrapped around mine, slow and sure. And something in me went still.

I shifted slightly, my shoulder brushing his, not even meaning to. He leaned closer. And then his lips were on my jaw, feather-soft, and barely there. He placed another kiss lower on my neck. A shiver rippled through me, quiet, private, and undeniable. He lingered just long enough to make my breath catch, and then he pulled back. I knew he didn't want to push it or ask.

He stood and extended his hand.

"We should sleep," he said, voice low as I took it. "There's more coming. We both know that."

I stared at him, eye to eye, the moons glowed from a window behind his head, throwing a glimmer through his dark hair. He looked mythic in that light, sacred and safe. And real, oh, so real. I slid my fingers into his and rose to my feet with no words—just the quiet promise of rest.

15

TRIAL OF STILLNESS AND REMEMBRANCE

I woke up swaddled in warmth, the kind that sinks into your bones and makes you forget you ever knew cold. The bed, if you call it that, was carved from smooth stone but somehow felt like memory foam. I blinked at the golden canopy above, embroidered with swirling symbols that shimmered like sunlight on turquoise.

Someone sighed contentedly across the room.

"Anyone else never want to leave this place?" Blair's voice drifted from her alcove, muffled by layers of blankets.

"I thought I had died," Parker mumbled. "But then I tasted that lemon scone again and figured the gods wouldn't serve Earth pastries in the afterlife."

I rolled over and sat up, hair wild, stomach already grumbling. "Seriously. Who made that food? It was even better than my mom's arroz con leche. Oh, thank you gods, I swear I smell coffee."

"Yes, you do, so breathe deeply." Sasha padded barefoot toward the long table, which now had breakfast items—eggs, hash browns, fresh bread, even sliced mango. "This doesn't seem like Aztalun food," she said, fingertips grazing the rim of a steaming mug of coffee. "It's food from back home."

"Maybe it was Zanira," Elijah offered, stretching until his joints cracked. His lean, muscled frame looked relaxed for once. "Or maybe the gods are just sentimental."

Denali chuckled from beside me, running a hand through his black hair. "If they're bribing us to stay here, it's working."

"Do you know where we're going next?" I asked.

"Judging by the etchings on this wall, I would say we're heading for several pyramids," Parker guessed, pointing to the large wall between the bed alcoves.

We eventually rose, packing what little we had. Outside, the shifting pyramid loomed in the distance—an impossible structure, angles realigning every few seconds like it was ever-changing.

"I guess that's our final trial," I said, voice steadier than I felt. My pendant pulsed faintly against my chest.

"I hope so," Blair muttered, shouldering her bag. "Because I don't think I can do another sacrifice."

I glanced at each of them. "Let's end this together nice and strong."

And we walked toward the living stone.

***

The desert stretched endlessly in every direction, flat and blinding beneath a sky scraped raw by heat. Our boots sank slightly in the sand with each step, grit clinging to our ankles like static. The six of us stood still, shoulder to shoulder, at the edge of something ancient, something watching.

Three pyramids loomed ahead.

Each was massive, each oriented toward a different horizon. One pointed true north, its tip bathed in the pale light of the highest moon. Another tilted eastward, its base half-sunken in shimmering sand. The third leaned west, but none of them aligned.

And between them, a temple hovered.

Suspended midair, it rotated slowly, shifting on an invisible axis in tune with the three moons above. Their glow passed through it like breath through bone, bending its reflection into strange arcs across the desert floor. The whole formation felt less like architecture and more like an echo of thought, built by intention rather than hands.

"It's like we're standing inside a pulse," Parker said beside me, his voice low and hesitant.

He crouched at the base of the first pyramid, where wind-carved sandstone steps gave way to a sunken platform half-buried in ochre sand. There, set into the stone foundation like a forgotten altar, was a wide panel—a celestial interface etched directly into the pyramid's base. Parker brushed away layers of dust with the corner of his jacket, revealing a series of dials arranged in a precise arc. The outer rings were made of aged bronze, dulled and pitted with time, but the inner components sparkled like polished orichalcum—an alloy that caught the moonlight in rippling waves. The glyphs engraved on them—some spiraling, others linear—seemed to adjust subtly as he touched them.

Parker's spiky blond hair was soaked at the edges with sweat, but his focus didn't waver. Carefully, he laid out his maps on the sandstone beside the panel, anchoring the corners with mineral chunks from his leather satchel—rose quartz, smoky obsidian, and a sliver of moonstone. The maps weren't ordinary: they were hand-sketched astronomical charts showing the orbits of Aztalun's three moons, with notations in Parker's looping script. I realized that's what he'd been working on at night when the rest of us were sleeping. He aligned them carefully with the engraved symbols on the dials, matching the crescent patterns and overlapping planetary nodes.

My pendant began to throb insistently, like a drumbeat, in sync with the moons. I knelt beside him and placed my hand over a small, curved panel just beneath the central dial. It was smoother than the sandstone, forged from a silvery metal that pulsed faintly under my touch. Its surface was engraved with a pattern of shifting geometric lines, some of which began to glow faintly copper-colored the moment my skin made contact.

"They're all reacting," I whispered. "The stones, the air, and even the sky is bending."

Parker adjusted one of the main dials. It clicked into a new alignment, releasing a subtle tremor beneath us. Smaller spindles spun beneath his fingers, aligning with indented notches shaped like moons in various places. "Gravitational oscillation. We're in a celestial corridor. The pyramid itself is the receiver, and the moons are the key."

Above us, the three moons shifted just a fraction in the sky, ever so slightly. A deep hum rose from the stone under our knees, and the panel beneath our hands glowed brighter, as if awakening. The pyramid's ancient heart began to stir.

I traced my fingers over the carvings embedded in the control panel—smooth, ancient metal set into the base of the pyramid like part of a buried machine. The equipment was massive and sunken, its edges fused into the sandstone, as if the structure had grown around it. The dials weren't just decorations; they were functional components—precision-forged, metallic, and covered in layered glyphs that shifted under my touch. My breath became shallow. The rhythm pulsing from the machinery wasn't random. It was patterned and older than time itself. It reminded me of petroglyphs I'd once studied in Sonora—spirals carved into stone, perfectly aligned with the solstice sun, symbolizing life, death, and rebirth.

I felt the same quiet certainty now. The energy thrummed through my fingertips, and I matched my movements to it instinctively, twisting one of the central dials a fraction to the right. It resisted at first, then clicked into place with a sound like a lock accepting a key.

A low hum rippled through the red sand.

Parker exhaled slowly, watching the light shift above us. "That did something, I'm just not sure what exactly."

The eastern pyramid rotated a fraction, barely noticeable, but enough.

The ground beneath it shook slightly, and grains of sand danced into mandala-like swirls. Each pulse from the pyramid seemed to awaken the others. The whole desert responded simultaneously.

"Sasha, Elijah," I called out, glancing toward them, "take care when the pyramids shift!"

They were near the second pyramid's base, entering what looked like a mirrored corridor. I saw a flash of Sasha's purple shawl before it dissolved into reflection. There were mirrors everywhere.

"I'll stay on this pattern," I said to Parker. "Keep tracking the lunar pulses."

He nodded, already back to his chart, mumbling to himself in mythic constellations and theoretical gravity arcs.

The mirrored chamber was like walking into glass that swallowed you whole. Walls reflected walls, and light refracted until nothing looked real. I watched from the control panel as Sasha stepped carefully across the patterned floor, Elijah behind her like a silent shadow. Each tile glowed faintly as they passed over it. Then Sasha veered left.

"No!" Elijah's voice rang out, sharp.

She froze mid-step.

A version of herself had walked toward an illusion—a corridor that wasn't there. I held my breath as Elijah surged forward and grabbed her wrist, yanking her back just as the tile she'd been about to touch flickered and cracked, breaking away and exposing a bed of knives.

The pattern reset.

She stumbled and caught herself, bracing against him. Her eyes were wide, frightened. "Thank you," she breathed, shaking.

He nodded, not letting go of her hand. "Don't trust your eyes, just listen to the rhythm, like Kata."

She breathed, then stepped forward again, this time letting Elijah lead. Together, they moved in tandem, tracing mirrored glyphs into the glowing floor with their steps. It wasn't brute strength, it was timing and trust, like a choreographed dance.

Sasha's tattoos pulsed along her skin—glowing birds and blooming vines flickering like living snakes. Her breathing had slowed, her movements sharper. She was hyper-focused. I caught myself admiring the calm in her chaos. The mirrored walls reflected not only their bodies but fragments of who they were: Sasha's childhood laughter, Elijah's broken moments stitched together with discipline.

Suddenly, the mirrored surface beneath them shimmered—not dangerously, but like a veil lifting. For a moment, I saw Elijah's reflection flicker into a child, fists up in a practice stance, and Sasha's become a swirling phoenix. Their deepest selves were unveiled. They couldn't see it, but I could.

I turned away only because Blair's absence suddenly pressed too hard.

"Where's Blair?" I scanned the ridges near the third pyramid where Blair and Denali had been exploring. "She was just—"

A sharp cry sliced through the heat, then nothing.

"Blair?" I turned sharply. "Blair?"

The air gleamed. A chamber had formed, walls like liquid origami folding around her, light bending and snapping with unnatural motion. A mosaic of color shimmered behind the barrier, trapping her like a painting half-finished and already alive.

She was trapped.

"Don't move!" I yelled, sprinting toward her, but the light hardened like glass between us.

Then Denali bolted around the corner. His black hair whipped in the wind as he raced forward, eyes locked on the illusion. He didn't hesitate or stop. His shoulder hit the wall of light, and it hissed, turning to smoke around him, searing his arm red as it opened. I screamed his name, but he was already inside.

The walls twisted, closed.

Outside I could only catch glimpses, flashes, of him running through corridors that shifted like paper caught in the wind. Blair lay inside a prismatic cocoon, face slack. Her painting canvas flaring beside her, leaking hues into the air. One of her figures had come to life and attacked her.

Denali reached her, tearing the canvas in half, and the illusion dissolved into glittering shards.

And then Denali emerged again. Blair was cradled against his chest, her breath shallow, face frighteningly pale. Denali shielded her with his entire body; his shirt scorched along one side. He looked dazed but resolute, like someone who'd just walked through fire and would do it again.

I froze, watching them. It wasn't jealousy that rose in my throat. It was something sharper, clarity. Denali wasn't just kind. He wasn't just soft smiles, jokes, and stories of glacial caves and carved flutes. He was fierce, loyal, and protective. He was a storm with a steady core. I saw him fully, maybe for the first time, and my heart steadied.

The chamber behind them collapsed into a curl of ash and silence.

I ran to them. "Is she okay?"

"She's breathing," he said. His voice cracked, low and strained. "Hopefully, she's just disoriented."

Blair blinked slowly and gave a faint nod.

I touched Denali's arm, then flinched; it was searing hot. "You're burned."

"I'm fine."

"You're not fine. I'll find Sasha for you," I promised.

But he met my eyes with such aching honesty that I stopped. I didn't press further. I gently wrapped a scarf around his injury, and he allowed me to.

"Thanks," Blair said weakly, voice barely audible.

"You were too close to the threshold," Parker added, coming up beside us. "Those chambers shift when exposed to erratic frequency, probably emotional surges. Fear might've triggered it."

Blair gave a quiet nod, still leaning into Denali's side.

Parker turned back to the central dial and called out a moment later. "We're close! The moons are aligning!"

Elijah and Sasha had headed toward us by then. "Let's place Blair over there," Elijah nodded a little further away from the pyramid structures, "while she regains her strength."

Denali carried her several meters away and set her down to rest. We regrouped between Blair and Parker, still at the controls, each of us breathless, dusty, and hearts drumming to different tempos but somehow still beating together. I felt my nerves jangling, but a calm had begun to settle in my chest, low and centered, now that we were no longer separated.

"I can feel it," Sasha whispered, holding her hand over a mirrored glyph floating above the smooth metal control panel, its light refracting like starlight on water. It wasn't floating in the sky—it was right there, above the panel, tangible, humming with old power, yet with a dimensional shimmer that made it look almost untethered.

The glyph had activated when Parker had turned the final dial. It wasn't painted or engraved—it *grew* from the surface, light-infused and reactive. Energy rippled through it in perfect rhythm with the moons overhead, as if some unseen event linked sky and stone.

"The hovering temple's moving faster now," Elijah added. "Do we have to synchronize all three pyramids at once?"

"Yes, that's it." I responded, then turned to Parker. "Let's sync time with rhythm."

He smiled, eyes gleaming with intensity and purpose. "Brilliant!"

Blair slowly moved to join us. The six of us, each drawn to a different point of activation. The dials had changed and were more intricate now, like the puzzles knew we were ready. My pendant glowed bright against my chest as I aligned the inner ring with a symbol I swore I'd only ever seen in dreams.

Moonlight poured through the air like liquid, and the pyramids began to rotate, slowly at first, then with increasing speed. I could hear it: the click of alignment, the music of purpose finding its place. The sound thrummed through my feet and into my chest.

Lines of golden light raced across the ground, linking each pyramid to the levitating temple in the center. The sand hissed as the heat rose, but we didn't move. We stood in it and let it burn.

The ground cracked in places as celestial veins of glowing ore emerged beneath us—ancient pathways, buried deep until now. The sand no longer felt lifeless but alive, like skin breathing. I could feel the rhythm in my bones.

A glyph above us cracked open like an eye. And then there was a clap of thunder. The final click echoed like the heartbeat of a god. The pyramids locked into place. And the temple descended.

It didn't crash or fall, it floated, settling lightly onto the sand like a memory returning home. Doors carved in gold and obsidian unfurled like petals revealing a pure white light within. A wind stirred that hadn't touched this land in eons.

We stared.

"I think we did it," Sasha breathed.

Parker said softly. "I think this is just the beginning."

I looked at each of them, lit by the glow of three moons and a million unspoken truths. We weren't the same people who stumbled separately into this realm. We were something else now.

"We go together," I said. "No matter what's next."

Denali nodded. "Together."

Blair gave a tired smile. Elijah placed a steady hand on Sasha's shoulder. Parker looked at his compass, even though we all knew it wouldn't help here. The space hummed like a song waiting to be finished.

We held hands and stepped into the light.

The moment we crossed the temple's threshold, the world changed. The oppressive heat gave way to a silvery chill, the sand beneath our boots turned darker and finer, almost like volcanic ash. It took a moment to realize the shimmer in the air wasn't heat distortion anymore. It was a shadow, moving of its own accord.

We had passed the trials and entered the Maze of Shadows.

Blair was still weak, her skin pale and her movements sluggish. She clung to Denali for a moment, but when her knees buckled again, Parker moved in without a word and swept her into his arms.

"I've got her," he said softly.

Denali gave a slight nod and stepped aside, rubbing at the burn on his shoulder. Blair didn't protest. Her head rested against Parker's chest, eyes closed, her breathing slow but steady. She looked drained, like someone who'd poured everything into something and had nothing left.

Sasha shifted toward Blair, her expression focused and gentle. She placed two fingers lightly on her temple and closed her eyes. A faint shimmer of violet light pulsed beneath her touch. "Her energy's low, but steady," Sasha informed us. "She's overextended herself, but she's stable."

Sasha reached into her bag and pulled out a carved crystal and tucked it into Blair's hand. "This will help recharge your well of energy," she said, rising with a glance at Parker. "Just keep her close."

The rest of us fell silent as we walked.

The path wound through dimly glowing corridors, the sand underfoot occasionally shifting to black glass, then to smooth stone. Strange silhouettes flickered on the edges of our vision, structures or perhaps illusions, too vague to be named. A wind blew from nowhere, cool and laced with the scent of minerals and something more ancient, like burnt incense.

We walked for what felt like hours.

Then, just when the fatigue began to settle into my bones again, we saw a hut made entirely of curved, smoked glass, sitting atop a raised obsidian platform. Pale blue light spilled from within.

The door was wide open.

Inside, six beds lined the walls, simple but clean. Individual trays of food had been left at the foot of each one. Not Earth food—no bread or fruit or meat we could name— but spiced roots that steamed with fragrance, glowing berries in carved stone bowls, and a kind of golden broth that gleamed when stirred.

We stepped inside hesitantly.

"Someone's expecting us," Elijah said, eyeing the room.

Parker laid Blair gently onto the nearest bed. She murmured something unintelligible but didn't open her eyes. He stayed beside her, his fingers brushing her wrist to check her pulse.

"It's unbelievably slow," Parker said, concerned.

"She probably just needs rest," Elijah said with a nod.

"I hope you're right," I said as I went over to squeeze her hand. "We're all right here with you, Blair," I told her softly.

Denali collapsed onto the edge of his own bed and let out a slow, relieved sigh. "Please tell me we're done with trials."

Sasha leaned against a glass pillar. "There were five trials mentioned. We've passed them, and the pyramids aligned. All of that was to get the maze to open, right?"

Elijah rubbed the back of his neck. "Yes, I believe so. There have been five. We must be done."

"I hope so," Sasha whispered. She sat next to Denali and gently touched his arm over the scarf I'd tied around his burn. She closed her eyes and breathed slowly and deeply. Opening her eyes, she smiled ever so slightly and confirmed, "You're fine." He nodded.

I sat on the edge of my bed, too wired to eat yet too exhausted to resist the lure of comfort. I glanced at my food tray—broth, a twisted green root steaming gently, and a bowl of glowing orbs that pulsed faintly, as if they were still alive. I poked one. It giggled.

Sasha raised an eyebrow. "The berries laugh?"

"Apparently." I smiled weakly.

Elijah bit into one of his glowing fruits and nodded. "Sweet. A little like a pear, if pears were made of lightning."

We all chuckled, the sound low but genuine. The tension began to melt, just a little.

"So, someone's been following our path," Denali said, stretching out on his bed. "Feeding us and leaving shelter. That's more than coincidence."

"Maybe it's her," Parker said. He didn't look away from Blair. "Calista. Maybe she's guiding us the only way she can."

We all sat with that thought for a long moment.

"I'd like to believe that" I said quietly, "but she's in prison, so how would that be possible?"

"Zanira?" Denali questioned.

"That's a more plausible choice," Elijah agreed.

A hush settled over us. One by one, we began to eat, slowly, tasting this strange food that warmed from within. The exhaustion hit heavier afterward, a weight pulling us down into stillness.

"I think we're close," Sasha said with a long sigh, curled under a silken blanket. "The prison has to be near here. All of this was leading us to her."

Denali reached into a pocket in his bag and pulled out a thin flute, carved from pale wood. He played a soft, brief note, one that echoed faintly in the glass.

"Let's hope she's still alive in there," he said and then continued to play. It lulled us all into a deep, satisfying sleep.

16

DESCENT INTO SHADOW

The air changed the moment we stepped closer to the maze.

It wasn't just cooler; it was cold in a way that made my bones ache. Tendrils of darkness seeped from the mouth of the Maze of Shadows, moving like ink in water. I couldn't tell if the shadows were smoke or mist or something alive. But I did know one thing: nothing good poured out of a place like that.

We stood in a loose half-circle, all six of us facing the entrance like we were about to step into a nightmare we'd been rehearsing in our sleep.

Zanira, wrapped in silver and midnight-blue robes that fluttered in an invisible breeze, stepped between us. Her eyes glistened with that unplaceable color, something between starlight and sorrow. "This is the last gate," she said softly. "Beyond this, truth bends, identity unravels. You may see yourself and then not recognize the seeing."

"I'm hoping we will be able to figure out what you're referring to," Parker said from beside me, voice tight but calm. His blond hair, usually neat, was wind-tossed. A thin scratch that had not been there when we first met, traced his cheek.

Zanira ignored the comment. She moved to each of us slowly, placing her warm palm against our foreheads one by one. Her thumb brushed my brow last. Her skin felt like fire meeting ice. "Remember who you are," she whispered, voice soft and firm. "Even when you are not."

Something flickered behind my eyes. For a second, I saw my own reflection in water, but then it wasn't me at all. My heart slammed in my chest. Then it passed just as quickly as it had come. And then Zanira was gone as if she had never been there.

Denali shifted beside me, his breath steady, but his eyes dark and fixed on the shadowed entrance like it might swallow us whole. His fingers twitched at his side like he wanted to reach for someone and wasn't sure if he should.

Blair, pale and freckled, stood like a sketch not yet colored in. Her red hair fluttered in the cold. She was holding her sketchpad, even now. "Does anyone else feel like we're being watched?" she asked, her voice a soft ripple.

"Definitely," Sasha said. She stood tall, arms crossed over her chest. The faint glimmer of her bird tattoo shimmered beneath her collarbone like it wanted to take flight. "The maze is watching and studying us."

"Testing us," Elijah added, voice low. His light blue-gray eyes scanned the entrance, always calculating and ready. His martial stance hadn't relaxed since we woke. "It's waiting for us to doubt ourselves."

"Too late," I said, hugging my arms close. I didn't mean to say it out loud.

Denali gave me a sidelong glance. "You've made it through everything so far."

"Yeah, well. What if I've already used up all my courage?" My laugh was sharp, brittle.

His brow furrowed. "Courage isn't a one-time thing. It's choice by choice and step by step."

"God, you sound like a wilderness guide," I said, but it came out too soft to be sarcastic. He smiled faintly.

The sand beneath us pulsed, and the maze beckoned.

Parker took a cautious step forward. "We've passed the trials," he said. "All five. Which means this isn't a test. It's a transition."

"Semantics," Sasha said with a slight smile.

"No," he said. "Symbols and thresholds. The maze is a liminal space. It's designed to undo us, so we can become something more."

"Like caterpillars?" Blair offered.

Elijah tilted his head. "More like ghosts."

Sasha groaned. "Wonderful. I just love it when metaphors start haunting us."

I adjusted the pendant around my neck. The metal— silver, copper, turquoise—felt hot and cold at the same time. My mother's voice flashed through my mind: *You're made for more than the surface of things, mi corazon. Trust the spiral. Trust your path.*

I squared my shoulders. "All right," I said. "We go together. No splitting up or hero moves, and no wandering off alone."

"That wasn't aimed at me, was it?" Elijah asked, grinning.

Denali let out a low laugh. "She means all of us, even the wanderers."

"I'm not a wanderer," Parker said. "I follow myth lines."

"You *named* your compass," Sasha replied.

Parker looked momentarily offended. "It's a sacred talisman."

I knew we were stalling. I stepped forward—one pace, two, and finally three. The cold slid against me like needles brushing my skin. I couldn't see the red sand anymore.

The others followed. Slowly. Quietly.

Blair clutched her sketchpad. Sasha rolled her shoulders like she was warming up for a battle of energy. Elijah's breath synced with some rhythm I couldn't hear. Denali moved forward so he was just behind me, a quiet strength at my back. Parker was last. I listened to the soft scrape of his boots against the stone.

The darkness swallowed our shadows first; the light behind us.

Zanira's voice echoed one last time, impossibly far away yet achingly near:

"Remember who you are, even when you are not."

And then there was nothing, only the maze.

I didn't know I had separated from the others until the silence became too personal.

There was no path beneath my feet anymore, just shifting stone tiles, some soft as sand, some brittle as bone. The air pressed against me like I was underwater, every inhale thicker than the last. I looked all around, searching for the others.

That was when I saw him: Vincent, my ex.

He was standing in front of a stone archway that hadn't been there a moment ago, perfectly real—palest green eyes too calm, posture too familiar. My stomach dropped so hard it felt like gravity had changed.

No! This was not real.

I took a step back. But the maze behind me shifted and closed in so that I could no longer move, and the only way forward was through him.

He looked exactly as I remembered with his button-down shirt, faint scruff on his jaw, and that smug tilt of the mouth that always danced the line between charm and cruelty. "You always come back to me," he said smoothly. "Even here."

"This isn't real," I said, even though it felt real. "You're not real." But I second-guessed myself because of the way he stood. I could smell his scent in the air—his cologne, subtle and distinctive. *God,* even my body responded to him. I hated that.

He smiled, stepping closer. "Isn't it? You know you never really left. You just buried me under work, ambition, and dirt. Dig deep enough, I'm still with you."

"No. I left you." I whispered to myself.

The maze was clever. It wasn't using Vincent, it was using *me*: my voice, self-doubt, guilt, and my shame, all dressed in *his* skin.

"You push people away before they can leave you," he said. "It's always been your pattern. I just had the misfortune of staying long enough to prove you right."

My fists curled at my sides, but I remained mute. I didn't know what to say.

"You're still angry," he said. "Not at me, but at yourself. You knew who I was, but you stayed anyway."

"I stayed," I snapped, "because I believed in you. And I thought that if I just gave a little more, bent a little further, you'd finally meet me halfway."

He paused, and for a moment, the illusion cracked. I could see something flicker behind his eyes.

"You desperately wanted someone to love you," he said quietly.

"And you wanted someone to control."

His face didn't twist or lash out. He just looked tired. Or maybe it was me that I saw reflected in his eyes. Perhaps this wasn't his ghost; maybe it was mine.

I looked around. The stone tiles now formed a perfect square—claustrophobic and deliberate—a trap dressed like a room.

I didn't owe this memory anything, not even a good ending. I realized I had really and truly put it all behind me. And so, I turned and walked away.

The world shuddered around me.

Behind me, I heard glass break, then stone, and then something like thunder, but softer and closer, like something inside my chest was cracking open.

I didn't stop, not when the voices started—his voice, my own, my mother's, Heidi's—all tangled up in echoes: *You'll regret this. You'll be alone. You're too much. You're not enough.*

I kept walking, and then the light appeared—warm, golden light, like late afternoon in the desert. I stepped into it, breath hitching. The moment I crossed that threshold, the stone floor crumbled behind me, and the air thinned. The scent of Vincent's cologne was gone.

I was alone, but I wasn't broken. In the dust beneath me was a spiral, drawn faintly, like someone had traced it centuries ago with the tip of their finger. I knelt to touch it. It was the same spiral on my pendant, on the temple door, and on Sasha's tattoo. My mother's voice rang inside me: *Trust the spiral. Trust your path.*

I touched it and whispered, "I remember who I am."

Something shifted in my chest. Not relief or closure. It was something even better. It was clarity.

I stood, brushing dirt from my hands. That's when I felt him, a warmth behind me, steady and quiet. I knew it was Denali before I saw him.

I turned, and there he was, still and strong in the lavender light, black hair pushed back from his face, eyes darker than midnight. He didn't ask what I saw. He didn't need to. His eyes moved over me with the gentlest urgency, like he was counting the parts of me that returned. I must've looked like a wreck—dirt on my hands and cheeks, scratches on my arms, my heart in pieces—but I was whole. I was myself.

"Alayna," he said, voice like breath. "Are you okay? We couldn't find you. We looked everywhere and called out to you. You simply disappeared."

I nodded. "I finally let go."

He didn't move toward me, not right away. He just stood there, honoring the space I'd reclaimed. But then he took a single step forward. His hands, rough and warm, found mine. Our fingers interlaced. We shared no words. There were no questions. I held on to him without fear.

We stood like that for a while, surrounded by silence and soft light, our shadows long and entwined across the stone. His thumb moved over my knuckle, once, barely, but it was enough to ground me.

"I thought I'd lost you in there," he said softly.

"I almost lost myself," I replied. "But the maze made a simple mistake."

He raised a brow. "What was that?"

"It showed me who I was with him, but it also reminded me who I am without him."

Denali's lips curved, just slightly, to reveal a quiet smile that didn't need a spotlight.

"I like the you without him," he said.

I gave him a look. "You barely knew the other one."

"Maybe not, but I know this version, and she's someone I want to keep finding out more about."

My chest tightened, but it wasn't fear; it was something else. I wasn't scared, not anymore.

I gave his hand a slight squeeze. And we walked together, deeper into the maze—not lost, but choosing the unknown—step by step and side by side. And whatever shadows came next, they'd have to face both of us.

The maze had quieted. No illusions, no shadows leaping from corners—just silence thick enough to press between ribs. Denali walked beside me, our boots scuffing across the uneven stone. My hand still tingled from holding his. I didn't bring it up, and neither did he.

"We've got to find the others," I said, scanning the space ahead. "Assuming this place lets us."

He nodded, eyes sharp beneath his dark lashes. "It's like it rearranges when we're not looking."

I blew a slow breath. "Yeah. Like a dream that's pretending to be solid."

We turned a bend, and there it was, unexpected, strange, and oddly beautiful. A massive tree, gnarled and silver, rose from the center of a cavernous chamber. Its bark shimmered faintly, and at its hollowed base was a small, circular door, wooden, with a carved spiral pattern I'd seen a hundred times before.

Denali moved toward it first, brushing dust off the edges. "Locked," he said, jiggling the knob. "Of course."

I stepped closer, staring at the design. The same spiral that matched the pendant at my chest. Zanira's voice echoed faintly in my memory—*"Your pendant is more than protection. It knows the old locks."*

I reached up, fingers wrapping around the metal. "Let me try something."

Holding the pendant out, I hovered it near the knob. A warm vibration pulsed through the spiral, humming like a tuning fork. Then—*click*. The door creaked open.

Denali looked at me like I'd just summoned lightning. "You really are full of surprises."

I gave him a tired smile. "Let's hope the tree's as cozy as it is weird."

Inside, it was warmer than I expected—a round room, walls of smooth root wood and moss, and a cushiony hearth. Blankets were folded neatly in one corner, like someone—or something—knew we were coming.

"Should we trust this?" I asked, but my legs were already aching. My head spun with exhaustion I'd been ignoring.

Denali dropped his bag beside the hearth. "Right now, I think resting is smarter than pushing forward half-dead. Besides, I don't think this maze is going to let us go any other direction for now."

I didn't argue.

We each claimed a blanket and lay close to each other. My limbs, still vibrating from the earlier confrontation, finally began to relax. I turned my head and caught the curve of Denali's jaw with my eyes.

"You okay?" he asked.

"Getting there," I whispered. "Tired, but my mind is very clear."

He nodded and shifted closer. His body radiated heat, a comfort more grounding than I realized. I turned toward him, propping my head on one arm. My face was inches from his.

Too close yet not close enough. His hand brushed a lock of hair from my cheek. I tilted my chin, caught in the space between instinct and decision. My pulse stuttered. And then his lips brushed mine, soft, hesitant, and asking. I didn't pull away. Instead, I kissed him back. Not tentative or careful but filled with fire.

His hand slid to my waist, mine curled behind his neck, and we lost ourselves in the hush of breathless wanting. His kiss deepened, and I let myself unravel, my body curving into his like it knew the shape already.

When we finally pulled apart, breath catching between us, he rested his forehead against mine.

"I didn't mean to rush that," he said, voice low.

"You didn't," I whispered. "I wanted it too."

He smiled, which tugged something loose in my chest. I shifted closer, head on his chest, heart steady now. His arm wrapped around me. We said nothing else. Our bodies stayed pressed together, breath slowing. For the first time since entering Aztalun, I felt something I hadn't let myself feel in months. *Safe.* We both slept, in warmth, in quiet, in each other's arms.

17

VAREK'S WARNING

Denali and I stood slowly, brushing ourselves off. He pulled me into a quiet hug, warm and steady, grounding us both. "We should go back to the others."

"Yeah… let's go."

The moment we rounded the bend I saw them waiting at the convergence of shadow and shimmer. Sasha walked over and gave me a quick hug. Blair clutched my hand for a moment before stepping back. Elijah offered a nod. Parker tapped the spiral on my pendant and gave a faint smile. Denali moved to stand beside me, our hands brushing. No one spoke right away. We simply regrouped, falling into step as if no time had passed.

The maze narrowed, then widened again, opening into a vast chamber lit by no flame, only by the strange, ambient glow of the labyrinth itself. The air glistened like a heat mirage, even though it was cold enough to turn breath into mist. We stepped forward together—me, Denali just behind my right shoulder, Sasha glowing faintly with the magic pulsing under her skin. Parker's eyes swept the shifting walls, mumbling under his breath. Blair clutched her sketchbook tight to her chest. Elijah flexed his fingers as if preparing for battle.

And then we saw him.

He stood like a monolith at the heart of the chamber, tall as a tree, broader than any man I'd ever seen. Cloaked in black shadow, he was both there and not there. His armor flickered between molten obsidian and cracked, starlit stone. His face was half veiled in darkness, but the other half, a ruin of beauty, was touched with something ancient. His eyes were dying amber suns.

There was no way I could have prepared myself for the Keeper of the Maze. He was the last thing standing between us and Calista. Varek wasn't just a man; he was a rupture, a wound in the world given form.

"You seek the goddess," he said. His deep voice vibrated through my bones when he spoke, not loud, but low, a kind of sound that didn't need volume to command attention.

"Yes, we have," I said before I could second-guess myself. My voice echoed, too, unbelievably steady. "We are the Hexad."

A smile curved the corner of his mouth, but it wasn't kind. "I am Varek, Keeper of the Maze and the Guard of Calista's Obsidian Prison. I am her warden, but if you seek to free her, then I will be your ruin." His voice cracked, briefly, like something fraying from within. Fury seemed to emanate outward in anger. "Turn around and go back from whence you came. I do not wish to harm you."

I couldn't stop staring at his hands. They were massive, calloused, veined with something dark, but they shook, just barely, when he said her name. He wasn't just her warden; he was her grief made flesh, her betrayer and her echo all in one. Yet, even in his fury, there was something fractured in him. The more I looked at him, the more I wondered if this was the real prison, the man himself, not the walls around Calista, and certainly not the maze.

Sasha took a brave step forward, tattoos bright across her collarbone. "You don't have to fight us. Calista will want to see us. She doesn't belong in a cage."

"Don't speak of belonging," he growled. "You, who've barely begun to understand what balance truly costs."

His presence weighed on me like gravity. The pendant at my neck pulsed once. I clutched it, heat bleeding into my palm.

"We're not here to destroy balance," Parker said gently, his fingers brushing a nearby rune. "We're here to restore it."

Varek laughed. A deep, hollow sound. "Restore it?" He paced a slow circle, boots dragging across the obsidian floor. "You think balance is light and dark holding hands under moonlight? No! Balance isn't sacrifice; it's silence. It is the tearing out of your own heart if the scales demand it."

Denali's hand brushed mine briefly. "Then why keep her locked away?"

"Because," Varek said, and the shadows around him rippled, "her freedom would unmake everything: the laws that bind gods and mortals alike, the veil between realms, and your very own souls."

"You're afraid of her," Blair whispered, her voice like paper folding.

The shadows recoiled, lashing out around the chamber in jagged lines of darkness. My heart raced, but we stood our ground.

"I fear her release. It would be an end," he snapped, but his eyes told a completely different story. I saw pain, memory, and guilt.

"You have not ended us yet," I said.

He stopped and looked at me, *really* looked.

And for just a moment, just a flicker, he seemed like a man lost in a dream he couldn't wake from.

"Elion forged the maze to bind her," he said at last. "But it was I who volunteered to hold the key. I, who let myself be broken. Her prison became mine."

My knees felt weak, but I spoke from my center. "Then help us undo it."

His jaw clenched. "You cannot undo what was done by divine decree."

"We're not divine," Elijah said. "That's the point."

Varek stared at each of us in turn: Sasha glowing with inner fire, Blair trembling but unbroken, Denali holding his sorrow like a shield, Elijah's fists curled at his sides, Parker watching everything with intense-blue eyes. And me, burning inside, not with fear, but *knowing*. We were here for a reason.

"If you open that prison, you don't save her," Varek said finally, "You invite war. The gods will not allow her to return. And you, little *Hexads*, you will shatter into dust."

I rose to my full height, not that I was very tall, but I was resolute, the pendant pulsing like a second heartbeat.

"Maybe," I said. "But perhaps it's time the gods learned they're not the only ones willing to bleed for balance."

He didn't move; he just watched me in silence. And then the shadows thickened, swirling around him. "Then come to me," he said as softly as a giant like him could speak. "Let us see if your truths are strong enough to survive the dark."

We fanned out instinctively, each of us taking a different direction across the shattered floor of the maze's heart, trying to circle Varek. The air trembled around him like heat waves on desert rock, except this heat wasn't warmth; it was distortion. Reality folded and stretched with every twitch of his hand.

He loomed at the center like a living storm, cloaked in shadow and crowned in cursed obsidian. When he moved, his limbs left afterimages of someone else, softer and barefoot. I glimpsed them in flickers and heard the name *Theren* in the wind. But Varek's body swallowed them up again, as if ashamed to let them linger.

"You seek to end all things," he growled, voice like gravel grinding on glass. "To free the one who would unmake the order." But the timbre cracked mid-sentence, just for a breath. A flash of remorse threaded through his syllables.

There was a tremor in the dark, and Sasha heard it too. She stepped forward, eyes burning like torches. "That's not your voice," she said. "That's not who you are."

He turned sharply, but Sasha didn't flinch. Her hand rose, tracing spirals through the air, silver and violet tattoos on her arms pulsing with light. I felt her reach out, not physically, but psychically, like an energy tether, delicate as thread and humming with intention.

The moment Sasha's tether brushed him, Varek staggered, just for a heartbeat. His whole body twitched like invisible hooks had yanked him, and in his eyes, black, endless pain cracked through.

He roared in pain. Magic exploded out of him, wild and unfiltered. The floor beneath us split open, revealing nothingness. In one corner of my vision, time spiraled backward: Parker's lips moved before his breath left them, Denali blinked and then hadn't yet. Everything lurched sideways.

"Sasha, stabilize the matrix!" Parker yelled, his hands glowing with glyphs as he raced to the nearest fragment of stone. "It's unraveling time!"

Runes blossomed beneath his fingers in golden light, sinking into the floor like roots, and for a second, the distortion eased.

Sasha swayed near the edge of a growing rift. "Ah—!"

Denali dove, caught her waist, and hauled her back just before the floor she stood on disintegrated into a swirling fractal maw. He didn't let go right away, and neither did she.

On the other side of the chaos, Elijah held up a crumbling stone wall with brute force, his muscles straining as debris rained down. "Blair, go!" he shouted.

Blair, smeared with charcoal, darted beneath the collapsing arch, clutching her brush like a weapon. A trembling sketch glowed on her palm, ready to unleash something living, if she had the space.

But space didn't exist anymore, not like it should.

The maze itself was rebelling. Its walls bent inwards, warping and cracking. Celestial light pulsed across the sky like forked lightning, and gravity spun in bursts. I felt it pull sideways, then drop out entirely, and for a second, I was floating.

Above, the moons—Aztalun's three guardians—crept into alignment. Their combined glow struck Varek like divine crosshairs. He screamed, low and guttural. Shadows coiled from his spine like wings. He sent a pulse through the air that felt like grief, pure and ancient.

And then—something else—a whisper. It came like a breeze through broken glass. It didn't belong to any of us. It was a voice softer than rain and heavier than realization.

"Theren," it breathed.

He froze. His head jerked slightly to the right. "No!" he cried out. "No, I am Varek. Varek, I say!"

But his body trembled, and his shoulder spasmed. Where the shadow coiled before now light bled through.

Calista's voice echoed again, not just in our ears but in our chests. "You were born of truth and tenderness. You are not what they have made you."

The battlefield went still, and even the maze held its breath.

A glow threaded through the cracks in the floor, golden and radiant, like sunlight breaking through stone.

I stood dumbstruck, unable to breathe. Around me, the others were still, eyes wide, chests heaving.

Varek looked down at his own hands. One was still shrouded in darkness, black veins writhing beneath the skin. But the other one glowed. The glow spread up his arm, over half his chest, illuminating ribs and collarbone from the inside.

He staggered back, fingers clawing at his chest as if to rip the light out.

"Get it out," he growled. "GET IT OUT!"

But the light wasn't leaving. It was claiming him.

Calista appeared above him, ghostlike and magnificent. Her form was translucent, with braided hair drifting like riverweed in slow water. She didn't touch him, only hovered there, face etched with ancient sorrow.

"You are still mine," she said. "Even now."

His mouth opened, but no sound came out.

And then my pendant burned. I gasped, stumbling back, grabbing at my chest. The spiral maze at its center twisted violently and then lifted on its own, tugged by an unseen force. It rose above my neckline, hovering in the air, and then shot downward.

It smashed to the ground with a deep, ringing chime. A pillar of light erupted from the impact, surrounding us all in a protective golden-orange ring. I turned in awe as the world peeled away from me.

The shadows broke apart.

Like skin sloughing from a serpent, the illusion dissolved, peeling back to reveal a chamber beneath, a crystalline sanctuary lit from within. Above us, a vaulted ceiling shimmered with obsidian glass, glittering with embedded stars. The walls pulsed like they remembered being alive.

At the center of the space, hovering above a prism of what looked like suspended crystal tears, was Calista.

The *real* Calista.

Her body floated serenely and radiantly. She was sleeping, glowing, her skin kissed with silver light. Her chest barely rose, as if she were dreaming still.

The others slowly stepped forward into the new space, breath caught in their throats.

Blair whispered, "She's beautiful."

"Is she alive?" Elijah asked, his voice hoarse.

"She's waiting," Parker said, eyes wide. "This place holds her heart."

But Varek—no, Theren—was still convulsing.

He dropped to his knees, clawing at the border between shadow and light on his chest like a fault line. One half of him radiated Calista's presence, the other half snarled in rage and despair.

And then the maze responded. For the first time, it turned on him.

The shadows recoiled, no longer obeying him. The fragments of wall he summoned twisted around him like a cage. Veins of light began piercing the stone, and the room trembled.

"He's losing control," Sasha said. "The maze was part of his magic—if it turns on *him*… "

"He won't survive it," Denali finished grimly.

But I wasn't so sure.

This wasn't just destruction; it was rebirth. And rebirth is always violent.

Varek—Theren—was curled on the floor now, growling, the crown of shadow on his head flickering between form and nothingness. One hand punched the stone, cracking it further. The golden light around us grew brighter, feeding on something more than energy—truth, maybe. Love and memory, certainly.

Calista's voice came again, and this time it sounded like mourning in harmony.

"Theren," she said, softer than before. "You are not the guardian of my prison; you are its key."

He lifted his head, eyes filled with tears, black and gold clashing like lightning in a storm.

"Help me," he rasped.

And then the maze screamed.

A great, twisting roar filled the crystalline chamber. The shadows lashed out—not at us, but at him. They didn't want to let him go, not their king.

But I saw it now. He was splitting.

The scream of the maze rose higher and sharper, until it wasn't just sound anymore, it was pressure. It pressed behind my eyes, curled inside my bones, a vibration of fury and unraveling truths. The shadows lashed again at Varek—no, Theren—recoiling from the light growing in his chest.

He tried to stand but stumbled. One knee gave way, and he hit the ground with a grunt, half of his body haloed in gold, the other still cloaked in writhing darkness. He looked up, straight at Calista's suspended form, and something changed in his expression.

Not hatred or rage. It was grief, like he'd just remembered what he'd lost. A tremor ran through the chamber, and obsidian cracked.

"He's not whole," Parker whispered beside me. "And the maze knows it."

"Then it'll destroy him," Blair said, backing closer to the ring of light. Her hands trembled, stained with the remnants of animated ink. "It won't let him change."

Varek bared his teeth and roared—not at us, not even at the maze—but at himself. The sound was raw, too human to be a monster, and too broken to be a god. The glow on his chest flared and then flickered, dimming as his other side surged forward. The darkness won out.

"No!" Sasha reached out instinctively, her psychic tether pulsing, but the connection burned away like paper in flame.

His body jerked backward, and then he turned. He didn't fight, and we watched his pain. A wave of shadow coiled up from the broken floor and swallowed him whole. One blink and he was gone, melted into the maze, and the fractures of a world unraveling around us.

"No—no, wait!" I shouted, lurching forward, hand outstretched toward Varek.

But there was nothing to reach for, just emptiness. That god-awful silence left behind when something vital slips away.

Denali caught my arm. "Alayna. He's gone."

I didn't pull away. I wanted to, but I couldn't.

"Where did he go?" I sobbed. "He's part of this maze. If it's rejecting him—"

"Then it's hunting him," Parker said grimly. "The very walls that obeyed him are going to crush him now."

Sasha took a shaky step forward, her eyes wide and wet. "He's not just lost, he's terrified. I felt it, through the tether when it connected. I felt his pain, confusion, and anguish."

"He was changing," Elijah said. "He was becoming something else."

"Calista called him Theren," Blair reminded us, clutching the edge of her cloak.

The name hung in the air like incense, sacred and damned.

My gaze turned to the place where he'd vanished. The shadow hadn't closed completely, so a thin slit of darkness remained, pulsing like a wound in the earth.

"I think I can follow him," I said quietly.

Sasha's head snapped toward me. "What?"

I stepped to the edge of the breach. The golden light from the pendant's blast still swirled faintly around us, but it didn't extend into the opening. That corridor was his—his alone. And the maze was alive now. Hunting for him. If we didn't—

"I don't think we're supposed to chase him," Denali said, stepping beside me. His voice was low, calm. "If we follow now, we'll trigger something worse."

"Then what?" My voice cracked. I was barely able to control myself. "We just let him disappear into that hellhole?

He was reaching for her, he was changing. We have to find him. We have to help him." I begged them with my eyes and tears.

"He was unraveling," Parker said gently. "And unraveling, people tend to run. That's their last defense."

The chamber groaned, a deep tectonic sound like the realm was shifting again. I looked up, and the cracks above us spread wider.

"Elijah," I said, "the ceiling…?"

He was already moving. "We need to find shelter. That beam won't protect us forever."

The floor beneath Calista's suspended prism began to ripple, like the chamber itself was bracing.

"Wait," Sasha said suddenly. "The maze is reacting to him. But Calista… she's still here. We stay. This place was hidden under illusion, maybe it's the core. It's solid here at the heart."

I looked up at the sleeping goddess, her limbs floating in weightless silence, her expression serene despite the crumbling world around her.

"But if the maze collapses entirely—" Blair started.

"It won't," Sasha said, surprising us all with her certainty. "She's still tethered here, and so are we."

Parker touched a hand to his heart. "Our arrival triggered something ancient. This place is shifting back to its truth. That illusion was Varek's defense. But now he's running, and the maze has reason to lie."

A pulse of power rippled out from the ground where my pendant had struck. It wasn't violent, it was rhythmic and deliberate—Calista's energy.

We were inside her heart now.

"He's afraid," I whispered, resigned to staying. "Varek or Theren. Whatever parts of him are still clashing. That light—her light—it scared him."

"Maybe it reminded him who he was," Denali said softly. His voice had a strange, reverent ache to it. "Maybe that's what broke him."

I felt a pang deep in my chest, not just sympathy but recognition. I knew what it meant to run from a truth too big to bear. I knew what it meant to be so tangled in your own past that the light felt like punishment.

"We're not done here," I said. "You all know that, right?"

"No," Elijah said, voice hardening. "We're not. But we've seen him bleed now. That means he's not invincible."

Blair lowered her head, brushing trembling fingers over the charcoal on her hands. "He's not our enemy anymore, not fully."

Parker nodded solemnly. "He's the door, and we need him to get to Calista. I don't think she'll ever wake unless he is here."

A wind rushed through the chamber, lifting my hair off my shoulders. It came from the slit in the shadows, where Varek had disappeared. The edge of it shimmered and then sealed shut with a sound like a blade sliding into a sheath.

He was gone, but not forever. The maze had turned on him, but it hadn't destroyed him yet.

We stood in the silence that followed, each of us shaped differently by what we'd seen—what we'd nearly touched. Calista's prism floated higher, and a wave of warmth spilled through the chamber. It was a heartbeat of confirmation.

We weren't done. We'd just stepped into the truth.

18

BREAKING OF THE CROWN

We were catching our breath. Facing Varek had felt like a battle that tore our nerves, and now we sat scattered around a clearing, all that was left of the maze. It had mercifully stopped shifting, for now. Elijah paced, Sasha meditated, Blair leaned into Parker's shoulder, eyes half-lidded, Denali stood watch near the corridor's bend, a hunting knife from his gear bag in hand.

"Do you think he'll return?" Blair asked quietly.

"Of course he will," came Sasha's response.

I exhaled slowly, heart still pounding. "But when?"

Parker opened his mouth to speak, and then the shadows split wide, and Varek erupted from the shadows like a wound torn open. One second, we were resting in a corridor that felt eerily calm, and the next, the walls screamed and folded in on themselves.

Varek's form seemed taller than I remembered, cloaked in black that rippled like smoke underwater. The moment I saw his eyes, pitch black and full of fury, I froze. Not from fear, exactly, but from recognition.

"Move!" Elijah shouted, stepping in front of Blair, her red hair plastered to her forehead with sweat.

Sasha raised her glowing hands. "I'm going to try and veil him."

But Varek struck first. His shadow-laced magic burst outward, not sharp like a blade, but *blunt*, like thunder with weight. It didn't slice—it *severed*. I felt something yank at my chest like my soul had been snagged and tugged sideways.

"Elijah, use your shield!" Sasha shouted.

He answered with a grunt, slamming his palms to the ground. A column of sandstone rose between us and the next blast. It held, for a moment, but then the corners cracked and buckled under the pressure.

Blair, panting, threw a handful of silver paint into the air. The particles formed winged glyphs that darted toward Varek like swallows, glowing with illusion magic.

They hit his obsidian armor and hissed, disrupting the shadows curling around him.

"Nice," Parker muttered from beside me. He twisted his fingers through the air, sketching runes in a strange, mirrored sequence. "We've got to fracture the maze. We damaged it before, and his control is rooted in the geometry."

I nodded. "Then let's uproot it."

Denali charged straight ahead, ducking a tendril of shadow, his blade slicing upward. "Over here!" he yelled, trying to pull Varek's focus off the rest of us.

It worked for a second.

Varek turned on him with terrifying speed, a wall of darkness lashing toward him like a wave.

"Denali!" I screamed.

Sasha leapt forward, arms outstretched. "Soul-bind!"

A radiant tether of violet light shot from her palms, snagging Varek's shadow mid-swing. The whip of darkness fizzled just before it could slam into the ice guide's back.

Denali looked over his shoulder and gave her a shaky nod. "Thanks."

Parker's runes flared silver. "We're pushing him and he's reacting without calculation."

That was when it hit me. "Varek's not aiming to kill us," I said, the realization sinking deep. "He's holding back."

Parker grunted. "This is displacement magic."

"What does that mean?" Denali asked, backing toward us again, his dark eyes still locked on Varek.

"It means he's only trying to scare us," Parker said, "drive us off, not destroy us."

He was right. Every strike Varek launched bent the maze, spun walls, and shifted the ground beneath our feet. We weren't being hurt; we were being *caged*.

Still, he looked feral, his thick beard matted, long dreadlocks wild around his face, chest heaving beneath armor carved from obsidian itself.

His voice growled through the chaos. "You don't belong here. You *don't understand* what she is!"

"Calista?" I echoed, chest tightening.

Then I felt it, a whisper, soft and mournful, like moonlight humming through bone. It was Calista. Her presence threaded into the air like silver silk, brushing against our skin, quieting the roar of magic around us.

"I think she's trying to calm him," Blair gasped. "Calista, we're here for you!"

The shadows around Varek stuttered.

"She is trying to soothe him," Sasha agreed, breathless, eyes wide with disbelief.

Golden light cracked through the air, just like before, slicing through the center of Varek's chest. He screamed, clutching it like it burned. But it wasn't fire. It was his truth.

His body staggered, shadows hissing like steam. His eyes darted to mine, just for a second, and I saw his pain and confusion, and deep sorrow.

"Theren," I whispered, "I know you're there. You don't want to stop us, not really."

Denali moved beside me. "He's fighting himself."

The maze shook again, walls groaning, and it seemed the realm itself was screaming.

Varek roared, shadows curling from his fingers like smoke with teeth, and the obsidian walls around Calista's prison trembled. His eyes, wild and black, too full of something timeless and broken, locked onto us. I barely had time to yell before he lunged.

"Parker!" Elijah shouted.

We scattered, but one of us was not fast enough.

A pulse of dark energy exploded from Varek's hand and struck Parker full in the chest. I saw the moment his body left the ground, arms flailing, mouth open but silent, before he hit the stone wall with a sickening crack.

"No!" I screamed.

He dropped, crumpled into a ragdoll of silence.

Blair ran to him first, her red hair flying behind her like fire. Sasha and I were right behind her, knees skidding on cracked marble. Somehow, Denali was already there, pressing his fingers to Parker's throat. Elijah knelt beside him, calm but sickeningly silent.

"Elijah," Blair whispered as my heart slammed against my ribs. "Tell me he's okay."

Elijah didn't speak; he just shook his head, jaw clenched, eyes glinting with a grief he'd never let us see before.

Blair covered her mouth. Denali's hands were trembling. Sasha dropped forward and gripped Parker's arm, her tattoos writhing like frantic birds trying to take flight. And I couldn't breathe. Not Parker! Not the one who saw through illusions and who always knew the way forward.

My scream tore from somewhere primal, and it wasn't just mine. Sasha's voice joined, raw and guttural. Blair's followed, cracked with anguish. Denali bellowed in fury. Elijah's growl shook the floor. We all screamed, not with words but grief, all of it pouring out like blood.

That's when it happened. Our rings ignited, Zanira's rings. Each one blazing at once, searing with power that wasn't ours alone. A wind surged from nowhere, circling us in a vortex of starlight, ash and the colors of the chakra. I could feel all of them: Sasha's pain, Blair's sorrow, Denali's fury, Elijah's guilt, and my own heartbreak. Our souls united in a spiraling energy.

We rose, literally lifted from the ground, in a perfect circle, our feet dangling a few inches in the air. Light poured from our rings and spiraled into columns of living memory. The air buzzed with a sound I can't explain, like a thousand whispered names folding into one truth.

"Channel," Sasha whispered. "Together."

And we did.

Without speaking, without moving, we unleashed something more primal than this realm. It wasn't a spell. It was ancient collective memory cast through unity, one voice in five bodies. Power burst outward, pure and glowing with the colors of flame, slamming into Varek and wrapping around him like molten chains.

He screamed, but he couldn't move. For the first time since we met him, Varek didn't look invincible; he looked lost. The dark crown on his brow sparked and hissed.

Parker still hadn't moved. I fell to the ground beside him, my hand on his chest. Still no rise or heartbeat.

And then, Calista's voice drifted on the wind. "Please… don't."

I froze. "What? Don't what?" I whispered aloud.

The air turned soft, spiraling like smoke, and the world tilted. I was being sucked out of the chamber and into something that had no shape or edges, just spirals—infinite spirals. I tumbled through them, weightless and breathless, until everything stilled. The space around me shimmered, silver and indigo, with no gravity or time.

Before me knelt a man. He was young and barefoot. His long, dark brown hair tousled and streaked with golden sunlight. His arms were chained, and he sobbed, shoulders shaking with the kind of sorrow that makes the soul brittle.

"Theren," I whispered.

He looked up, startled. His eyes were amber, not black like Varek's, not full of rage, but soft and searching. I stepped closer. The spirals moved with me, stretching and echoing like mirrors. When I reached out, my fingers brushed his, and I felt his heart, not just the beating of it. I felt who he was inside with every ache, and every moment he'd been twisted into something monstrous. I felt every second he'd loved Calista and was punished for it, and my heart wept for him.

He was never the enemy. He was simply a pawn in the game of the gods against Calista. Varek was a weapon forged from devotion and rewritten as wrath.

Tears burned down my cheeks. "Oh, Varek," I whispered. "You're not the monster."

He looked at me, confused, and hope flickered behind his pain. I knew it was Calista showing me this, but why?

The spirals around us pulsed, and I felt the spell tug me back, toward the chamber, toward my body, but I gripped his hand tighter.

"I know who you are, Theren," I whispered.

Then the light shattered, and I woke gasping on the stone floor beside Parker, who was still lifeless.

When I looked up, the others were surrounding Varek, who stood at the center of a broken altar, shadows writhing around his feet like serpents sensing blood. His crown pulsed with jagged veins of obsidian. Every breath he took sent tremors through the maze. Denali's chest rose and fell like a storm barely held at bay. Sasha's fingers sparked with psychic light, her eyes unreadable. Elijah's muscles were taut, his stance poised to strike. Blair clutched her side, pale and shaking, but resolute.

My heart thundered like a war drum. I didn't know what to do. If we didn't kill him, he would regain his strength and not let us pass through to free Calista, and quite possibly, he might end up killing us. But if we killed him, Calista would be lost in grief, and this would all be for naught.

"We end this," Elijah growled. "Now."

"No," Denali said softly, almost to himself. "That doesn't feel right."

"It *has* to be him," Sasha told us. "It's his death or her freedom. We have no choice."

I looked at the crystal structure now visible behind Varek, which was sharp, translucent, and pulsing with pale blue veins. Calista's body floated within, suspended.

My pendant burned against my chest. It wanted resolution, justice, and balance, but something felt terribly wrong.

Varek stumbled, shadows flaring. "You think I care what happens next?" His voice fractured mid-sentence, low and wrathful, and then suddenly human—*Theren.*

"Do it," he spat, stepping forward. "Free your goddess and finish me."

Blair's whisper broke through. "Wait, he's no longer covered in shadow."

Suddenly, a shimmer of silver light bloomed before us, and Calista appeared in spirit form, glowing and impossibly still. Her wheat-blond braids floated like silk in water, her green eyes soft and sorrowful.

"Stop," she whispered, her voice echoing in every one of us. "Please… do not kill him."

We froze as her gaze landed on Varek, or rather *Theren,* and something ancient and fragile passed between them. I saw recognition, devastation, and *love.*

"That man… he is mine," she said, a tear gliding down her cheek like liquid crystal. "My beloved, Theren."

Sasha's lip trembled. Elijah cursed under his breath.

"If you take him from me," Calista continued, "you may shatter my prison, but you will chain my soul in everlasting grief. I would rather remain entombed than awaken to a world without him."

"Calista—" I stepped forward. "He tried to kill us all."

"No. He tried to protect me."

Theren collapsed to his knees. His shadows vanished like mist under moonlight as the dark crown on his head cracked and fell to the ground with a loud *clank.* Somewhere from deep inside him, a shuddering breath escaped, a sound too haunted to ignore.

"I think he's dying," Sasha said, her voice breaking.

"Please, I'm begging you. Please don't let my beloved die. I would weep for a thousand years," Calista said, her eyes never leaving his face.

Theren looked at Calista now with understanding.

"No," I whispered, heart thudding. "We won't kill him. But we will bind his rage. Hexad, hold your rings high."

Our rings, silver and warm, glowed at once. Each of us focused our energy and will on them. I said a spell in my mind, and it rippled outward like a net made of starlight.

Varek screamed—no, *Theren*—as the remaining shadows were drawn from him, sucked into the rings until all that remained was a man: breathless and trembling, eyes wide with grief and confusion.

"I… Calista… " he rasped as his eyes settled on her.

She reached for him, her light barely brushing his cheek. "Theren, my love… You are found."

And for the first time, he wept.

And so did we.

Calista turned to us, her eyes shimmering. Her voice, low and radiant, seemed to resonate with the very air around us. "Because you showed mercy to my Theren," she said, "because you did not strike down the one I love, though you had every reason to… I will show mercy in return."

I felt my breath catch as her gaze shifted to Parker's still form. Blair ran to his lifeless body and clung to him like she could anchor him to this world by sheer will alone.

"I will restore his breath, his strength, and his spirit," Calista said softly.

Sasha exhaled a stunned gasp. Elijah took a reverent step forward. Denali gripped my hand.

Calista knelt and pressed her palm to Parker's forehead. A quiet ripple of light poured from her fingers, spreading like water through dry soil. Parker arched slightly, gasped, and then breathed.

Blair sobbed, laughter and tears mixing.

Parker's eyes fluttered open, dazed but alive.

I looked at Calista. "Thank you," I whispered.

She smiled, not like a goddess, but like a woman who knew what it meant to love deeply and be loved in return.

We rushed to him like gravity had pulled us all at once—Blair still on her knees, clutching him; Sasha dropping beside him with wide, tearful eyes; Denali helping ease Parker upright while Elijah steadied his back. I reached for his arm, just needing to feel the warmth return to it.

Parker blinked, eyes glassy, lips parted. "Did I fall asleep in the middle of something?" he rasped.

A laugh burst from Sasha, choked with emotion. "Only a cosmic battle with a time-fracturing sorcerer."

Blair wiped her eyes, cupping his face. "You really scared me."

He looked at her, then at each of us. "I remember fire and then everything went quiet."

"Yeah, well," Elijah said gently, "quiet doesn't suit you."

Parker shared a knowing smile. "It feels good to be alive then."

"You are alive," I said, voice thick, "thanks to her."

He glanced toward Calista, awe and confusion flickering across his features. "Guess I owe a goddess a thank-you."

"You owe us all," Blair teased, even as fresh tears fell. "Especially me."

He kissed her hand. "I'll start with you, then."

Once we all felt secure that Parker was alright, we turned our attention to Theren, who was still on his knees, shoulders shaking as the last shimmer of Calista's spirit dissolved into the air. The chamber felt strangely hollow without her, like the echo had been sucked from the world. His head hung low, tangled hair falling across his face, and the shadows that had once obeyed him like hounds curled around him like lost things.

"She loves you so deeply, Theren," I said gently, stepping forward. "It echoed across centuries."

His face lifted slowly, eyes swollen and wet, and for the first time, he looked truly human instead of a monster or a cursed guardian. "I'm sorry I tried to kill all of you," he choked. "I forgot who I was. Who I am."

"No," I said, crouching so we were level. "You didn't try to kill us. You tried to scare us. There's a difference. You were just doing what you thought you had to." I didn't know where the words came from—maybe from Calista, or maybe from something more profound—but they felt true.

That seemed to knock the wind out of him. His eyes softened just a fraction. "I thought I had to protect her. That was the only thing that made sense."

"We know," Denali said, his voice a low rumble of empathy behind me.

Sasha stepped forward, fingers clasped before her heart. "Zanira told us that freeing Calista isn't just about her. It's about restoring all the realms, ours too."

Theren swallowed hard. "I'm sorry to tell you this, but I only knew how to open the obsidian door when I was Varek. Without him, I have no idea how to get to her."

I glanced down at the pendant around my neck, now warm against my skin. "Maybe I do."

Strolling to the towering translucent door, I held the pendant close, its metal buzzing faintly. "Come on," I whispered. Nothing happened.

I closed my eyes and reached inward, not just with thought but with feeling. *Calista, let us in. We saved Theren, please. Let this be enough.* The spiral flared hot, and the door gave a deep groan.

Stone shifted while the seal cracked, and the door slid open.

We all froze, breath caught. But when we walked inside, we saw that she was still encased in that terrible crystalline cage. She was still asleep and unreachable.

"I don't understand," Blair whispered behind me. "I thought she was awake. We heard her and saw her spirit."

"She's right there," Elijah said, fists clenched. "So, how do we wake her?"

I turned to face them all, heart pounding. "We opened the door, but I don't know how to break the crystal prison and wake her."

Theren stood beside me now, taller than I remembered, taller even than Denali, his voice rasping with awe. "You need to go into her tomb and solve the puzzles there." He pointed to a room off to the side.

We walked toward it, turned to each other. I took a deep breath "It's not over yet."

19

THE LANTERN AND THE TOME

The chamber hummed before I even stepped inside. It was massive, wider than a cathedral, its floor an endless grid of square stone tiles stretching into darkness. The ceiling was impossibly high, vanishing into shadow. Suspended above, slowly rotating, was Calista's Lantern. Its silver flame flickered like a heartbeat in the void, throwing thin beams of light that swept across the tiles in gentle, rhythmic arcs.

The doorway across the room was sealed tight, with no bridges or markings, just this tiled floor between us and whatever came next.

"We'll have to cross it," I guessed, more to myself than anyone else.

I raised the lantern. The flame responded, glowing brighter. A handful of tiles directly in front of us shimmered faintly as the light brushed over them. I took a tentative step forward onto one, and it held solid beneath my boot. The tile behind me dimmed again.

Sasha moved next. She stepped onto a tile slightly to the left, one that hadn't glowed.

A flash of blue light shot upward from the floor, and she cried out. Ice crept up her leg, crystallizing her boot to the tile. She couldn't move.

"Sasha!" I tried to reach her, but Elijah stopped me just in time before I touched the wrong tile.

"I'm okay," she said through clenched teeth. Her voice trembled, not from pain, but from fear. "Just stuck."

Blair placed her hand on Sasha's shoulder and closed her eyes, channeling warmth. Elijah knelt to carefully strike the edges of the ice with his fists, just enough to weaken it. Denali and Parker studied the lantern's light, noting the pattern of its movement.

"We're being timed," Parker informed us quickly. "The lantern is cycling through a pattern. It's showing the path, but only for a moment."

"We have to move as a group," Denali said, watching the pulse of the flame. "Wrong tile, wrong time, wrong emotion, any of those might lock us down. This isn't just a puzzle. It's about alignment."

We stepped back to the start. Together.

Tile by tile, we followed the rhythm. At first it felt manageable, watch, step, breathe. But the deeper we moved into the room, the more unpredictable the lantern became. Its rotations sped up. Tiles began to flicker out faster, some disappearing mid-step. Denali barely caught Blair when one under her foot began to sink. She gasped and threw her weight into his arms as the tile vanished below.

"Blair, wait for the light," I whispered, heart pounding.

Parker was scanning the floor with frantic eyes, fingers twitching. "There's a harmonic sequence. Every seventh tile pulses on a longer beat. But we've been breaking that rhythm."

"We're out of sync," Sasha said, frowning. "I can feel it."

"Feel it how?" I asked.

"The way the tiles react. Some respond to fear, while others respond to calm. They're tuned in to us."

I closed my eyes for a second, just to feel. Beneath my boots, the floor hummed faintly, not with sound, but something more profound. Resonance? The lantern wasn't just guiding us visually. It was measuring our internal states.

"This isn't a path of logic," I said. "It's a path of trust."

No one answered, but something shifted. We stopped trying to race ahead. We started moving more deliberately, listening to one another's breath, and aligning our pace accordingly. Denali watched the lantern; Parker called out timing; Sasha focused on emotional attunement; Blair used color magic to mark our past safe steps; Elijah steadied our balance. I became the anchor, holding the lantern and listening for its quiet changes.

Still, we nearly failed. One tile, three steps from the end, flickered so fast that we all hesitated. It glowed, dimmed, glowed again, and then disappeared. We froze and no one spoke. Then Elijah misjudged the beat and stepped too soon.

His tile lit for a split second, then turned black. He gasped as the light around his legs pulsed violently—a shimmer of dark ice formed at his ankles.

"No, Elijah!" Blair dropped to her knees beside him, placing both hands over his boots.

Parker calculated something under his breath, then shouted, "We need to be in sync, now!"

Without thinking, I raised the lantern. Its flame sputtered, and I closed my eyes, centering every emotion I had fear, hope, guilt, and courage. I let them all pass through me, unhidden, and the flame steadied.

"Step on the tile together," I said.

One by one, we all moved onto the same tile Elijah was trapped on. The moment we did, the lantern flared white-hot, and the ice cracked. Elijah stumbled forward, and the tile beneath us expanded, revealing a path to the final platform.

We didn't hesitate. As one, we ran.

When we reached the far side, panting and shaking, we turned around quickly. The lantern descended into my hands, its flame no longer flickering. Instead, it glowed strong and steady.

The sealed door in front of us creaked open.

No one said anything for a long time. We just looked at one another—blistered, bruised, exhausted—but deeply and undeniably closer. We had almost failed. But we didn't because we trusted each other. And that, I thought, was what the lantern had needed to see.

The clearing opened before us like a dream unearthed, wide and circular, carved with celestial symbols that mirrored the sigil on Calista's tome. The sky above shimmered strangely. The stars, usually non-existent, began to shift, clustering into a rare triad I recognized only from ancient myth. My breath caught.

"Wow, there are actually stars here," Blair commented, looking up in awe.

"It's so nice to see them again," I said with a smile.

"I missed them," Denali agreed.

"I believe this is the Trine Constellation," Parker whispered. "That's not supposed to exist anymore."

"It does tonight," Elijah said, his gaze lifted. "Aztalun remembers."

In the center of the clearing sat a stone dais etched with a six-pointed ring. It appeared to be a place of significance, power, and ritual. As we approached, Calista's tome seemed to float in the air, lifted by an unseen force. It hovered above the center of the dais. Six seats encircled it, each one facing inward, as if designed for this exact moment.

"I'm assuming we're supposed to sit," Denali said, brow furrowed. "Since there is a seat for each of us."

"Based on archetype," I nodded, pointing to the subtle engravings on each seat. "They match the ones Zanira spoke of."

I stepped forward, drawn to the sigil marked *The Explorer*. The stone was warm beneath me as I sat. Around me, the others followed: Denali at *The Lover*, Elijah at *The Hero*, Blair at *The Creator*, Parker at *The Sage*, and Sasha at *The Magician*.

As soon as we were all seated, the tome pulsed, and a low vibration stirred through the ground.

Then, it opened.

Pages—dozens, maybe hundreds—spiraled into the air like fireflies, each one glowing faintly as it hovered. One by one, the pages floated toward us, each finding a path to our hands. Mine tingled with heat as it touched my palm.

"Are these… glyphs?" Elijah asked, squinting at his page.

"I don't recognize any of this," I said, scanning the page. The symbols danced and shifted, rearranging with every blink. I could feel the meaning in my chest, but not in my mind.

"They're in the celestial script," Parker said softly. "But it's encoded."

"Then, how do we read it?" Blair asked.

"We don't," Sasha said slowly. "Not until we stop trying to do it alone."

I looked at her. "What do you mean?"

"Look." She held her page up. "Mine doesn't settle. It keeps flickering. But when I close my eyes and just trust—" she inhaled, shaking slightly "—it stops."

She exhaled, and the glyphs settled.

"But I can't interpret them alone," she added. "I need… "

Elijah knelt beside her without a word and placed a hand on Sasha's back. "Breathe with me."

They inhaled and exhaled together, their rhythm syncing. Slowly, Sasha's eyes opened—and she began to speak. "In motion and stillness, the veil divides the seen from the unseen. Magic and healing is not taught. It is remembered." As soon as she finished speaking, we heard a click at the far end of the room, where a wheel dial was located. The hand must have been pointing upwards on the symbol corresponding to her archetype, but now it was pointing to the Sage.

"Your turn," Sasha smiled as she turned to Parker.

He stared at his page for a long moment, unmoving, lips pressed tight. Blair glanced at him and said, "Hum with me."

Parker blinked. "What?"

"Just… trust me." Blair closed her eyes and began to hum, low and measured, almost like a heartbeat in sound.

The glyphs on Parker's page began to realign, line by line, following the cadence.

Parker spoke: "Logic alone cannot unravel the infinite spiral. Only when sound becomes pattern does truth emerge."

Blair grinned. "Told you."

Parker chuckled under his breath. "You didn't *tell* me anything. You just hummed."

"Same thing." She shrugged.

Denali turned to me, nodding gently. "Your hands are shaking."

"I can't read mine. It's all pulses and light and, ugh, it's *frustrating*," I admitted.

"Let me try something." He reached out and placed his hand over mine.

The moment our skin touched, the glyphs on my page stopped pulsing chaotically. They began to thrum in rhythm, almost like a heartbeat.

"You're grounding me," I whispered.

"You ground me every time you look at me," he said, quietly enough that only I heard it.

My voice caught, but I pushed forward. "From shifting sands the seeker steps forward, not to conquer, but to uncover. What is buried is never truly lost."

His eyes didn't leave mine. "That's the most *you* thing I've ever heard."

"I'll take that as a compliment."

Next, Blair stepped forward, her page held like a sacred relic. "Mine's blank."

"Impossible," Parker said, peering over. "It's glowing."

"But I can't see the symbols."

"Try painting it," Parker suggested. "Not literally. Imagine the strokes."

She closed her eyes and mimed painting with her fingertip as if she were brushing over a canvas hanging in the blank air. As she did, the glyphs formed in strokes of glowing ink.

Her words came slowly: "Creation is the echo of the eternal. It does not begin, it continues."

She opened her eyes, stunned. "I think I felt her voice."

"Calista's?" I asked.

Blair nodded.

Denali reached for my hand and read, "Never alone, the Hexad is bound through eternity, and the Lover holds the tether." He nodded to Elijah, "Looks like you're last."

"I've been reading mine this whole time," he said, shaking the page. "But the order keeps changing."

"Try giving up control," Sasha offered.

"Have you *met* me?" Elijah smirked. Still, he exhaled, closed his eyes, and dropped his shoulders. The glyphs reordered again, this time coherently.

He read: "The warrior's task is not to destroy but to protect. Even from himself."

Silence settled over the circle.

Then, the tome in the center flared, its pages returning to it in streaks of light. The book sealed with a snap, and a soft chime echoed in the air like a bell made of starlight.

Glowing symbols hovered briefly over the dais, glyphs like the ones we'd just read.

"They match the ones on Calista's crystal prison," Parker breathed.

"They're not locks," I whispered. "They're a resonant equation."

"An equation?" Sasha asked.

"Not to be *spoken*," I said. "To be *enacted* with trust."

The sky above us pulsed. The Trine Constellation shimmered, connected, and then faded.

But the truth remained, etched into our hearts. This wasn't about unlocking a book. It was about unlocking each other.

—

The Obsidian Fortress once again loomed before us like a monument to silence. Towering walls of black crystal reached into the lavender sky, their surface carved with shimmering glyphs that pulsed faintly, like breath caught in stillness. At its base hovered the cage—no, the prison—where Calista slept, suspended in a cradle of silver light and blue crystal. Her eyes were closed, her face serene, but the air trembled with tension.

I stepped forward, drawn to her as if gravity had shifted.

My pendant flared against my chest but then dulled. The lantern in my hand, once a steady beacon, flickered dimly as though confused, disoriented in this place. Only the tome responded now. It drifted from Parker's hands and opened midair, its pages fluttering wildly before slowing and glowing.

"Do you see that?" I breathed.

The words lifted from the pages, curling into the air like ribbons of starlight. Celestial glyphs danced above us in a circular spiral, weaving themselves into patterns I didn't recognize, yet somehow understood.

"I think it's speaking," I said. "Not in words, exactly."

"Meaning what?" Elijah asked, his voice low.

"The glyphs on the prison, they're not locks. They're more like *notes in a* kind of cosmic musical equation."

Denali stepped beside me, squinting up at the glowing cage. "You're saying it's not just about what we do. It's about *how* we are."

I nodded slowly. "The frequency only works if each of us is tuned to our truest form. If we're misaligned, even slightly, it collapses."

Blair tilted her head. "Like a song played off-key."

"Exactly," I said. "Calista's sleep isn't a curse—it's a *sustenance*. This whole prison feeds off imbalance and disharmony. We need to find the harmony and balance within ourselves."

The tome turned another page. More glyphs swirled into the air, then shimmered and aligned above each of us.

"These symbols," Parker began, "are individualized. This one's mine, I recognize its equation."

"The one above me is a paint stroke, by my own hand," Blair said, mesmerized.

Sasha's eyes welled up. "Mine's breathing, deep and slow. It's the same rhythm we used in the Tome Circle."

Elijah reached up, hand hovering beneath the glyph above him. "Mine is movement. A strike followed by stillness."

Denali looked at me. "What's yours?"

I stared at the glyph above me, curved like a spiral staircase leading into a star. "Exploration, but not outward, it spirals inward."

We all stood there, six fragments of a forgotten harmony, suddenly understanding our place in the composition.

"I think we have to *become* these fully," I said. "Not pretend or perform, we have just to be who we are."

The tome glowed brighter, throwing a warm light on the obsidian surface. The glyphs on Calista's crystal prison pulsed in response, like strings being tuned.

Parker stepped forward first. "I'll anchor the structure."

He knelt, whispering numerical patterns under his breath. His glowing silver glyph spun and clicked into place above him like a lock turning.

Blair closed her eyes and stretched her fingers as if painting the air, soft colors flowing from her palms. Her glyph pulsed vibrant green, then sank into the crystal surface.

Sasha stood tall, hand on her heart, breathing in time with Blair. Her glyph shimmered violet and threaded into the lattice.

Elijah moved with grace and precision, striking an invisible pattern. The moment he finished, his glyph flashed red and struck like a spark into the crystal wall.

Denali turned to me. "You're the center, Alayna. You always have been."

He pressed his hand to his heart, his other reaching toward the sky. His glyph, a glowing blue arc, floated down and melted into the floor, humming deep and warm.

My fingers closed around the lantern's base. It was glowing again, faintly, but with purpose. It lit a single glyph near Calista's suspended form—golden-orange like a single flame spiraling up to the star.

The final note.

I stepped closer, every breath synchronized with the others. I didn't command the light, I followed it. The lantern pulsed in time with our group, our breath, our hearts, and our bond.

"I see it," I whispered. "It's not about unlocking her. It's about unlocking *us*."

As I touched the blue arc glyph, the others pulsed in harmony with it. The air thrummed, and the fortress itself seemed to sigh.

A sound, low and achingly beautiful, rippled through the clearing. It wasn't music, exactly; it was *Resonance*.

Calista stirred, her fingers twitching. Her chest rose, just slightly, and her lips parted.

The crystal softened, not shattered, but liquefied—one layer at a time, like ice melting beneath the sun.

She wasn't awake yet. But she was *listening*. And for the first time, we knew we were part of her, and she was a part of us, not because we were powerful, but because we were finally in harmony and balance. We were finally in tune.

20

THE REUNION

I didn't realize I was holding my breath until Calista finally opened her eyes. They were the most impossible green, like the first moss after winter. Her lashes fluttered as she blinked up at the world, her long ash-blonde hair falling in luminous waves over her shoulders. She drew a single breath, and the light in the chamber pulsed, as if the fortress itself recognized its mistress.

None of us spoke.

Blair's mouth parted, her fingers trembling against her own arm as the spiral birthmark shimmered faintly. Parker's lips moved silently, probably trying to form some ancient word none of us knew. Sasha placed one hand over her chest, right above her tattooed maze, grounding herself through breath. Elijah stood tall, but his storm blue eyes glistened, shining with emotion he didn't dare let fall. And Denali's hand brushed mine.

Then Calista stood.

The shards of her prison fell away like petals, vanishing into mist before they hit the ground. Her gown was woven from starlight and silk—silver-white, shimmering like moonlight over snow. She stepped forward carefully, like someone relearning how to move.

We all stepped back instinctively to give her space.

Her gaze swept over us, slowly and tenderly.

"You are the ones," she said, her voice like wind over water, clear, soft, and yet echoing in my bones. "I have felt you in dreams. Threads of you, emotions tangled across time. I called you and knew you were coming to me."

Her eyes locked on mine, and suddenly I couldn't move.

Calista's smile was slight but radiant. "Alayna," she whispered. "You are the fire beneath the sand, the intuition that dares to love what it cannot explain."

My chest tightened. I didn't know whether to bow or speak. "You know me?"

"I know what you carry," she said gently. "As I know all of you."

She turned to each of them, and with every name she spoke, something ancient inside me stirred.

"Sasha, breath of spirit, weaver of wounds into wonder."

"Elijah, courage cloaked in calm, and the roar beneath the mountain."

"Blair, maker of meaning, and gentle mirror."

"Parker, map-reader of myths, and quiet storm."

"Denali," she said last, her voice catching slightly as she smiled. "Heart of hearts, the anchor between the stars."

Denali blinked fast, looking down.

Calista placed a hand over her chest. "Thank you," she said, eyes sweeping over all of us now. "You woke me from the silence. I felt your steps through the maze. I felt your joy and your pain. You were my lantern in the dark."

She looked down for a moment, as if gathering something inside herself. Then her gaze rose again, and this time it shimmered with apology.

"I did not wish to summon you so harshly," she said. "But the veil is thinning and Aztalun frays, while mortals cry out. The gods draw swords now, so I could not remain still." Her voice faltered. "I could not bear to let this realm unravel without trying."

None of us spoke.

And then her eyes shifted toward the edge of the chamber, toward him. Theren, who stood in the shadows, broad shoulders tense, head slightly bowed, as if unsure whether he had the right to witness this. His dark hair was loose, catching stray beams of light, and his shadow-drenched form, so often terrifying, looked… lost.

Calista's breath hitched. "Theren," she whispered. The name seemed to ripple the very air. He raised his head slowly, his amber eyes meeting hers. And for a moment, the world held its breath.

Calista moved toward him with measured steps, her bare feet soundless against the obsidian. Her hands trembled slightly at her sides. When she reached him, she stopped only inches away. The chamber felt like it had shrunk to just the two of them.

"You may not remember, but I do," she said softly. "You are not Varek. You never were. You were taken and twisted. But the truth, our truth, it waited."

He shook his head once, his jaw clenched, as if her words hurt more than any blade.

"I don't know who I am," he rasped.

She reached out and cupped his face with both hands. Her touch was trembling and sacred. "Then let me remind you."

She leaned forward, her forehead resting against his. A single tear slid down her cheek. And then he followed. His large frame buckled, and he collapsed to his knees before her, hands fisted at his sides, breath ragged.

"I failed you, my queen," he gasped. "I tried to keep you safe, but I couldn't kill them."

"No," she whispered, kneeling with him, her arms wrapping around his shoulders. "You were trying to protect me. Even twisted by lies, you still guarded me."

"I didn't know—" he choked out.

"But you do now." Her words were a balm. "And that is enough. I love you and always will."

Theren stood then, his eyes looked into hers as she grazed her lips across his. He took her hands and said, "I love you too."

And then they wept together. Not loudly or with drama, but with the slow, devastating tenderness of two souls stitched back together after centuries apart.

Blair wiped her eyes beside me. Parker turned away, jaw clenched in reverence. Sasha let out a soft exhale, touching a glowing symbol on her wrist. Elijah placed one hand against his heart, the other brushing a silent blessing toward them.

And Denali was crying. I felt his fingers curl into mine, and I looked up. His eyes were glistening, not with grief, but with something bigger. And in that moment, it was like a wall inside him dropped. All the gentleness he usually masked behind strength, all the longing he tried to tuck beneath leadership was right there, open and unashamed. He looked at me as if I were something holy. And just like that, I forgot how to breathe. I didn't need words, not when his eyes already told me everything. I squeezed his hand and closed my eyes as my heart swelled.

And even with Calista's light warming the air, with magic trembling in every breath, with the very laws of gods and mortals bending around us, I knew that moment would stay with me forever. The moment we all remembered who we really were. Not just travelers or summoned saviors. But the Hexad—a living truth, born from imbalance and held together by choice. And for the first time in this strange, spiraling world, I felt like maybe we were finally whole.

Theren's tears still shimmered on Calista's shoulder when she finally drew in a steady breath and stood.

Something shifted in the air as she rose—not just around her, but inside us too. It was as if the room had realigned itself to accommodate who she was, now fully awake and divine.

Calista's hand lingered on Theren's chest, and then she stepped forward to face us. Her presence was no longer fragile or uncertain but glowing with that unshakable grace that only someone ancient and sacred could possess. Her silver gown drifted behind her like mist, though there was no wind. And her eyes—those wild, bright-green eyes—held galaxies of knowledge we weren't ready to understand.

I couldn't move.

We were all still standing in a loose circle around her. Blair leaned lightly against Parker, who stood like a carved statue, unreadable except for the way his throat bobbed. Sasha's eyes were closed, one hand to her solar plexus. Elijah bowed his head. Denali hadn't let go of my hand. His thumb brushed across mine gently, like he needed that tether as much as I did.

"I have been asleep too long," Calista said at last, her voice a delicate chime threaded with iron. "And in my absence, balance has shattered."

She lifted her hand, and suddenly the room responded. A radiant beam poured down from the center of the ceiling, illuminating her entirely. She didn't command or conjure it. The light wanted to be near her.

"I see now that the gods—my brothers and sisters—they feared not just my power, but what I chose to do with it. I believed in truth, even when it hurt. I believed in balance, even when it required sacrifice."

Her eyes met mine, and I felt that strange pressure in my chest again. Like her gaze was reading the parts of me that even I didn't understand.

"But I see now what I could not accept before," she continued. "Balance cannot be imposed. It must be chosen."

She stepped slowly toward us, and every step left a faint shimmer on the obsidian floor, like moonlight pressed into glass.

"I sought to protect mortals by shielding them from knowledge. I erased truths and silenced wars before they began. I thought I was sparing the world pain, but in doing so, I stripped it of its voice."

The guilt in her voice struck me. It wasn't performative; it was real. And it made her seem even more powerful.

"I failed to trust you, all of you. And now, I ask your forgiveness."

"No," Sasha whispered, eyes opening slowly. "You don't need forgiveness, you just needed to remember."

Calista's lips trembled with the softest smile.

"Aztalun suffers," she said. "Its boundaries weaken, realms bleed into one another, war festers among the divine, and mortals grow desperate, turned into pawns by forces they cannot see. But I—" her voice tightened—"I am no longer the only one who can tip the scales."

She raised both hands. "You are the balance now."

I shivered.

"The six of you," she said, "are not mere bearers. You are fragments of my essence. You are pieces of the harmony I once divided and lost. You were born to restore what I cannot do alone."

Calista closed her eyes, and for a long moment, the chamber filled with glowing symbols, floating spirals, geometric constellations, fragments of divine script I couldn't decipher but somehow understood.

"You were not summoned," she said softly. "You were called home."

The air pulsed, and everything stilled, as bright light filled the room.

Her eyes opened again, fierce and crystalline. She turned to us; her eyes filled with a quiet flame. "And that is why I ask if you will stand with me?"

I didn't hesitate. "Yes," I breathed.

Sasha nodded, voice steady. "Yes."

Elijah stepped forward. "With honor."

Parker's voice was quiet, but certain. "Always."

Blair's whisper carried like a song. "For you… Yes."

Denali squeezed my hand. "We never left your side."

Calista's smile was luminous. "So, it begins."

She reached behind her and lifted something from the mist—a silver lantern. "I return now with no throne," she said. "Only light. Let it guide us." Then she turned, and slowly, her eyes met Theren's.

He had stepped forward during her decree, his tall frame caught in the edge of her glow. His expression was quiet and humbled. As if every word she spoke had etched itself into the core of who he used to be.

"What will you do?" she asked him gently.

He looked at the rest of us. At the world he once defended in shadow. And then at Calista. "I will follow," he said. "Not because I am told but because I want to remember what light feels like."

Calista walked to him and pressed her lantern into his hands. "Then carry it with me." They stood together, side by side.

Behind me, Denali whispered, "You okay?"

I turned. He was still holding my hand, but his other hand came up to tuck a strand of hair behind my ear. It was such a small gesture, but it burned through me like wildfire. "I don't know if I've ever been this okay before," I said, stunned by how true it felt. His forehead pressed gently to mine: a promise and a new beginning.

And around us, Calista's light rose higher, opening a skylight above the fortress, revealing the sky of Aztalun—three moons now aligned, casting their pale halos down like blessings. Balance hadn't been restored; it had been reborn.

Calista stood in the center, the silver lantern in one hand, her living tome cradled in the other, its pages whispering as they turned themselves in slow rhythm.

She didn't speak at first. She simply looked at each of us with those radiant green eyes that seemed to hold every thought we hadn't said aloud.

"I am Calista," she said at last. "Born of Elion, the First Word. Forged from knowledge and balance. I was not made to rule, only to know and guide."

Her voice wasn't loud, but it didn't need to be. It moved through the air like wind through ancient trees—soft, inevitable.

"For centuries, I walked the realms of Aztalun as a presence, not worshiped or feared, only listened to. I held the lantern so others might see what they would not look at. I carried the tome so no truth could be lost."

I felt my pendant warm faintly against my chest, responding.

"But as I watched civilizations rise and fall, I saw the same pattern repeat," Calista continued, turning slowly as she spoke. "Knowledge was never the problem. It was the refusal to accept it. Mortals demanded comfort over truth, and gods demanded loyalty over justice."

Her grip on the lantern tightened. "And so, I interfered."

Sasha tilted her head, eyes narrowing thoughtfully.

"I began to shift the scales," Calista admitted. "I silenced wars before they started and unraveled destinies that I deemed too dangerous. I took memories from tyrants and gave them to orphans. I thought I was being merciful."

Blair stirred beside me, her expression softening. "But others saw it as control."

Calista nodded slowly. "The gods grew afraid, whispered that I had forgotten my place, and no longer observed balance. Instead, I dictated it, and perhaps they were right."

Her gaze dropped for a moment, and I saw it, regret, etched into her perfect features like a quiet storm. "I erased too much. I silenced voices I should have let speak and turned knowledge into a blade."

"And then there was Theren," she said. Every breath in the room caught.

Calista's lips parted as if a song were trying to escape. "He was a mortal—a philosopher and a dreamer. He did not worship me; he challenged me. He questioned the paradoxes of my design and made me laugh when no one else dared."

She smiled, but it was a fragile smile.

"We loved in silence, not hidden, but sacred. The kind of love that seeks no witness."

Calista smiled at him. "But he wanted to know too much and believed there was a truth even I had not seen, a flaw in the fabric of existence. I warned him. I begged him not to go."

She stepped toward the edge of the circle, then stopped herself. "But he went anyway, and died, or so I believed."

Her breath caught, tears glistening in her eyes. "What I didn't know was that the gods had taken him. They tore him from his body, reshaped him with cursed memory and shadowed thought. They turned my love into my jailer."

Theren stirred in the shadows behind us now, silent and listening.

"They called him Varek," Calista said, her voice trembling. "A creature of darkness, the Guardian of the Maze, and he became the very warden of my prison."

She turned toward us fully now, holding up the tome. Its pages had stilled.

"And I was brought here, not with force, but with illusion. They told me I had made the world too fragile, and that I was unraveling divine order. They sealed me in this fortress, not with chains, but with paradox."

My brow furrowed. "Paradox?"

She looked straight at me. "The prison can only be undone by accepting that not all things can be balanced, truth itself is not always healing, and imperfections must sometimes remain."

Sasha exhaled shakily. "But you couldn't accept that."

"No," Calista said softly. "Because my very being is balance. I am logic and pattern. To accept chaos would mean shattering myself."

"Then how did we free you?" Blair asked, her voice almost a whisper.

Calista stepped into the lantern's glow. "Because I am not whole anymore."

We blinked at her.

She smiled, and this time, it was a warmer smile. Brighter.

"I divided myself long ago," she explained. "Fragments of my essence—my emotions, my contradictions, and my untamed truths—I scattered them across distant stars and secret earths. And those pieces became you six."

Sasha's eyes widened. "Wow."

"Yes," Calista said. "You are not my servants, you are my echoes, and my evolution."

She looked at each of us slowly.

"Sasha—healing and transformation. Blair—imagination and expression. Elijah—courage and integrity. Parker— wisdom and perspective. Denali—connection and empathy."

Then her eyes met mine. "And Alayna… compassion and intuition. You are the center of what I forgot."

I felt my throat tighten. My hand found Denali's again, grounding me.

"You were drawn to Aztalun not to save me," Calista continued, "but to complete me and teach me what I was never designed to understand."

"Which is?" I asked quietly.

Her eyes glistened. "That balance is not always the answer."

For a moment, the whole world seemed to pause.

"The leyline spirits chose you because you were imperfect and imbalanced. You were full of longing and pain and contradiction, but also full of love. And that love—that harmony among disharmony—is the only force strong enough to break the paradox that held me in my own chains."

Parker let out a breath. "So, we weren't summoned, we were remembered."

Calista nodded. "Exactly."

Theren stepped forward at last, his voice low. "And now?"

She turned to him, gently.

"Now," she said, "we begin to mend what was broken. Not by force or erasure. But by truth shared freely."

She lifted her lantern and placed it on the ground before us.

A beam of light erupted, not blinding but warm and inviting.

"We will face resistance. The other gods will not easily surrender their illusions. But you were not chosen to fight them. You were chosen to reveal them."

Sasha stepped forward first, placing her palm over the lantern's beam. Her tattoos glowed, alive.

"I'm ready," she said.

Blair followed; her fingers trailing starlight, "Me too."

One by one, we joined. Elijah. Parker. Denali.

And finally, I stepped forward. The pendant at my chest pulsed softly, and I felt something rise inside me—not certainty, but peace.

Calista smiled. "This won't transpire soon. There will be learning and preparing. The time will be revealed to you, and you will know it when it comes."

And in the silence that followed, I finally understood. We hadn't freed a goddess. We had freed ourselves.

"The Gods will be angry that you have freed me. They will hunt my rescuers. You will be tested repeatedly. Will you still stand with me?"

We all nodded, and I didn't feel scared. I felt ready.

21

THE FINAL TETHER

The air shimmered around us, silver light pulsing from the ground like breath returning to the land. Calista stood at the center, not quite touching the earth, glowing, steady, and eternal. Her eyes met mine, and I felt my heart still, not from fear, but from recognition. This was not an ending. It was a beginning.

She turned to me first.

"Alayna," Calista said, her voice both thunder and hush. "You crossed thresholds with nothing but your truth and your heart."

She raised the pendant that had guided me from the beginning, no longer flickering in panic but steady, luminous with warmth. She placed it against my chest, and I felt its power surge gently through me. "What you gave, you now carry," she whispered, brushing my cheek. "Your heart is now the bridge."

I didn't cry. But I did feel something in me exhale, finally.

Then Calista stepped toward Denali. "Your strength has always been in what you protect." She held her hands over both of us, drawing light from my pendant and the steadiness in his chest. The energy wove between us, becoming a glimmering shield across his back, light that bent and breathed with him. "Love forged your bond," she said. "Let it shield you now from danger."

He looked at me then, and I knew we were tethered in ways I couldn't explain. I reached for his hand and held it tight.

Next, Calista turned to Sasha. "You carry silence like a blade. But your voice has always been the cure." She unfurled strands of silver light that wrapped gently over Sasha's shoulders, forming a veil of shifting shimmer. "You may now cloak or reveal truth as needed," Calista said. "But speak with mercy. Each truth leaves a mark."

Sasha gave a slight nod, her fingers brushing the veil with quiet reverence.

Then it was Elijah. "Fire has walked beside you since birth," Calista said. "But now, it lives within your hands." She summoned a single ember—no bigger than a coin—and placed it in his palm. It pulsed with a soft, living glow. "Let it burn injustice," she said. "Let it warm what was broken."

Elijah bowed his head, the flame reflecting in his stormy eyes.

Calista crossed to Blair, bathing her in a soft light that oscillated between pale green and peach. "Your palette has no limits. You will create all manner of beauty fed by your love of life and all living things." Blair's eyes were moist yet steady.

And finally, Parker. Calista summoned a thin obsidian disc, unfolding into a glowing orb of layered maps that hovered at his shoulder. "You read the land's sorrow like scripture," she said. "Now let its stories rise through you."

The orb spun softly, showing glimpses of forgotten temples, buried grief, and healing paths.

We stood together, all six of us, forever changed.

The maze behind us began to dissolve, its walls turning to mist, its shadows lifting like a long-held breath finally released. Light surged from the ground beneath our feet, not blinding, but whole and complete.

I looked at each of them—my friends, my new family—and I knew. We hadn't just survived Aztalun. We had become part of it. Forever.

<hr>

The light beneath our feet softened, no longer the stark silver and black of the maze, but the golden blush of something warm and alive.

Calista turned, her gown sweeping behind her like a current, and extended her hand. "Come," she said gently. "There is something I wish you to see."

Theren—no longer Varek, walked beside her. He didn't speak, but his presence was different, less shadow, more peace. I didn't know if I'd ever trust him fully, but I believed her love had steadied something in him. For now, that was enough.

We followed them along a ridge path that had once been tangled with thorns. Now it bloomed, little blue flowers unfurling wherever Calista stepped, and golden vines chased after her hem as if eager to touch her.

The wind had changed, too; no longer whispering in fractured riddles, it moved like a lullaby. The maze behind us dissolved into mist, and ahead, the world opened like a sigh.

We descended slowly, and just over the subsequent rise, a village came into view.

It was smaller than I imagined. Tucked into a crescent valley, its stone homes were nestled between glassy streams and pale silver trees that shimmered faintly in the light. Children ran barefoot through fields of luminous wheat, and laughter drifted up to us like a song remembered.

It wasn't just alive, it was joyful.

Denali slipped his arm around my waist, and I leaned into him without thinking.

"I thought this place would feel haunted," Sasha said from beside me. "But it doesn't."

"It's vibrant. The land renewed itself," Elijah said.

Calista nodded. "You feel that because it has. The moment balance returned, the seals broke, and life began to move forward again."

As we reached the edge of the village, people looked up and gasped, not in fear, but in wonder. An elderly woman dropped her basket and touched her chest as if she had seen a miracle.

I could feel her heart swell with praise. I smiled, and I saw it reflected in her eyes.

Calista smiled, serene and glowing, as villagers poured forward in awe and reverence. Children whispered her name like a secret, and older men wept without shame. Theren remained beside her, quiet, gaze downcast, but no one recoiled from him. Perhaps time would give space for healing but today was not about punishment. Today was about light.

Just then, the sky shifted as the violet color vanished. A hush fell over everything as warmth bloomed across the clouds—pink and honey-gold streaks spilling like ink into a pale blue canvas.

My breath caught in my throat as a massive sun crested the horizon.

It wasn't like Earth's sun. It was much larger, burnished copper rimmed in white-gold flame, with three rings orbiting slowly around it like halos. And it pulsed—softly and steadily—like a heartbeat waking from a long, dreamless sleep.

Calista turned to us. "The sun vanished the day I was imprisoned. Without balance, the realm could not hold it. Its light fled from the wound in the world." Her voice caught slightly. "But now it returns. Thank you. Aztalun thanks you."

The villagers fell to their knees, and a few sang. I just stood there, staring up, and feeling the warmth kiss my skin.

I looked at Denali. "It's beautiful," I whispered.

He smiled, the glow of it reflected in his eyes. "So are you."

And as the sun climbed fully above us, I realized something. I never even asked Calista if we were going home.

The village glowed like a dream. Lanterns hung from every tree branch, their lights like floating stars drifting just above our heads. Music echoed from wooden flutes and crystal drums, a melody full of rhythm and joy, as if the land itself had been waiting to sing again.

We sat around a massive fire in the center of the village, its flames a swirling mix of amber and soft blue. Children darted between benches, carrying trays of glowing fruit and breads that steamed with a sweet and citrusy scent. Someone passed me a cup of warm nectar that tingled all the way down. I wasn't sure what it was, but I'd never tasted anything so alive.

Blair was laughing as she painted streaks of shimmering light into the sky, creating pictures that danced above us like fireflies. Elijah and Parker sat with a group of villagers, listening to an older man spin a tale about a singing mountain. Denali had one arm around me, the other passing Sasha a skewer of flame-grilled root vegetables.

"I could get used to this," Sasha said, her veil glinting faintly in the firelight.

So, could I. I had to swallow back my tears of sadness and the farewell that I could feel was coming, deep in my heart. These people had become so dear to me, especially Denali. I sucked in a sharp breath. Would we ever see each other again?

But as the laughter rose, and the village pulsed with celebration, I felt a presence behind me, so gentle it barely stirred the air.

"Walk with me, Alayna?" Calista asked, her voice soft.

I followed her through a narrow path lit by stones that glowed under our feet, past gardens bursting with color, and toward a quiet bluff overlooking the valley.

The sun had long since dipped beneath the horizon, but the sky still shimmered with the memory of it, pink and golden threads painting a realm reborn.

Calista stood still, her gown rustling slightly in the breeze. "I wish I could let you believe this peace will last forever."

My stomach turned slightly. "It won't?"

She looked at me then, eyes deep and sorrowful. "The gods will feel the shift. They will know I am free, and Theren too. They will not act immediately. Some will doubt, others will debate. But once they decide…" Her voice trailed off.

"They'll come for you," I said quietly. "For Theren, and maybe even for us, because we freed you?"

She nodded. "Possibly. You released what they bound. Not all will see that as righteous."

A knot formed in my chest. "What can we do?"

Calista reached into a fold of her sleeve and pulled out a thin silver ring. It was simple, unadorned—except for a faint rune etched along the inner band. "This is my last gift to you. It is a ring of return. It will open a doorway from wherever you are to wherever you need to be. I hope that return will sometimes be here, to visit with us. You are all part of me, and I wish to spend time reconnecting with each of you. Whoever you are touching when you wear the ring, and summon a portal, will be able to travel with you. Do not be a stranger."

I held it in my palm. It hummed quietly. "Thank you, Calista. It has been a pleasure helping you, and we hope to return to visit, as you say."

"You'll feel it activate when the time is right. Use it to flee, to fight, or to find others. It was Zanira who wanted me to give it to you. Thank you for trusting in her and letting her guide you to me," she smiled then, a genuine, mischievous smile.

I laughed, surprised. "You're giving me a magical friendship ring?"

She tilted her head. "It's a very *serious* magical friendship ring."

I slipped it onto my finger. It adjusted to my size instantly, calm and comforting.

"You carry the bridge, Alayna. Don't forget, you're never alone. You will always be connected to me, and you will always be able to find me when you need to."

In the distance, the music swelled again. The stars blinked. And I knew, no matter what was coming, we would be ready.

The house was small but glowing with soft light radiating from its stone walls. The windows were open, letting in the music and laughter that still floated through the village. The air smelled like roasted citrus and honeyed roots, and the blankets had the faintest scent of lavender and Ashwood.

We all sprawled in the central room, limbs tangled, shoulders brushing, laughter blooming in uneven waves. A fire crackled quietly in the hearth. Someone, probably Elijah, had dragged in a pile of cushions big enough to swallow a moose, and Blair had claimed half of them.

"I swear," she said, flopping backward with a dramatic sigh, "if anyone wakes me before the sun's second blink tomorrow, I will hex your eyebrows clean off."

"That's oddly specific." Parker laughed as he stretched out on a woven mat near the door.

"Don't think she won't," Sasha said, eyes half-lidded as she rested her head on Elijah's shoulder.

"Yes, beware," Blair shot back, grinning.

Elijah chuckled, then looked at me. "Do you think it's really over?"

I shifted where I sat, curled against Denali's side, the ring Calista gave me warm on my finger. "I don't think it's ever truly over. But for now, yeah. I think we've earned a pause."

Sasha nodded. "I don't even know what I'll do when we go home. My apartment's going to feel like a shoe box since everything here is so vast."

"I think mine's *actually* a shoe box," Parker said, and we all laughed.

Denali looked at me, voice soft. "Would you want to go back right away?"

I hesitated. "Part of me does. My students, my work, my cat. But the other part... I feel like we're not done here."

"There's so much we haven't seen," Blair said, rolling onto her stomach. "The floating cliffs, the Singing Dunes, that giant library I dreamed about. What if it's real?"

Parker's brow furrowed. "It might be. Aztalun's resonance is still stabilizing. We might be feeling places call to us."

"That sounds exactly like something you'd say," Sasha teased, tossing a cushion at him. He didn't dodge in time.

"That is exactly something I did say," Parker smirked.

We all cracked up again.

I looked around at them, at Elijah, arms crossed and eyes soft; at Sasha, veiled and smiling in a way that made her look younger than I'd ever seen her; at Blair, glowing in the firelight like a portrait of laughter; at Parker, quiet and steady; and at Denali, whose heat was radiating through me like fire.

"I don't want to lose this," I said.

"You won't," Denali assured me.

"I've got a magical ring now," I added, wiggling my fingers. "I can drop in on any of you at any time."

Sasha groaned. "Oh god, she's going to become the surprise guest friend."

"Mid-shower visit," Blair warned.

"I'll bring snacks," I said, and the whole room dissolved into laughter again.

And when it finally faded into quiet, and the fire softened to embers, we didn't move apart. We just stayed there, in a nest of cushions and blankets, tangled together in warmth and quiet.

The world had changed, and so had we, but whatever came next, I knew this: We would face it together.

BEFORE THE FAREWELL

The aurora skies stretched above us like a living river, green and violet, gold flickering at the edges, and ribbons of light twisting across the midnight sky of Aztalun. I'd seen celestial events in the Sonoran Desert, but nothing like this. This sky felt alive, as if it were watching us, blessing us, perhaps even grieving for us.

Denali and I lay side by side on a bed of soft moss and woven blankets atop the ancient terrace, hidden just above the village. Denali's arm curved beneath my neck, his other hand slowly trailing down my arm. His body, all lean strength and quiet heat, pressed along mine. We hadn't spoken for a few minutes, just listened to each other's breath, and the soft wind weaving through silver grass. Calista's village celebration still echoed below.

I turned slightly to look at him, his face bathed in pale green light. His black hair spilled over his brow and shimmered at the ends. His obsidian eyes reflected the sky, but when he looked at me, they held something deeper, something that clutched at my ribs and made breathing a challenge.

"How are you feeling?" I asked softly.

"I think we did something outstanding," he reflected out loud.

I swallowed hard. "I think so too."

He brushed a strand of hair from my face. His fingers trembled slightly. "What if this is the only time I ever get to hold you like this?" His voice faltered.

A lump rose in my throat. We both knew this was temporary. We didn't say it outright, but the silence between us had been heavy with it for days. We were from different parts of the world. Once Calista helped us return home, we'd be gone, separated by distance and reality.

My fingers curled around the collar of his jacket. "You know, this won't be easy for me."

"I know," he whispered. "But I won't let the fear of losing you stop me from loving you tonight."

His honesty broke something open in me. "I'm terrified of loving anyone again," I admitted, voice raw. "Everything before was twisted—what I thought was real and what I thought was safe."

"You're safe now." Denali cupped my cheek. "You've always been stronger than he ever deserved. And you don't have to carry that weight alone anymore. I know you said goodbye in the maze. I know you let it go."

Something in me unraveled, and when he kissed me, it wasn't hesitant or possessive. It was as if he were offering a prayer to something bigger than either of us.

We shed our clothes slowly, the moss warm beneath our skin. His hands memorized me with tenderness and fire, my body arching and trembling under his. The stars swirled above us, echoed in the way he touched me, as if he wanted to write constellations across my skin.

I pulled him closer, breath catching in my throat. "I don't want this to end."

"I know." His voice broke. "But if I only get tonight with you, Alayna, then it's enough. It'll have to be enough."

And when we finally came together, it felt like time held its breath. Like even Aztalun—the strange, haunted, beautiful realm—had stilled for us. His mouth found mine with aching hunger, hands trailing fire as they moved across my skin. My fingers twisted into his hair, pulling him closer, needing more. He kissed down my neck, my chest, every inch of me like he'd been waiting for lifetimes.

"I need you, Denali," I told him in ragged, shallow breaths.

"I want you, Alayna, today, tomorrow, and always."

Our bodies pressed flush, heat building with every breath, every grind of hips, and every whispered moan. We didn't rush. We moved slowly and deliberately—his rhythm matching mine as if we were tethered to the same pulse. The way he looked at me, like I was both salvation and surrender, made the world vanish. Nothing existed but us, and the wild, sacred way we fit together.

"You're so beautiful," Denali's voice was low and rough in my ear. "I'll never stop wanting you."

We moved slowly, then fast, then slow again, like waves cresting and breaking, like neither of us wanted it to end. His skin was hot against mine, slick with devotion. When I arched beneath him, he held me like I might disappear, like I was something sacred, and in that moment, I was.

Afterward, wrapped in the curve of his body, his chest rising against my back, I stared up at the sky. The aurora had softened into waves of blue and lavender, stars piercing through like tiny truths. Denali traced circles against my stomach, then kissed my shoulder.

"Alayna?" he whispered.

"Yeah?"

"No matter the realm," he said, voice barely audible, "I'll find you again."

I turned to face him, heart aching so much I thought I might break open. "Promise?"

"I promise." He touched the spiral pendant around my neck. "Even if we never meet again in this form, I'll recognize your spirit. I'll know you."

A breeze lifted my hair. I pressed my palm to his chest, over his heart. "I'll know you too. Always."

We laughed softly at that, but the tears still came, quiet ones, the kind that slip down your cheek while someone you love watches without wiping them away, just holds you tighter.

And so, we lay there, skin cooling beneath the dawn-warmed stone, our breath slowing in unison. One night. One impossibly perfect, impossibly sorrowful night, painted in firelight, auroras, and the ache of something we couldn't keep.

We stood together one last time, eight souls bound by something none of us could name but all of us felt. The air in Aztalun was rich with memory and magic, humming with unshed tears and the weight of what we'd survived. Behind us, the village shimmered beneath twilight mist. Above, stars blinked through a sky that had forgotten what it meant to be dark.

Sasha stepped forward first, her black curls wild in the breeze, her tattoos shimmering faintly in the moonlight. "We'll stay in touch," she told Blair with a nod. "I want to see what happens when your paintings meet my meditation room."

Blair's laugh was quiet but warm. "Only if you let me paint you in mid-spell." She stepped in and hugged Sasha, then whispered something I couldn't hear.

When they parted, Parker rolled out a map across a flat stone. "Leyline echoes," he explained, tapping points with his fingers. "They pulse where our energy merged. If the veil ever shifts again, we might find each other here or here."

I leaned in, memorizing one near South America and another near the Scottish Highlands.

"You planned this?" I asked him with a small smile.

"Mapped it while you were all sleeping," he replied. "Old habits."

Elijah crossed his arms, the red glow of the realm catching on his dark skin and close-shaven beard. "You know we're going to see each other again," he said, glancing at each of us. "Spiritually or not. But what if we didn't wait for the next miracle?"

Blair blinked. "What do you mean?"

"I mean," Elijah said, grinning, "Let's have a reunion every year. We can pick a sacred site on Earth and show up, no excuses."

Denali chuckled beside me. "Even if I have to dog sled across the ice to get there?"

"Especially then. I dare you," Elijah said.

"I'm in," Sasha added, her voice soft. "That would mean everything."

Blair turned to me, her blue eyes glassy. "We never would've made it without you." She hugged me hard, burying her face in my shoulder. "I'll paint it all, every fragment of light, every shade of shadow, but only in colors we'd recognize."

I swallowed back emotion. "Good. I'll be the one sobbing in front of it."

She let out a watery laugh. "Promise?"

"I promise."

Sasha stepped beside Denali and flicked a teasing wink at him. "Take care of her," she said, and her voice dropped low, "She's fire wrapped in calm, that one."

Denali's arm wrapped around my waist, his voice steady. "I know."

Then Calista stepped forward, tall and radiant, her green eyes gleaming with some emotion too ancient to name. Her silver lantern glowed at her side, the living tome floating behind her in a gentle orbit.

"You are more than echoes," she said. "You are balance reborn." Her voice rang like wind through glass. "I thank you, each of you. Your journey has not ended; it has only shifted."

Theren stood at her side, hand in hers. His amber eyes now held softness and a kind of weariness that only love could heal. He bowed slightly. "I don't remember everything, but I remember enough to know you've given me back my truth."

Calista's gaze met mine. "We shall meet again," she said with a wink. "Much sooner than you think."

That did it. The tears came.

The hugs blurred together after that, arms wrapped tight, words half-whispered through tears. Parker squeezed my hand and said, "Keep reading the Earth, she listens to you." Sasha kissed both my cheeks and told me to "breathe with purpose." Blair pressed something into my hand, a folded piece of handmade paper inked with swirling paint. I didn't open it.

Elijah pulled me into a bear hug. "Keep looking up, Alayna. That's where the path starts."

I nodded, unable to speak. Every fiber of me wanted to stay, to cling to the magic we'd created. But I knew better. Explorers don't stay. They witness, they remember, and they move forward.

Denali's fingers laced through mine. I turned to him, our foreheads touching.

The sky shimmered in pale gold as Calista stepped forward, her ash-blond braid gleaming like a silver thread against the growing light. She reached for Theren's hand.

"I am not what I was," she said, her voice gentle, timeless. "But I know what I choose now. I choose Theren. And I choose freedom, not for power, but for peace."

Theren looked younger now, his features softening as if the truth itself was restoring him. The wind teased his long, dark hair, the blond streaks catching sunlight that filtered through the thinning mist. His eyes—once black voids—were a rich amber again. Alive.

He brushed her fingers with his lips. "I would walk through every illusion again to find you at the end."

They stood at the cliff's edge, where starlight poured like a waterfall into the great spiritual veil beyond. Their hands entwined, bodies close, and hearts aligned.

Calista turned, her eyes full of sorrow and grace. "The six of you were the breath that stirred a still world, and the fire that burned away illusion."

I squeezed Denali's hand, feeling the heat of his skin steady me. "We didn't do it alone Calista," I said, barely above a whisper. "You helped us become who we needed to be."

She smiled then—radiant, ageless, and luminous. "You were always meant to find each other."

A soft pulse of light rose from the ground around them, the spiral glyphs glowing beneath their feet. Calista raised her lantern one final time. Its silver light bathed Theren's face, and for a breath, I swore the whole realm sighed.

Then, they began to dissolve—not violently or in agony—but with serenity. Their forms shimmered, unraveling into threads of starlight that danced upward, weaving into the sky.

As they vanished, Calista looked back one last time. "You are no longer echoes," she said. "You are balance reborn."

And then they were gone.

I didn't cry, none of us did. It wasn't an ending, not really.

Denali wrapped his arm around my waist as I stared at the sky, where Calista and Theren had become part of the stars. Lavender light bled into blue above us, auroras rippling like breath across the heavens. I felt his chest rise against my back, grounding me.

Parker was the first to speak. "I thought I understood myth," he murmured, brushing a hand through his short blond hair. "But I've never seen it come to life like this."

Blair nodded, her blue eyes shining with quiet awe. "They weren't just stories. They were love, and loss, and truth painted across the stars."

Sasha stepped closer, her tattoos softly glowing like embers. "I felt their spirits pass through me. Like they left something behind."

"Hope," Elijah said, his deep voice resolute. "They left hope."

I turned toward them—my friends, my fellow explorers in a realm we didn't choose but somehow belonged to. "We survived a collapsing maze, spectral jaguars, trials of fear and fire. We became more than who we were."

Sasha laughed, wiping her eyes. "And we didn't kill each other in the process. That's the real miracle."

We all burst into laughter, the kind that shakes off sorrow and draws people closer. Blair stepped in first, wrapping her arms around me. Then Sasha, then Parker, Eli, and finally Denali. One big, tangled, tear-streaked hug beneath the dissolving light of gods.

We held each other for a long time.

I looked up at the sky again, heart full. Maybe it wasn't about where we came from, or even where we were going.

Maybe the only thing that ever mattered was who we became, together.

And that was truly just the beginning.

23

THROUGH THE SPIRAL GATE

The vortex shimmered open again, a swirling breach of violet and gold against the lavender sky. We stood on the edge of it, the six of us, wind tousling our hair and clothes like even the realm didn't want to let us go.

Sasha wrapped her arms tightly around herself, her soft curls wild in the breeze. "What if… what if centuries have passed back home?"

"Or only days," Parker added, adjusting his spectacles. The cut on his cheek had nearly faded, but his voice still carried a quiet rasp from the battle. "Time doesn't run straight here."

Blair stood barefoot in the dirt, her palms open to the wind like she was trying to paint the moment in her mind. "It feels like goodbye," she whispered.

"It's not," Elijah said, clapping a hand on her shoulder. "It's home."

Home. The word landed differently in each of us.

"I left my Jeep at the dig site," I said suddenly, trying to sound casual, though my stomach was in knots. "I wonder if it's been towed."

"I bet it's waiting exactly where you left it," Denali said with a soft chuckle beside me. His dark eyes sparkled, framed by the strands of his long black hair caught in the breeze.

Sasha turned to the vortex. "Well, we won't know what's on the other side if we just stand here chit-chatting about it."

Before I could say anything, she stepped forward and vanished into the swirling mass.

Elijah followed her with no hesitation. "See you on the other side."

Blair took one long breath, then smiled and said, "Let's not wait another lifetime," and stepped in.

Parker went last of the four, pausing just long enough to nod to me. "Alayna. Thank you."

And then it was just me and Denali.

I stared at the vortex. It pulsed softly, almost breathing. My heart pounded. What if the portal dropped us into chaos? What if my parents thought I was dead? What if everything had changed?

Denali took my hand.

"I'm not letting go," he said gently.

My voice came out smaller than I meant. "But what if you can never make it home again?"

"I don't care, Alayna. My life is with you now. Maybe we can try to find my home together."

"I would love to see where you're from, and what your life was like."

"Good, let's find your life first, then mine."

I looked up into his face. His wind-chapped cheeks, the burn scar on his shoulder peeking from his torn shirt, and his eyes so steady and full of quiet devotion.

I nodded once. "I love you, Denali." I had to say it just in case.

"I love you, too, Alayna. For now, and forever."

We held tight to each other and stepped into the vortex together.

The world spun inside out. Light, warmth, and sound collapsed into silence. My grip on Denali tightened until I couldn't tell where his fingers ended and mine began. We weren't falling, we were being remembered.

And then the sunlight hit, intense and warm. We rolled out of the portal like we were rolling down a small hill. I gasped as I blinked up at a deep blue sky, and my stomach jumped like when you've swung too high on a swing. The scent of dry earth and creosote hit me like a welcome slap.

"I know where we are," I whispered. "We're in Mexico."

We lay in the sand, side by side, under the afternoon sun. The familiar swirl of desert heat shimmered around us. Just beyond my elbow, petroglyph spirals faintly glowed on the red rock.

We were back. I looked around and sat up. We were exactly where I was when I had left, in precisely the same spot.

Denali sat up, brushing dust from his jeans. "We made it."

I stared at him. "We really did."

He looked down at our joined hands and smiled. "You didn't let go."

"I didn't want to," I said with a smile.

A breeze rolled across the desert floor, rustling the mesquite nearby. It smelled like home, like dust and scorched stone.

"We brought the magic back with us," I whispered. "I can feel it."

He raised our hands. My pendant shimmered with an inner light, throwing a turquoise hue across my skin. Denali's ring—the half Calista gave him—glowed to match.

I reached with my free hand and pulled my pendant forward.

Together, we pressed the two pieces against each other. A soft, golden warmth bloomed outward like a sunrise beneath my ribs.

It wasn't heat, but something ancient and steady.

Denali leaned in and kissed me, slow and sure.

When we pulled back, I rested my forehead against his. "We're not just part of the story anymore."

"We've become its beginning," he said and smiled.

***

The desert heat hit me like a memory—dry, warm, a little dusty, like the earth itself was exhaling. Warm for the time of year, we were exactly where I'd been before everything changed: crouched beneath the overhang of a red rock ledge, the spiraled petroglyphs still faintly glowing behind us. Denali stood beside me, his hand still in mine.

"Well," I said, glancing around the scrubby landscape, "welcome to Sonora."

He squinted toward the horizon, where saguaros were scattered where the ridge sloped down toward the dig site. "It's much drier than Aztalun."

I let out a laugh. "We'll get you some water and sunscreen. You'll survive. I'm so relieved that everything is the same as when I left. I had so many worries while we were away. I imagined so many different scenarios. I'm glad this is the one I came home to."

"Think they'll believe I'm your long-lost ice-cave boyfriend?"

I gave him a sidelong glance. "No. But they might believe you were simply lost in the desert, maybe dehydrated and confused."

Denali raised an eyebrow, amused. "And just happened to be found by you?"

"Exactly," I said, grinning. "Weird stuff happens out here all the time."

Denali stuffed his parka into his gear bag. We started walking, my boots crunching over gravel and sage. Denali's steps were quieter, even in the clunky hiking boots he'd somehow conjured during our return, thank you, Aztalun magic. The closer we got to the dig, the more real it all became. Back to Earth and my reality. And yet it didn't feel like I'd left the magic behind. I felt it pulsing in my chest.

A few tents came into view first, then the scattered crates of gear and equipment. The flap of the main canopy rippled in the breeze. We were thirty yards out when a tall figure in a wide-brimmed hat stood up from behind a folding table and froze.

Jake.

His brows furrowed beneath his hat as his gaze flicked from me to Denali and back again.

"Oh no," I cringed. "Here we go."

Jake walked toward us slowly, his body language a mix of caution and confusion.

"Professor A," he called out, stopping a few feet away. "Is everything okay?"

"Yes!" I said, too quickly. "Totally fine. This is—uh—Denali. Denali, this is Jake."

Denali gave a soft, polite smile. "Hello, nice to meet you."

"He was… lost," I added. "In the desert, and I found him."

Jake blinked at us, processing. "Lost?"

"Yeah," I said, lowering my voice just a little. "I think he's been out here a while. Probably wandered off the trail and has no ID. He was only a little dehydrated but fully coherent."

Jake's lips parted, but he didn't press. God, I loved him for that. He just nodded slowly and looked Denali over once more. "Well… you found him, so that's lucky."

"Very lucky," I agreed.

"Jake," I said, slipping into Professor mode, "I'm going to help him get checked out and cleaned up; I'm going to have to head back to Tucson early. One of the crew can drive you home, if that's alright with you?"

Jake hesitated. "Of course. Don't worry about anything here. We've got it covered."

"Are you positive?" I asked, though relief was already flooding my chest.

"Absolutely. I can finish the analysis notes from Sector Three and work with the crew."

I smiled at him. "See? I knew I trained you too well."

Jake allowed a small, proud smile to form. "I'll also make sure to text or email you if anything weird comes up."

I stepped forward and gently touched his arm. "You'll be fine. And if something does come up, I'm only a call away."

Jake's eyes flicked to Denali again. He didn't ask any more questions, just offered a wary, "Take care, okay?"

As we turned to leave, Denali exhaled next to me. "That went much better than I expected."

"Jake is good at letting people have their stories," I said. "He's loyal and probably far more curious than worried."

"I like him," he said. "He reminds me of my brother, Silla, calm and capable."

"He's the best grad assistant I've ever had," I said, meaning it. "And probably a better human being than I am on my best day."

We walked side by side through the rocks and cactus, and the sun had clearly passed its zenith. I could feel the warmth on my shoulders and the familiar ache in my boots. But this time, something was different. The air didn't feel quite so heavy.

"That's my jeep," I nodded toward my favorite orange trail beast.

"I definitely could have guessed that," Denali bumped my shoulder gently with his. "So, where are we going?"

I smiled, glancing up at him. "I hadn't thought of that, actually. First, we will go to my motel room, and then we can figure out where to go from there."

By the time we made it back to the motel, the late-afternoon sun had turned everything gold. The saguaro shadows stretched long across the desert, and I could feel the familiar grit of desert dust settling into my boots again. Somehow, it felt both surreal and completely normal to be walking the edge of my own life with a man who technically shouldn't exist here.

Denali walked beside me, his black shoulder-length hair tied back with one of my old bandannas. The desert heat clung to us both, but he didn't complain. He just kept looking around with that quiet reverence I was sure he always had in wild places.

"This is where you live?" he asked, squinting at the distant adobe rooftops just visible beyond the ridge.

"No, this is the motel we're staying at while we're on the dig," I explained, pulling my ponytail tighter. Tucson's a couple of hours' drive across the border. "This is home base for now. At least I'm not sleeping in a tent somewhere."

We stepped into the lobby, the air-conditioning hitting our sun-warmed skin like a welcome shock. Denali looked around, his eyes sweeping across the adobe archways, wrought-iron light fixtures, and terracotta tile floors like he wasn't quite sure if this was real.

"Smells like cinnamon and bleach," he said as he looked around.

"It's Sonora's version of comfort," I said, flashing a tight smile at the front desk attendant and leading him straight toward the elevator. "Come on, my room's on the second floor."

As soon as we stepped inside, I leaned back against the cool elevator wall and let out a long breath. Denali stood across from me, his broad shoulders more tense than I expected.

"I can't believe no one questioned us," I said, glancing up at the slow-moving numbers. "I guess I look just unbothered enough to make dragging a mysterious man out of the desert seem normal."

Denali gave me a quiet smile. "You do have a way of looking like you belong anywhere."

The elevator dinged, and I led him down the hall, my boots clicking on the tile. The keycard beeped green, and I pushed the door open into my temporary home away from home.

I kicked off my boots and dropped my field pack by the door with a sigh that felt like it came from my bones.

Denali leaned against the edge of the dresser, arms crossed, his black eyes scanning the room. The overhead light buzzed faintly, throwing a yellowish glow over the beige walls and the stack of half-sorted excavation notes on the desk.

He turned to look at me, eyes deep black and unwavering, searching mine like he was still half in Aztalun. "Is it hard living away from your home so much?"

I nodded. "Sometimes, although I've gotten used to it."

I walked to the small kitchenette and filled a glass from the filtered water tap. Wordlessly, I handed it to him.

He took it with a grateful nod, watching me over the rim as he drank. That same stillness, that steady quiet I'd come to recognize in him, hadn't faded with the shift back to Earth. It made something flutter in my chest.

I sat down at the edge of the bed, rubbing my temples. "Okay. We need a solid plan. One that doesn't make anyone call the cops or think I've lost it."

"I trust you," Denali said, setting the glass down gently.

"Thank you for that," I said, cracking a wry smile. "We should talk about where we go from here."

Denali gave me that crooked grin that made something in my chest go soft and stupid. "I figured you'd have a plan."

"I always have a plan," I said, with a wink. "I just rarely share it until the last second."

His hand brushed mine, and for a heartbeat, I almost forgot what world we were in.

Focus, Alayna.

"Okay," I said. "I know I joked that you had no ID. Border humor. But *please* tell me you do have your ID on you?"

He looked slightly uncomfortable. "Unfortunately, no. I'd left it in my locker at base camp, just before I headed out on that solo climb into a newly exposed formation in the Mendenhall Glacier near Juneau."

"Hmm, that might pose a problem for us."

Denali chuckled. "I won't be able to travel home until I have my ID. It means you may be stuck with me for a while. Is that a problem?"

"More than you may realize." I sighed. "We'll never be able to *legally* drive across the border into Arizona without showing at least our driver's licenses. A passport would be even better."

Trying to distract myself until a better plan formed in my head, I flopped onto the bed and stared at the ceiling fan. "I wonder how it's going for everyone else. I'm glad we remember everything. Imagine if our memories of Aztalun were erased?"

Denali sat beside me, our shoulders barely brushing. His warmth was grounding, even when my brain felt like it was still spiraling through celestial mazes. "I guess if that happened, we wouldn't remember what we were missing, so it wouldn't really affect us," he said gently.

"I suppose you're right." That's when I remembered the ring. I shot upright. "Wait! The ring! Zanira's ring!"

Denali blinked. "What about it?"

"Calista said it could take us to where we need to go." I looked at my hand. The gold band pulsed faintly, warm in my hand. "I didn't even think about it until now."

He tilted his head. "Does that mean what I think it means?"

I let out a dry laugh. "I think so. I guess all we can do is try it."

Denali raised a brow. "Did Calista tell you how to use it?"

"Not really. She did say that whatever I'm touching will go with me, so I guess I had better get off the bed."

Denali chuckled. "That would be funny, watching you travel around with a bed attached to your hip.

We both stood up, and he wrapped his arms around me. "Mind if I hold you like this while we try it?"

I reached up and gave him a long, sensuous kiss. "Not at all."

"Do you think we can end up right at my house?"

I shrugged. "Only one way to find out."

I looked at the ring and said, "Okay. So, think about your home and focus on where everything is located. Visualize it."

He gave me a crooked smile. "You're an archaeologist, not a sorceress."

I grinned. "Let's pretend I'm both."

He continued holding me wrapped in both arms. "Alright. I'm thinking of my cabin. The ridge line and the moss on the porch—the smell of spruce."

The ring pulsed once—twice—then warmth flooded through me. A tug in my chest, like gravity was sideways. The room bent and I gasped.

And we were standing outside in the middle of a rainstorm. Within seconds, we were drenched. "Why couldn't you have thought about being *inside* your cabin?" I chastised him softly.

"Sorry. I guess this will take some practice."

I shivered, blinking against all the cold raindrops. Cedar clung to the air, tinged with a trace of smoke. A soft amber glow lit the wraparound porch of Denali's cabin, which was nestled along a forested ridge. Aged wood gleamed beneath the rain, softened by moss that crept across the edges like a blanket.

I turned to Denali, who was staring at his home with a stunned expression.

"You didn't think it would work, did you?" I asked.

He shook his head, then reached for the door.

Inside, the cabin was like stepping into his soul. A wall of windows framed a dense stretch of dark trees, rain threading softly down the glass. Wool blankets were draped over a low couch, and the scent of cedar lingered warmly in the air. Hand-carved shelves lined the walls, filled with stones, worn books, and a bit of driftwood that was polished smooth by time. A weathered journal sat open on the coffee table.

I walked in slowly, taking it all in. "It's beautiful, Denali."

His smile was quiet. "Thanks. I tried to make it cozy and welcoming."

Denali retrieved his passport from a drawer tucked beneath a shelf of tea tins and began packing a small suitcase: a few lightweight cotton and linen shirts, two pairs of breathable hiking pants, a wide-brimmed hat, his worn leather journal, trail mix in a tin container, a reusable water bottle, underwear, socks, shorts, his favorite paperback of Tlingit stories, a slim bag containing sunscreen and lip balm, toiletries, and a pair of well-worn sandals. I watched him in silence for a moment, then turned toward the window again.

"I guess we'll never know how long we were in Aztalun. Like if you calculated the time in Aztalun in Earth minutes," I said absent-mindedly.

Denali zipped his bag, thoughtful. "It felt like it was months." He trailed off.

"Being back here makes it feel almost unreal that we were ever there. Do you think that if we tried, the ring could take us back to Aztalun? And if it could, I wonder what we'd find. With time moving so much faster there, who knows how much has already changed?" I wondered.

"You certainly are full of questions," Denali said as he moved toward me and held me.

"I know. I wish I had asked Calista or Zanira about the time thing. I feel a little unsettled. Being home is wonderful, and I'm so relieved we didn't miss anything here, but I'm also experiencing some homesickness for Aztalun. Is that strange? What about you?"

"More questions," he teased as he leaned down to kiss me. "Any chance I could convince you to the bedroom?"

I laughed. "You could, always, but I feel like we should go get your driver's license and figure out what comes next."

He nodded, walked over to the front door, and pulled on a jacket. "My driver's license is at the tour locker. It's not far, just through the woods to the highway. Want to come with me?"

"Lead the way, Juneau." He laughed at my nickname for him, grabbed a sweatshirt off a wooden peg, and tossed it to me. It was like wearing a tent, but it was warm.

We stepped back outside. The rain had stopped, and the forest glistened under the pale moonlight. I followed him along a narrow trail lined with wet, leafy ferns until we reached a low building set into the trees. The front faced the highway, but we had approached from the back of the building. He unlocked the door, retrieved his wallet, license, and a few folded papers, then looked at me.

"This is really nearby. Is this where you work from?" I asked.

He nodded as he tucked the papers into his bag. "Yeah. It's my space before every tour—gear, maps, emergency kits, everything lives here."

Curiously, I looked around. A long wooden bench stretched beneath a wall-mounted rack lined with neatly organized climbing gear—crampons, ice axes, coils of rope. Above it, laminated topographic maps were pinned in careful layers, some marked with faded red pencil lines that traced old routes through the glacier.

To the right, a low shelf held waterproof bins labeled in Denali's clean, looping handwriting—*first aid, thermal bags, flare kits, spare gloves.* A pegboard displayed more tools than I could name, everything arranged in a kind of functional harmony that somehow made the place feel peaceful, not cluttered.

"I love this place. You must have so much fun on your tours."

"I do. I would love to take you sometime."

"I would love that kind of adventure."

"I'll look forward to it then." He looked into my eyes and added, "I can't wait to discover so many things about you and get to know you better. I was really worried for a bit there when I thought we would be separating forever."

I slid my arms around his waist and leaned my head on his chest. "Me too. I'm so glad you didn't let go of my hand."

"We should lock up and head back to the house. You're shivering." Denali put an arm around my shoulders.

"I was under the impression it was Springtime," my teeth chattered.

"It's *early* Spring, and that's definitely rain outside, not snow," Denali smiled.

We headed back through the woods and into the firelit warmth. Denali set his belongings down and jerked his thumb toward the bedroom. "I'm sorry, I can't wait any longer. I must make love to you on Earth!"

That made me laugh, and he picked me up and carried me, and dropped me on his bed. We dissolved into a fit of laughter, leaning into each other until the space between us disappeared. His hands framed my face, gentle at first, then more certain as his lips found mine. The kiss deepened slowly—like a question asked and answered in the same breath—until my pulse drowned out the world. Rain dripped from the eaves outside, but in that moment, all I felt was his warmth, his breath, and the way his fingertips grazed the curve of my neck and sent heat spiraling through me. He peeled away the distance between us with each touch, each murmur, like he was rediscovering something he already knew by heart.

We moved together with an urgency that was somehow soft, like we'd waited long enough. His mouth explored the skin below my collarbone. He murmured my name against my neck, his breath sending shivers down my spine as his lips traced a path lower. When he sank into me, everything else—worries, time, the real world—faded. Our bodies wrapped around each other, slow and consuming, and an unspoken conversation of trust and tenderness passed through us. It was connection, elemental, and raw. We made love like we were stitching ourselves back together—slow, deliberate, and breathless.

Denali opened his eyes and said, "We should get back to your motel."

"I know you're right, but this place is so cozy!"

He smiled and kissed my nose. "We can come back here any time we want."

"It's kind of exciting, right? I hope it's okay to use the ring for personal reasons."

"Calista didn't say anything to make you think you couldn't, so why not?" His eyes glistened with mischief.

An hour later, I slid the ring back on, and we were back in the motel room within seconds.

I staggered slightly from the shift, laughing despite myself. "Okay. That's going to take some getting used to."

24

SOMETHING STILL CALLS

A month later, I woke to the smell of bacon frying and freshly ground coffee beans. "I hope you didn't put bacon in the *chilaquiles* I was saving for breakfast," I called toward the kitchen.

Denali walked into the bedroom carrying a steaming mug of coffee, "Your breakfast is safe from this carnivore, but if you keep looking so beautiful in the morning, I can't promise the same for you." He placed the mug on the nightstand and nibbled my earlobe.

I sighed with contentment. The initial analysis from the dig was drafted, Spring break was already forgotten by my students, and Denali and I had settled into the start of a familiar routine in my little Tucson bungalow, less than two miles from the University. Opening the door to head to campus, I found a small, flat package on the steps of the front patio—tied with twine and sealed with a pressed heather blossom. I smiled the second I saw Blair's handwriting. Inside was a sketchbook unlike any I'd ever seen. The cover shimmered faintly, and as I flipped it open, her illustrations moved gently, like breath—waves rippling, trees swaying, a flock of painted birds lifting into the margins. On one page, she'd drawn the six of us standing in a spiral, palms glowing, and my throat tightened.

I showed it to Denali, and he smiled and kissed my forehead. "That is really gorgeous."

An hour later, sitting at my desk in a tiny basement office in the archeology building, I found Parker had emailed me an encrypted file. "Thought you might want to hold onto this," the message read. I opened it on my laptop. A map of Aztalun unfurled across the screen, layered with topography, myth symbols, and shifting constellations. It pulsed, alive with meaning. Of course, he'd found a way to chart the unchartable.

I forwarded Parker's email to Denali, then my inbox dinged again.

I looked at the screen and saw an email from Sasha. There was no subject line. Just a poem in the body of the message. It was titled *Echoed Flame*. Her words—raw, lyrical, and beautiful—unraveled the tragedy and tenderness of Varek and Theren in a way that made me ache. I read it twice before saving it to my desktop.

Echoed Flame

by Sasha Kahn

> He was not born in darkness—
> he fell into it,
> a slow descent dressed as duty,
> cloaked in the silence of forgetting.
> His name split like stone,
> Theren to Varek,
> love twisted into law,

light devoured by the very truth he swore to
    guard.
But still—
beneath the ash of his fury,
a coal remembered warmth.
Her name.
Calista.
The syllables lit caverns in his mind,
a ghost of touch,
a breath that never left.
She waited—
not in fear,
but in knowing,
that even broken gods leave trails of gold
through their ruin.
Their love was not a blaze.
It was ember,
eternal,
flickering beneath the frost of rage.
And when the world forgot him,
when he forgot himself—
she remembered.
She always did.
So let the cosmos shift.
Let time collapse and rebuild.
Let the veil lift once more.
Because love,
true love,
doesn't burn out.
It echoes.

I sniffed when I finished reading it. "This is so beautiful. We're still part of something bigger, aren't we?" I said aloud to myself.

Each message was a thread—woven across continents, across realities. Proof that what we shared wasn't confined to that realm. It lived in us. In ink and pixels. In memory and magic.

And no matter how far we scattered, the tether held.

Three months later, the lecture room buzzed with the low hum of shifting chairs, the rustle of papers, and the faint click of laptop keys. I stood behind the podium at the front of the university's anthropology hall, heart steady, voice calm. The topic was a new one for me, setting the stage for a future research grant, I hoped: "Nonlinear Time in Sacred Geographies." On the surface, it was academic, but for me, it meant so much more.

"We often speak of time as linear—past, present, future," I began, scanning the room. "But across ancient cultures, especially those tied to sacred landscapes, time is a spiral. It loops, layers, and returns. Sites like Uluru, The Fairy Glen of Skye, Mount Shasta, Kaieteur Falls, Sedona Arizona, and the Mendenhall Glacier—they're not just geological marvels, they're temporal membranes. Thresholds, if you will."

A few audience members nodded. A couple scribbled notes. A few blinked slowly, clearly lost or wondering if they were in the right lecture. But I kept going.

"Petroglyphs aren't just stories; they're timestamps layered across dimensional understanding. When we stand at these sites, we don't just stand in space, we stand in folded time."

My pendant warmed against my chest, like it knew I wasn't just theorizing. I glanced up and caught the eye of a man near the back. Mid-fifties, salt-and-pepper beard, sharp eyes beneath wire-rimmed glasses. He wasn't nodding like the others. He was watching, *really* watching, as if he knew something was hidden beneath my words. I moved on quickly.

Afterward, as people filed out, a woman brushed past me. Short-cropped hair, sun-lined skin, leather bag over one shoulder. She didn't stop, she just whispered as she passed: "Spiral energy is rising in Peru at Machu Picchu."

I turned immediately, but she had already vanished into the chattering crowd like smoke.

Later that night, back in my home, rain pounded, and thunder rattled the windows during a summer monsoon as I sat beside Denali watching the lightning. He was stretched across the couch, bare feet propped on the second-hand coffee table, relaxing. My little gray fur-ball, Kiva was curled up beside Denali, and I smiled to see them together even though Denny insisted he had never been a cat-person and never would be.

"She said *spiral energy?*" he asked, eyes boring into mine curiously.

"Yes," I said, pacing. "At Machu Picchu. And then she was gone. She gave me no name, and she moved so fast I didn't see her face."

He gave a low whistle. "Do you think it was Zanira or Calista?"

I nodded. "I think so, but I can't be sure. I wish I could have seen her face."

I stopped near the window, arms crossed, thoughts spinning like galaxies. "If the spiral's active there, maybe something's opening, or something needs to be opened."

"Machu Picchu's one of the places on Parker's map." Denali watched me quietly. "You want to go, don't you?"

I turned to face him, my expression probably conveying everything. He smiled, soft and knowing. "It's not over, is it?"

I shook my head slowly, heart thudding with a quiet thrill. "No. Not even close."

"I don't want to go right now, but I'm going to send the others an email to let them know about it."

"Wise idea."

"Or scary," I said, a little hesitant.

That night, when the storm had moved on and made way for a brilliantly clear sky, I held the pendant in the moonlight.

The copper spiral flickered to life, soft and rhythmic, like a sleeping heartbeat. The glow wasn't as fierce as before, but it didn't need to be. It pulsed with quiet insistence, just waiting.

Denali sat beside me on the front steps of the house; one arm draped loosely around his knee. The moon cast silver rays along the lines of his jaw, and his black hair shimmered faintly in the breeze. I didn't say a word. I just turned the pendant toward him.

He leaned in, eyes narrowing with wonder. "It's awake."

"Yeah," I whispered. "It's changed."

"How so?"

"Watch it and you'll see," I told him.

We watched together as the spiral rotated—slow, deliberate turns, almost imperceptible at first. Then one direction reversed, and the shape expanded inward, not outward. I caught my breath. "It's like it's turning toward something else," I said.

Denali's hand found mine. "Or drawing something back."

A silence settled over us, thick but not heavy. The desert stretched out around the house, hushed and wide. I could hear cicadas buzzing and smell mesquite smoke in the distance, as a neighbor was grilling something in their backyard. The wind touched my skin with warmth that still carried a trace of cold.

The spiral pulsed once more, then stilled.

And somehow, I knew, it was time to start planning.

I put the pendant back around my neck and looked at Denali. He was already watching me. Without a word, he smiled. And I smiled back, heart racing, because I knew he knew it wasn't over.

Six months later, my pendant wouldn't stop glowing. I held it in my palm, the silver and copper spiral so bright it lit the room in soft pulses. It wasn't just light, it was humming, a low, rhythmic sound that vibrated through my bones.

"Denali," I said, turning toward him. "Something's happening!"

He looked up from his tea, his black eyes narrowing as he crossed the room to me. "It's never been this bright?"

"Never," I whispered. "And it won't stop. I can also feel it pulling."

"Pulling where?"

I hesitated, my breath catching as a memory flashed— stone, heat, glyphs in the desert sun. "The Sonoran site. I don't know how I know, I just do. Are you in for a small road trip?"

Denali didn't argue. He never did when it came to instincts like this. He simply nodded once. "Small?" We both laughed.

On the drive, the sky melted from dusty orange to violet, the road unraveling beneath us like a ribbon through ancient land. We didn't talk much at first. The silence between us had never been uncomfortable; it just allowed space to breathe and think.

Denali finally glanced over at me, a faint smile tugging at the edge of his mouth. "Do you think this will be another quest in Aztalun?"

I let out a dry laugh. "I don't know. It feels different this time. It's almost like it needs us to go there to receive a message."

"How do you know that?" Denali asked as he drummed his fingers on the steering wheel.

"Intuition?" I looked down at the pendant resting against my chest, still warm. "Maybe not what, maybe who, or when. I'm not sure, but I can feel Calista."

He nodded slowly and turned the radio down so we could talk. "Every time I think we've closed that chapter, the pages keep writing themselves."

We didn't need to say it out loud, but we both knew someone needed us to do something.

A few hours later, we stood together on the rise of warm sandstone, the Sonoran Desert stretching out around us in shades of honey and rust. Heat shimmered on the horizon, and the air was heavy with summer's hush. I could hear cicadas in the distance, their buzzing like static against the quiet pulse of the Earth. My boots crunched faintly over grit as I stepped forward.

Beneath our feet, ancient glyphs shimmered faintly across the rock. Swirls and spirals, carved by hands long gone, whispered something familiar. They pulsed—not bright, not showy—but just enough to say: *I'm still here.*

"Well, this is new," I said, eyes wide with curiosity. I looked over at Denali. The wind tugged at a loose strand of his black hair, which had fallen from behind his ear. He reached down and took my hand, his grip warm and steady.

"Do you feel that?" I asked.

He nodded, slowly. "Yeah, it's pulsing under our feet."

I knew it was the tether to Aztalun. I could feel it like a quiet chord humming beneath the ground, echoing between worlds. The same energy that once wrapped around us now vibrated faintly through the desert stone.

"Alayna," Denali said quietly.

I followed his gaze.

Across the hot sand, a light warped just past a stand of ocotillo, a unique desert plant with a spiny, stick-like appearance. The air sparkled, not with heat exactly, but something else. Memory, maybe. And within it stood a figure, cloaked, still, and waiting.

I recognized her immediately. It was Zanira.

She wasn't fully solid. Her outline wavered like a reflection off the water. Her cloak moved with no wind. But her silver eyes were clear as moonlight. They locked with mine across the distance, and in them, I saw a spiral, but not the same one from before. This one curled inward, deep and sharp like a map not yet drawn.

My chest tightened. "Denali… "

He didn't move. "I see her."

"She looks different," I whispered. I couldn't believe how nice it was to see her and how reassuring it was to know she was still out there.

"She's in spirit right now," he said, voice low, "but she's real."

We stood there, hand in hand, the heat clinging to our skin. Sweat beaded along Denali's temple.

"Do you think… this is what that woman meant?" I asked. "The one after the lecture?"

"Spiral energy rising," he echoed. "She knew something."

Zanira lifted her hand slightly—not a wave, not a beckon, just a motion—the air around her pulsed and folded in on itself like ripples in a memory. A soft breeze stirred the desert floor, sweeping dry petals across the glyphs. They pulsed again, this time stronger. I could feel the vibration in my chest.

She stepped forward, her silver eyes catching the golden haze like mirrors of twilight. Her voice, when it came, was soft but carried weight.

"I apologize for the interruption," she said, her gaze flicking between us. "I know you've just returned to your world. I'm only here to offer an update, not a summons."

I was conflicted when she made that statement. I truly wanted to be at home and experience life here with Denali, but there was also a pull toward Aztalun since we were part of Calista's spirit, and I also considered Aztalun home.

Denali stood tall beside me, his hand finding mine again like it always did when something strange began. "We don't mind," he said quietly.

Zanira's mouth curved into something resembling a smile. "I'll be brief."

She looked out over the desert, as if gathering the right words from the wind. "I've had a premonition. The gods now know about both Theren and Calista's freedom. It did not go unnoticed, and they are not pleased."

I felt the breath hitch in my throat. "Should we be worried?" I asked.

Zanira turned back to me, head tilting slightly. "Not while you remain here on Earth. The gods will not interfere with life on Earth. It's a law even they cannot break."

Relief trickled in but didn't settle. I glanced at Denali, who nodded slowly.

"I believe Theren and Calista will be visiting your plane," Zanira continued. "They are in hiding. I don't know where, but I can feel their energy moving through your leylines. You may be contacted by them very soon."

Denali exhaled. "We think we already have."

Zanira's eyes sharpened. "You're perceptive. Good. But worry not, nothing is in dire straits at the moment. I merely wanted to prepare you. You may be called upon again, though not now."

Denali raised an eyebrow. "In Peru, perhaps?"

Her grin returned, sly this time. "Peru would be a lovely place to visit and get the 'ley' of the land, so to speak."

I couldn't tell if that was a hint or a suggestion. It confused me.

He chuckled, and I felt my face heat up when she added, "It might make a nice honeymoon location."

We both blushed like school kids. I glanced at Denali and caught the faintest smile tugging at the corners of his mouth. He was already looking at me.

Zanira's expression softened. "Solidifying your bond will unite you in a way no god can break. The universe has noticed. Your love is a thread stronger than magic."

My throat tightened. The way she said it seemed like it was a prophecy, but if it was, I didn't want to know about it.

"I'll see you at your wedding," she added with a wink, and then—just like that—she was gone—a shimmer of heat, a fold of air, and silence.

Denali stared at the space where she'd stood. "She's a funny one, all that teasing about a wedding."

I gave him a sideways glance. "Perhaps she's not teasing," I said, a little hopeful.

The desert was quiet again, except for the soft hiss of sand shifting in the wind. The glyphs had stilled, but I could still feel their hum deep inside my ribs. A low, living rhythm that hadn't gone silent, just quieted, waiting.

"I hope Calista and Theren know they can trust us," I said softly.

Denali moved beside me, his arm wrapping gently around my waist. "They know."

I leaned into him and closed my eyes. "We'll protect them," I whispered. "As much as we possibly can."

He didn't answer with words—just rested his forehead against mine.

And the desert, still pulsing beneath our feet, held the promise of whatever came next.

Beside me, Denali slipped an arm around my waist. His body was a comforting weight against mine, his scent warmed by the desert wind. "Whatever comes next, we'll be ready when the time comes. But right now, I want to focus on how much I love you."

I tilted my head, heart rising. "You're kind of good at this whole love thing."

"I've had the best practice partner," he whispered, brushing his lips along my temple. "And I want to make it permanent."

I blinked up at him. "What do you mean?"

He didn't answer with words. Instead, he pulled back just enough to reach into his jacket pocket, then dropped to one knee in the golden dust of the desert.

I gasped. "Denali… "

"Shh!" He chuckled, and then his black eyes locked with mine, fierce and steady. "You're the story I didn't know I was searching for. You've taught me that love isn't just something to feel and hold on to fiercely, every single day. Alayna Archuleta, I don't want to go on another adventure, face another realm, or sip another stupid herbal tea without you as my partner in all of it. Will you marry me?"

Time unraveled and twisted all at once. The pendant pulsed against my skin, each glow echoing the thrum of my pulse. For one beat, I couldn't speak. And then I laughed, full, breathless, and amazed.

"Zanira knew!" I blurted. "She was talking about weddings because she already knew this was going to happen, didn't she? She was teasing me!"

Denali's smile deepened. "She might've nudged me, just a little."

My hand trembled as I reached down and pulled him up. "Yes," I breathed. "Yes, I'll marry you, Denali Kwaan."

The sun had dipped far enough that dusk had begun to rise. Colors bled across the sky like oil into water, blending into each other: orange, teal, and gold. The desert held its breath as if it too recognized something sacred unfolding here. I leaned into Denali, and his arms wrapped around me again, solid and sure. Our lips met once more, sealing something ancient and new at the same time.

Denali turned to me, his fingers brushing mine. "I'm glad I fell off Earth long enough to meet you, Alayna. I will follow you to the ends of the universe where time bends and stretches. I will keep you tethered to me as long as we both take a breath."

I looked into his eyes and felt the tears glistening in the corners of my eyes. "I love you and I will be here for you physically, emotionally, mentally, spiritually, and magically for all the days we are together."

I stammered, "But first, I need to call Heidi and tell her the good news. And we need to visit my parents in Albuquerque. And get to Juneau before winter buries it, so I can meet your parents."

He pulled me close, his chin resting on the top of my head. "Anywhere you want to go, as long as it's together."

"Always." I sighed.

And somewhere in the distance, I thought I saw the faint flicker of silver eyes watching through the dusk. I shook my head and laughed. That was a story for another day.

The spiral on my pendant glowed brightly once more, and then it went completely black…

ACKNOWLEDGMENTS

I must thank many people and risk leaving someone out. First, I thank my loving husband, Randy, and our Children, Alyssa, Alex, and Daniel, for their support and belief in me. Additionally, I would like to acknowledge the many family members who provided encouragement and inspiration, including June, Bud, Penny, Connie, Kayleen, Sharon, Steve, Will, Doug, Caleb, and too many others to name (I come from an extensive family). I also thank my writing consultant, editor, and designer: Raven, Evelyn, and Michael.